THE KILLING KIND

SARAH K. STEPHENS

To my grandfathers, Charles and John

CHAPTER ONE

She spotted him across the crowded room and knew instantly he was her mark for the night. The music vibrated through her body and mixed with the top-shelf gin they were serving to create a special kind of alchemy. Under the right circumstances, it translated into what for Trina served as courage. Under the wrong circumstances, it ruined lives—mainly hers, but other people's too.

Tonight, she wasn't sure yet which it would be.

He was different from her type. Trina usually liked them with a whiff of post-football fraternity brother, thick and meaty like a lamb chop. But this guy was long and lean, with a half-finished tattoo sleeve of roses and skulls on his right forearm and a glittery pink bow tie. In the dark of the banquet hall, his attempt at a beard read as a meager scrubby patch under his chin.

The DJ cued up "Dancing Queen" by ABBA, and Trina was almost swept into a swirl of pink organza as the bridesmaids swarmed the dance floor and made a circle around the bride.

He stayed at the bar, sipping on what looked like a vodka tonic, but turned to watch the gaggle of women link hands and belt out the chorus. Trina pulled at the tight fabric of her dress and smoothed it over her thighs. It was a royal blue that brought out the rich black of her hair, which she'd had blown out yesterday. She knew she looked good tonight. Under the kaleidoscope lights of the dance floor maybe she could even pass for vibrant. That's why she loved weddings. Mood lighting and free booze and happy dreams rattling around everyone's heads, if only for the day.

Hard living was forgiven with the temporary suspension of reality.

She finished her drink, set it on a nearby table, and made her way over to the bar. As she got closer, she realized he was younger than she'd originally thought. Probably ten years younger than her, maybe fifteen. Not that it mattered. She'd never see him after tonight.

She took the spot next to him, shifting her hip over to his side and purposefully making contact with his leg. Trina noticed he'd sweat through the armpits of his plaid shirt.

"Vodka tonic." She leaned over the bar, pushing her cleavage together, and flipped out a hand to catch the bartender's attention.

"Bride or groom?" he asked. She'd been expecting some kind of lame opener, and he didn't disappoint.

Trina snatched the drink that appeared in front of her, turned around and leaned her elbows against the bar. In her head she tossed a coin.

"Groom," she told him. "Old family friend. And you?"

He smiled, and Trina couldn't deny how handsome he was despite the hipster vibe. "Bride. Childhood friend."

Trina took another sip. She hated vodka—would have preferred gin—but this point in the evening depended on some basic mirroring.

"Enjoying your drink?" she asked.

"I am now." *Ick*, she thought. She took another sip.

It was easy to get him dancing. She moved to the music,

grinding against his leg while the DJ played Today's Top Hits. His hands left wet smears on the fabric of her dress, and when he nuzzled up to her ear and asked if she wanted to get out of there, the sweat from his face left drops of moisture on her cheek.

She still told him yes.

Trina noticed some people, including a few twenty-somethings with primary colored cocktail dresses, casting nasty glances their way as they stumbled off the dance floor and out the door of the banquet hall. As he reached for her hand, telling her in sloppy half-speech that he'd rented a suite upstairs and she should really try these little special cookies they had in the minibar, she heard cheers echo out from the wedding guests. She pulled back on his arm, leaning into the doorway to see what was happening and catching the bride and groom as they delicately fed each other cake.

Trina smiled. She always liked that part.

He pulled her back in towards the hallway and kissed her hard. Trina had to fight not to recoil from his lips, which were surprisingly blubbery. She caught one of the dress brigade staring back at her from across the hall, judgment clear in her sunken eyes.

For one moment, Trina paused and considered what she was doing. She could leave. Just go and call an Uber and forget any of this ever happened. No one knew she was here. She didn't even know this guy's name, and he didn't know hers. He'd barely remember her in the morning.

But she did go with him. She spent the night with him.

The night that would cleave her life into a beginning and an end.

Before the murder.

And after.

CHAPTER TWO

TRINA

Trina woke in the morning, a complicated combination of sounds, tastes, and smells ricocheting around her head. She tried to open her eyes, but the light already streaming through her bedroom window made starbursts in her mind and so she groped for her phone blindly. She usually set it on the bedside table, but she'd crawled into her apartment during the early hours, casting everything off her body like a plane crash, and so now she had to sift through the wreckage.

Her phone buzzed again, insistent, and her head pounded.

She should have gone to the wedding at the Belamar instead of the Marriott. But she had been lazy and didn't want to bother traveling across town when it was frigid out. Everyone knew the Belamar always skimped on the top shelf booze, which would have helped Trina drink less. Theoretically.

Really, she shouldn't have gone to a Sunday night wedding in the first place. They were for couples who couldn't afford the more expensive Saturday night bookings, and the crowd was always more subdued with Monday looming over the horizon. But sometimes the loneliness was the worst for Trina on

Sundays, and she needed to go somewhere that felt alive, if only a cheaper version of it.

She tried to open her eyes again, pulling her hand as a shield against the light. Her clothes were strewn in a scattered line from the door of the bedroom to her bed, and she was wrapped in her comforter with only her bra and panties on. Trina thought she glimpsed her purse slouching next to one of her nude high heels.

Like an animal, she pulled herself halfway off the bed, balancing her arms over the floor but keeping her legs tightly knit in the covers, and triumphantly grabbed her purse and pulled it back under the safety of her duvet.

Trina screwed up her eyes to read the screen. It was him.

She'd let it go to voicemail.

She needed a glass of water desperately.

It was Monday morning, wasn't it? Trina glanced at her phone. 9:23am, so yes, late for work but still morning. Thankfully. She had a meeting with her department head today. There were a few times in the past where she'd slept through an entire day after a particularly rough night out.

The bubble popped up indicating she had a new voicemail, and she hovered her thumb over it before discarding her phone and shifting back down into the covers. But the curiosity of why he was calling—again—mixed with a certain type of loneliness, tugged at the back of Trina's mind, and so she pulled it out again and clicked the recording.

The voice, familiar to her, blasted out from the speaker, making her temples throb.

"I know you don't want to hear from me, but I need to talk to you. Call me. It's important. Please, Catriona. Call me."

The recording ended, and Trina slowly rose from her bed, filled a glass of water from the kitchen sink, and plunged her phone into the water.

Then, and only then, did she fill a second glass and drink it down in one satisfying gulp.

———

Monday kept rolling in like a semi-truck, all angry clouds and a brittle wind lashing at Trina's throat. She should have worn her warmer coat, but a guy she met at a Greek wedding a few weeks ago had vomited on it as they made their way to the back of his car, and she hadn't taken the time to have it dry-cleaned yet. It was still sitting on a hook by her apartment door, and every time she walked by she caught a slight whiff of sick mixed with honey.

So she was wearing her shorter, thinner coat with the pink lining and fur-trimmed hood. Which was fine. Her legs were freezing, and she regretted choosing tights and a skirt today, but she needed to look put-together. Driving onto campus was always a hellhole, even with a faculty parking permit, and Trina had failed to account for delays in buses running from the extension lot to her building on campus. As a result, she was five minutes late for her meeting with her department head, and she showed up with bright cheeks, a runny nose, and her coat still wrapped around her. The meeting was for 11:30am, and there's nothing quite like having a disciplinary meeting with your superior that lets them know you haven't yet settled into work by the time many of your colleagues were eating lunch.

"Trina, sit down." Her boss pushed a plastic Tupperware of salad to the side of her desk.

Liz Turley was really the best kind of department head. Charismatic, intelligent, a good communicator. Everybody in the department loved her, including Trina.

This meeting was going to be awful.

"I'm sorry I'm late. The traffic was obnoxious."

Liz nodded. A stack of research articles lay on the chair next to the one Trina was sitting in, and a small part of her was touched to see that Liz also preferred hard copies.

"A student has complained." Liz folded her hands and gave Trina a steady look.

Trina knew this was coming.

"I'm sorry that you're having to deal with these issues, but we all know students complain. It's part of the work we do."

Trina immediately knew it was the wrong thing to say.

"I wouldn't have asked you in here if it was a typical issue," Liz replied. She leaned forward in her chair. "And you're right. I shouldn't have to be dealing with issues like this."

Trina waited. Her stomach growled audibly. She'd skipped breakfast, and it looked like it was going to be a liquid lunch.

"It seems that you connected with some of your students on social media." Liz clicked something up on her screen, turning it towards Trina.

There it was. She'd deleted the post, but someone had done a screenshot and now the Department Head of Psychology at Dickinson College had it up on her screen. Last week Trina went home with a guy she met in the smaller banquet hall at the Marriott. She'd passed out across the fluffy white bedspread, her tight dress rucked up around her hips and her period-stained panties on full display. Nothing happened with the guy—she could tell when she woke up, running over her body in her mind like a lover—and nude-colored menstrual panties were a good deterrent to any douchebag. Which is probably why he swiped her phone and posted that picture of her onto her Instagram. Trina should have stayed home that night, but sometimes she felt like she couldn't breathe and so she went out and shouldered herself into a group of people who were happy. Her first pick, a gorgeous twenty-something with boy-band good looks, had rejected her, pulling her close to him and whispering in her ear that she was a drunken hag. The guy she ended up back at his hotel with was young, too, but a mean kind of desperate.

Trina discovered the post the next morning, scrolling through her phone over a huge coffee and sticky counters at the Dunkin' Donuts down the street from the Marriott.

"It's not me," she told Liz, who immediately gave Trina a disappointed look.

"It's not just the social media," Liz went on. "Students are saying that your classes have been canceled repeatedly. That you've been ill-prepared for lectures. That exams have not been graded."

Trina thought about the faces looking back at her from the chairs in her classroom. She was teaching Intro to Adolescent Development this semester. And an abnormal course that had the odd title of Developmental Problems. Who sat in the front row?

She couldn't recall a single student's name. One face came to mind, a doe-eyed girl with black hair and eyebrows like apostrophes. Maybe she was the one complaining?

"I've been ill," Trina tried.

"Then perhaps you should take a leave of absence."

Trina knew what that meant.

"I need this job." She also needed the paycheck.

Liz's face softened. "I know you care about your work, and that it's been a difficult time for you ever since Simon."

Trina flinched at his name. She hadn't expected Liz to know about all that, let alone bring it up in this meeting.

"Simon has nothing to do with my work." Trina cocked her chin up. She was very close to saying "I'm a professional," but she caught herself.

Liz stood up. "This is a formal warning, Trina. You won't have another chance to fix things. Get yourself together, do your job, and we won't have to revisit any of this."

Trina was still sitting, and self-consciously she followed Liz to the door. She thanked her boss for meeting with her, walked down the corridor and into her office, and pressed her back against the closed door. The lights were still off, and the air smelled of damp. A stack of papers from last semester lay on the side table like a carcass, run through with red ink that Trina vaguely remembered marking after a night of Chinese take-out, best intentions, and eventually several bottles of wine.

Leave of absence. She couldn't manage that.

Weeks of lazing around her apartment—unpaid—hoping to find something special in the day that brought a glimmer of hope. Not being able to do that and then putting on a too-tight dress and finding somebody getting married and crashing into their happiness until someone agreed to take her home.

Trina clicked on her computer and logged into the college's teaching portal. Scrolling through, she started to organize materials into folders for her courses. She consulted the syllabus and sent out an email reminding students of an upcoming deadline of an assignment she'd totally forgotten she'd ever assigned. She prepared for her lecture that afternoon, primping her content and including a few fun photographs on the PowerPoint slides.

The class roster showed student ID photos, and she clicked on a few to see if she could learn some names. The doe-eyed girl was called Evelyn.

Her office phone rang next to her keyboard while she worked through her email inbox, and she picked it up absentmindedly.

"Professor Catriona Dell." God, she still loved the ring of that. In a breath, she resolved to stop drinking, picking up random men and ruining lovely couples' weddings, and to Start. Taking. Care of herself.

And then the caller spoke.

She'd forgotten he had this number. But—come on, Trina—it was listed on the department's website, for Christ's sake. Of course he had it.

"Catriona." He said her name the way he always had. She was never Trina to him. Always so formal, so proper.

"Simon."

"I tried calling your cell, but I couldn't get through."

Trina pictured the glass of water where she'd doused her

phone, now replaced with a bowl of rice to hopefully resuscitate the device.

Sometimes she did things without thinking them through.

"What do you want?"

"It's coming up on the one-year anniversary, and I wanted to see how you were doing." He cleared his throat. "You know. Check-in. Make sure you were okay."

"I'm fine. You don't have to call."

"I don't think you're fine."

"I'm at work. I really don't have time to talk."

She heard a rustling on the other end. A siren blared in the background. It sounded like he was walking along the street. Or perhaps from his office to his car. Trina glanced at the time.

A late lunch with his wife? They liked to meet on Mondays.

"I went to one of your classes," Simon went on. Something icy ran up Trina's neck.

"You shouldn't do that."

Trina tried to recall if he'd been there. Surely, she would have noticed him, even if he was in the back. Although, lately, she'd been avoiding eye contact with her students. It was easier to get through class without seeing them, seeing her.

She reached down and smoothed the edges of her skirt absently with her hand. Her hair felt tangled, her hands chafed.

"It had been canceled. I ran into a student who was leaving. She thought I was your supervisor, coming to check on you. In fact, she seemed happy to tell me all about the problems you've been having in your class."

Evelyn's soft, dull face hovered in her thoughts for a moment. Smiling in her school ID picture, baby bangs making her face rounder.

"Why would my supervisor come check on me?" But she caught herself playing into him. "I need to go."

"Please don't hang up. Let me help you."

"The last time I did that, I ended up at the police station."

"That wasn't my fault."

"Of course it wasn't. Nothing is ever your fault." Trina couldn't stop herself. She should just hang up the phone, pack her things, and go teach her class. "Your wife calls the police to say that I'm stalking you and your family and you do absolutely nothing to defend me. I'm questioned like a criminal. Somehow, my department head knows about you?"

Something pinged in her mind. "Did you talk to Liz? Is that how you know my schedule?"

Oh fuck. What does Liz think happened?

"I didn't talk to your boss." There was a weighty pause. "But I did make some inquiries around the college."

"You had no right to do that." Trina was acutely aware that she was raising her voice, and that the walls between offices were thin. She could hear someone having a conference call somewhere in the warren of offices, tinny voices streaming out of the speaker.

"You wouldn't talk to me." Simon sounded suddenly pathetic on the other end of the line, sheer as a gauzy curtain in the breeze.

She hung up. Trina glanced at her watch.

She was late for class.

CHAPTER THREE

SIMON

His wife leaned her long, yoga-toned arms against the white tablecloth. She hadn't touched her cod fillet, and a few capers languished in the white wine sauce so meticulously trickled over the flaky piece of fish. She tapped her wedding rings against her glass of wine and glanced aimlessly around the room.

Simon ate his steak in three huge bites, swallowing each piece down with a slug of red wine. He'd kept his hands in his lap once he was done eating, but he caught a wave of bravery and reached out to take Joyce's hand and steady it.

"Aren't you hungry?"

She gave him a look back that was built on twenty years of marriage, and all the love and hurt and soft, well-meaning lies that go into keeping two people together for that length of time.

"It seems you were." She looked pointedly at his plate.

Simon blushed. He'd always been able to compartmentalize, and keep one crisis sectioned off from other, smoother pieces of his life. Joyce wasn't the same. She felt everything so intensely, one issue bleeding into the other. It made her reckless, and often cruel.

It's something they'd worked on during their marriage, trying to find a balance between each other. Sometimes it worked better than others.

"Do you want to talk about it?" Simon asked, already knowing the answer.

"No, I don't." Joyce picked up her fork and poked at her lunch.

"Shall I get the check?" He scanned the room for their waiter. The restaurant was one of their usual lunch places, and they'd shared many meals within its dark wood paneling and soft recessed lights.

"Do you love her?" Joyce asked suddenly, meeting his gaze.

Simon wasn't used to this type of pointed question from his wife, and he fumbled over his reply, stalling.

"Do I love who?"

Joyce stood up, laid several large bills on the table, and walked out.

Simon finally caught the waiter's eye, ordered a double Scotch, and after it was brought to him Simon sat back in his chair and sipped it thoughtfully. Joyce would take the car home, and he'd have to call a cab to get back to work.

They had dinner plans tonight, he remembered. With the Worthers, who were equal parts bland and reliable. It would be a nice dinner, more than likely. He recalled Joyce was planning to make duck.

He considered calling Trina again, but their last conversation had gotten out of hand.

Simon sipped his Scotch. He didn't plan to go to her classroom last week, but he couldn't get her to reply to any of his calls, and he knew that she'd been struggling lately. It was hard to believe that it had almost been a year since it happened. Anniversaries crept up on a person, baring their teeth and sinking into your soft flesh before you even knew you were in danger.

Joyce knew the date was approaching. They hadn't talked

about it, which was no surprise since they rarely talked about anything unpleasant anymore, but Simon was certain her more regular outbursts were a part of the days ticking down.

Simon paid the check, got up from his seat, and headed outside. He considered smoking one of the cigars he kept in a special case in the pocket of his jacket, but the car he ordered pulled up quicker than expected and he didn't have a chance.

"Good afternoon, Dr. Morgan. Northside hospital?" The driver was a young woman, tucked neatly into a black-and-white uniform with a driving cap sat on top of her dark curls.

"Yes, as quickly as possible." Simon checked his watch. He had surgery in an hour.

CHAPTER FOUR

TRINA

Trina needed a coffee, desperately. Her hands shook as she laid the bills and coins down on the counter for the barista, not wanting to log on later and see her credit card balance growing even more grotesque.

How did Liz know about Simon? Had he come poking around her department, sticking his nose in like a dirty fish and ignoring the boundaries they'd set once upon a time? Simon looked dapper, commanding. He could have passed himself off as a fellow professor. Or administrator. His three-piece suits and delicate hands.

She took a sip and waited for the surge of caffeine to bring her back to baseline. Class had been abysmal, her information disjointed and careless despite her best attempts to bring it together the few hours before. Some students left in the middle, and she ended thirty minutes early.

Trina took another sip and scanned her surroundings. Campus was small, even for a private school, and she could walk from one side to the other easily in just about ten minutes. A large glen of elms stood watch over the center of campus, and she walked underneath their branches now to drink her coffee and think.

Students were traveling between classes, and Trina let her eyes fall on a group of girls walking arm in arm towards the science building. The middle girl had a bright pink coat, flanked by her two friends in black. It reminded Trina of being that young and carefree, before her shoulders started to hunch from burden instead of adolescent angst.

What she wouldn't give to go back to that time in her life.

Trina caught sight of two other figures walking, the couple not seeming to fit with the rest of the campus traffic. They wore dark coats, but carried none of the sloppiness of students or, alternatively, pert professionalism of professors and staff. White shirts, dark pants, and trim hair for both the man and woman, although Trina could tell the woman had hers pulled back into a tight bun. Nobody wore their hair like that anymore, not even librarians or gymnasts.

She stood up and started walking away, because Trina was certain these two were police officers and they'd trained their eyes on her. Simon was right—it was getting close to the anniversary. Perhaps they were opening the case again, or they had a lead. She'd always felt it was more than a freak accident.

Maybe that was why these police officers were here.

But why ambush her on campus? Why not set up an appointment? Trina's phone was drying out at her apartment, but she could still get notifications on her laptop, which she'd just closed down in her classroom a few minutes ago. Something roiled in Trina's gut. She wasn't about to stick around and find out. After everything with Tom had come to nothing, she'd lost her trust in the police's ability to do anything besides bring further misery into her life.

Trina's heels clicked along the sidewalk, making a tattoo that echoed along the path leading out of the elms. But she was too late.

"Professor Dell," the female officer called out. "Wait a moment, would you?"

Trina clutched at her bag and walked faster for a few seconds before turning and facing them.

"Are you lost?" she asked them. She tried to push for an open expression but felt her mouth pucker unattractively instead.

"I'm Officer Kirkpatrick and this is Officer Bechdel, Summitville PD. Do you have a few minutes?" The male officer's eyes were a vibrant green.

"I was just heading back to my office," she lied.

"We can talk there," Bechdel said.

"I'd rather not." Trina took a sip of her coffee. Her hand no longer shook.

"Where were you Sunday night?" Kirkpatrick had taken out a notebook and flipped it to a clean page, pen poised like a Boy Scout.

"I was at a wedding. And a few other places." Her heart scudded inside her ribs.

A few people drifted by, casting longer glances at the trio. Trina caught the eye of one woman, who quickly turned her head and walked on.

"Did you meet a man named Dermot Carine?"

"I don't know that name."

Bechdel pulled out her phone. "Do you recognize him?"

Staring back at Trina was the man from Sunday night, smiling in a bright orange T-shirt with a waterfall in the background. It was a standard profile picture, all sunshine and big smiles.

"What's happened?" Trina asked.

"Do you know this man?"

"He was at the wedding. We danced a little." Trina shifted her bag to her other shoulder. "It's hard to remember."

"Had you been drinking?" Bechdel asked.

"It was a wedding." Trina forced herself to breathe. "What is this all about?"

"Maybe it'd be better if we talked at the station?" Kirkpatrick gestured with his arm vaguely towards somewhere behind him, and Trina's mind skittered along to wondering where they'd parked. Would they need to ride the bus in from the commuter lot too?

"No, that's not necessary. What happened to him? Why does it matter that I danced with him on Sunday?"

"Do you go to a lot of weddings?" Bechdel asked.

A dark pit formed in her stomach. Two cops wouldn't come to find her and ask questions about the last man she slept with just because he had outstanding parking tickets. Something was terribly wrong.

"This conversation is over." Trina started to walk off in the direction of her office, craving the quiet dark of her own space.

"Don't you want to know if he's all right?" Bechdel's voice came white hot across the sidewalk.

Trina kept moving, at first swallowing the response that rose in her throat.

"You wouldn't be here if he was," she blurted out over her shoulder, the wind chafing her voice on its edges.

Tom had always loved her spark. It was the reason he'd left with Trina at the party all those years ago, even though he had a girlfriend (one who he quickly broke up with to be with Trina). A bunch of high-school friends had come back together on a break from college for the party, and Trina couldn't stand the fact that the nastiest guys in high school were still making anyone they didn't like feel small. When they tried to pull the pants down of one guy who was back from his full scholarship at Carnegie Mellon for engineering but was still painfully shy—Trina wasn't sure why he'd come that night—she couldn't stand it. She shoved one of the offenders into the pool and emptied the slew of half-empty Solo cups on the counter over the other three. Tom had loved it. Meanwhile, his girlfriend was a girl Trina knew from high school who stood by and defended the popular guys, saying they were just having fun.

It might be why Trina sought out frat-boy bros now for one-night stands. Like somehow being around them might conjure Tom back.

But her "spark" also translated into Trina having trouble controlling her impulses.

Which was the reason the police were looking for her in the first place.

CHAPTER FIVE

JOYCE

She'd take the car home. Simon didn't need it, didn't deserve it.

Joyce pulled out into traffic and settled into the soft leather seat, wrapping her coat tight around her shoulders. She kept picturing her husband's face across the table, that hang-dog expression he got when something didn't go his way. Joyce used to think it was cute, back when they were in college and he'd hang around outside her classes. She was always one of the last students out because she liked to ask the professors questions after lecture rather than during—she'd been a bit shy back then— and Simon would get upset sometimes, waiting for her to finish up.

Joyce pulled into their long driveway, hearing the satisfying crack of pebbles under the tires as she turned off the main road.

Clara was inside vacuuming when Joyce arrived home. Joyce went into the kitchen and set the kettle to boil. She and Clara liked to have a tea and a chat on Monday afternoons, catching up on their weekends and reminding each other about the various dramas of their lives. Joyce didn't know if she could call Clara a friend, because she paid her to be there in a way, but it was the closest relationship Joyce had with another woman.

Simon had suggested at one point that she might be friends with Trina. Joyce could barely stomach the thought.

Joyce already had her hobbies. She didn't need more friends.

It was coming up on a year now, and Joyce remembered how last year the biting cold crept into her bones after the accident and wouldn't leave her until forced to by the obscene heat of summer. She'd stand by the fire, or soak in a scalding bath, but she'd still shake from the chills that wracked her body. All she would feel was the bite of ice on her skin.

"Is the tea ready?" Clara stood in the doorway to the kitchen, her maid's uniform fitting neatly against her round hips and sharp waist. Clara told Joyce once that, back in Croatia, she'd been a dancer in a nightclub. Her parents threatened to disown her, but she'd made enough money with her waspish figure to manage to leave and move to the US. Now a grandmother, she still had the same silhouette and Joyce found herself wishing she hadn't trained her body into boyish thinness.

"Almost. I bought some strudel from Straufmann's." Joyce set down a plate of the pastry on the round dining table in the eat-in portion of the kitchen. Not that she'd eat any of it, but Clara enjoyed a sweet treat with her tea.

"Tell me about your day." Clara settled herself in one of the chairs, crossing her feet at the ankles like a debutante.

Joyce poured the tea. Her phone thrummed in her purse on the counter, but she didn't move to get it. She knew it was probably Simon, calling for an apology for how she acted at lunch. She'd give him one, but not yet.

"Not much to report," Joyce said.

Clara took a sip of tea, her face expectant.

"What is it?" Joyce poured a dash of milk into her cup to mix with the Earl Grey. Drinking from the delicate porcelain, the heat of the tea snaked its way pleasantly down through her chest.

"The police stopped by earlier today." Clara said it as though it were a confession.

"Why was that?" Joyce forced herself to ask the question, and then followed up with, "Has one of our neighbors been robbed?"

"No, nothing like that. They were asking about a woman." Clara paused. "*The* woman."

"Trina," Joyce said, and Clara nodded in confirmation.

"She's gotten herself into some other kind of trouble. They wouldn't say specifically, and I was lucky they even mentioned her name when they were here. But they asked if you or Mr. Morgan were home, and I told them you were both out, and then I demanded—oh yes, I demanded—" Here, Clara balled her hand into a fist and set it firmly on the table, fixing her eyes on Joyce. She had very little traces of her accent left, but it came out in softer vowels and clipped consonant pairs when she got frustrated or angry. "I demanded to know if any of it had to do with *that* woman, and they wouldn't confirm anything but they also wouldn't say it wasn't about her. That's how I knew she was coming back into your life."

Simon was always a fool in that way. He thought he could save the world, when he couldn't even take care of himself. He never should have stopped that day to help Trina. Joyce could picture exactly what he'd said when she'd gone to him at the hospital to find him slouched on a gurney, his shirt soaked in blood and holding his head in his hands.

"I thought I could help." Simon's shoulders shuddered as he collapsed into sobs. Joyce held him, her heart going out to her husband, her dear friend in so many ways. But she'd also spoken to the police before going to Simon, where she was told Simon had killed his patient. That he'd done something wrong while trying to save the young man.

"Did they leave a card?" Joyce asked.

Clara reached into the pocket of her white apron and

produced a business card printed on cheap cardstock, the police department insignia stamped in the top left.

"They asked you or Mr. Morgan to call and set up a time to talk."

Joyce snatched a piece of strudel and took a huge bite. The sugar icing mixed with the cherry filling, flavor exploding in her mouth.

She knew what to do now.

Joyce took another bite, finishing the entire piece and licking her fingers afterwards.

CHAPTER SIX

LAURA

"What's the name again?" the woman asked.

"Dermot Carine," Laura repeated. It was the fifth time she'd called, but the first time someone picked up. A keyboard clattered in the background.

They wouldn't let her see the body, let alone take it home, which was absurd because she was the closest to family Dermot had. He'd listed her as his emergency contact, which was why she got the call early Monday morning from the police.

Laura leaned against the thin windows in the trailer and looked out at the bare woods. It was finally cold enough outside today that the creek might freeze over.

"Oh, here it is. Do you have the name of the funeral home we're sending him to?"

"Can't I just come and pick him up?" Something heavy pressed on Laura's chest, and she balled her fist and pushed into the center to try and relieve the pressure. Laura hadn't been told anything about a funeral home.

"No, honey," the woman explained patiently. "You can't just come and take his body. He needs to go somewhere people know how to prepare him." Laura wasn't used to people being so kind to her. Except for Dermot.

Who was dead.

Laura heard a thump come from the bedroom. Terry must be up. She balanced the phone on her shoulder and plugged the coffee maker in. She'd put the grounds in last night, so it'd be ready in the morning.

"I've never been to a funeral home before," Laura said. Two years ago, her sophomore chemistry teacher had a massive coronary in the teachers' lounge and Dermot had offered to take her to the calling hours at the funeral home, but she'd said no. The idea of seeing Mr. Kimble when he wasn't Mr. Kimble anymore made her queasy.

"I can give you a few names and numbers," the woman at the morgue said. She paused. "If you can't afford it, you can have him cremated. That's a lot less expensive. Or if you can't do that, the hospital will take care of things, but you won't be able to bury him."

Terry came into the main room of the trailer, shirtless and scratching at his crotch. "Where's my coffee?"

"I'm on the phone," Laura mouthed, but Terry ignored her and gave a huge yawn, moving past her to grab the creamer from the fridge.

He was like a scraggly dog, her brother. He'd been doing his twelve steps, staying off the booze and pills for the most part, but what Laura had discovered was that her brother was still an asshole even when he wasn't drinking and getting high.

"Can I get those names?" Laura asked the woman, grabbing a pen and pad of paper courtesy of Courtyard Marriott. Sometimes she brought toilet paper or fresh towels home from work too. She'd stopped taking the mini shampoos when her friend, Rosie, almost got fired for doing the same thing.

There were three options she'd have to call before her shift at the hotel started.

The woman explained that the funeral home would handle transferring the body.

"So I won't have to call here again?" Laura asked.

Terry flopped onto the faded navy sofa and turned on the television. It blared one of the local channels, which had a morning show on. Two women in soft pastels and matching glossy haircuts sat chatting at a table. And then Dermot's face was smiling back at Laura from the screen. It was the picture they'd taken when they went hiking together at Blue Falls Creek.

"No, honey. You won't."

"Okay, thank you." Laura hung up, slipped the phone into her back pocket, and stood at the back of the sofa watching as the morning show cut to another reporter holding a microphone in front of a building.

In front of the Marriott.

"The body of a young man was found dead in one of the hotel rooms at the Courtyard Marriott on Sunday. The police are saying little about the case, but it has been reported that the man's name is Dermot Carine, a twenty-five-year-old social worker from Beacon Hill. Sources indicate foul play appears to be involved. We'll be keeping you updated on this story as more information materializes."

"Who the hell were you talking to? And either sit down or fry some eggs up for me. You're making me nervous just standing back there." Terry took a huge swig of coffee.

"They're talking about Dermot." Laura couldn't believe she needed to explain this to her brother.

"Who the hell is Dermot?" Terry gave a thin smile.

"Stop it." Laura's instinct was to reach out and slap him, but she still had bruises from their last fight, and she didn't have the time or the endurance to do it again.

"I'm glad he's dead," Terry said.

"Stop it." Laura forced herself to walk away. She pulled the accordion door for the bathroom and flipped the lock. She made it to the toilet before the sob leaked out of her body.

Dermot was too young, too kind, too handsome to be dead. She'd just seen him Sunday morning, smiling over her at the diner in town where they liked to meet for lunch or sometimes just a milkshake.

Another image of Dermot popped into her mind, but Laura pushed that one away. She couldn't handle that. Not now, not with Terry shouting at her like some wench and nothing to look forward to other than her cigarette break after cleaning up other people's piss off toilet seats.

She'd call the funeral homes on her break from work today. Laura had a little money saved up in an account at the credit union Terry didn't know about. She'd been stupid after their parents died and put Terry as joint account holder on her original savings and checking account, which he'd drained to buy booze and pot.

Laura couldn't stand to think about Dermot's body being burned up into ash. Or worse, burned up and mixed with other unclaimed dead people at the county morgue.

She let the sob come again, hard and fresh through her body. She'd had plenty of practice learning how to make her pain silent. The TV blared on in the living room, some happy jingle wrinkling the air in the trailer.

The reality landed on Laura for the first time. Dermot wasn't just dead. He'd been murdered. Burying him wouldn't be the end of it.

The police would be coming, asking questions. Sniffing around the trailer, judging her life.

She had to get her story straight.

Terry shouted from the living room. "What's wrong? Do you have the shits? And where are those eggs?"

"Coming." Dermot was supposed to be her ticket to a better life.

Laura flushed the toilet. The cheap mirror above the sink made her look old, her skin dishwater grey.

All of this was so incredibly awful, because Laura was fairly certain of one thing more than any other: Dermot Carine could hurt her more now that he was dead than he had when he was alive.

CHAPTER SEVEN

TRINA

Trina poured herself a tumbler of vodka and slugged it down, the liquor a hot flash in her throat. Her phone sat in the container of rice on the counter. A satisfying sprinkle of grains tumbled over the counter as she pulled it out. She powered her phone on, the screen brightening after a few seconds of indecision.

The notifications came accordioned, one on top of the other. Two calls from Simon. Five texts from him. Nothing from the police.

Trina scrolled through. She had a voicemail from Monica.

"Call me as soon as you get this. It's not good."

They'd met at a tedious wedding that was trying way too hard to be classy—a jazz band and chocolate cheesecake instead of wedding cake and cookies. No one was dancing, and the bar was only white wine and lite beer. Monica spotted Trina leaning on the bar and sidled up to her like an old friend, whiskey on her breath and her dark tendrils pulled into a half-up chignon with a dragon-tipped spike thrust through the knot of hair. The dragon had fake ruby eyes that glowed under the fluorescent lights of the hotel ballroom. "Want to get out of here?" she'd asked Trina, and when Trina demurred, explaining that she wasn't into women, Monica laughed hard and loud, explaining to the surrounding guests desperately trying to get drunk on room temperature Coors Light that neither was she, "but she'd gladly try if it meant leaving this corpse of a party." Monica liked to search out parties, too, although she was braver than Trina with seeking out bar mitzvahs and retirements, anniversaries and family reunions. She worked in insurance, somewhere beige and bloodless. That's how she'd described it when Trina asked her over tequila shots at the bar they went to after the wedding. That's why she went out to parties: Looking for blood.

Monica picked up on the second ring.

"Where have you been?" Her voice sounded stretched. "This is crazy."

"My phone broke." Trina looked at her empty glass, and then shoved it and the bottle away from her. The glass skidded along the counter and fell onto the kitchen tile, smashing as it hit the floor. Trina stood still, aware of small shards of glass near her stockinged feet. "I just got back from campus. Two detectives cornered me while I was walking after class."

"They called me at work. I have no clue how they even know we're friends."

"What were they asking you?"

"About your weekend. About what you usually do on Sunday nights. They wanted to know if you drank, if you did any 'recreational' drugs." Trina could hear the quotes as Monica said the word "recreational."

"What did you tell them?" Trina drank, sure, but she didn't use drugs. Well, except for some high-end pot she smoked by herself after a long day of grading. Or just a long day.

"I didn't tell them anything. I didn't even admit I knew you."

"So you hung up on the police?" Trina was incredulous. The option never occurred to her. She should have walked away, without a word, today on campus when they cornered her.

"No. I stayed on the line and told them 'no comment' for everything."

"You've got balls." Trina was impressed.

"Let's just say it's not the first time I've been questioned by the police." Monica sighed. "Are you going to tell me what's going on?"

Trina explained what they'd asked her, about the guy she met at the wedding and the picture the cops showed her from his social media profile. "I don't know what happened to him, but I swear to you, he was fine when I left his hotel room last night."

"I know," Monica replied. Trina heard some voices in the background, and then the click of a door closing. "You'd never hurt anyone."

Trina paused, thinking about what to tell her friend next, but Monica pushed on. "Look, I've got people coming in for a meeting. I have to go in a sec, but I'll call you later, okay? Everything's going to be fine. Just don't talk to the police without a lawyer. I know a good one through a client—I'll text you her details."

"Thank you," Trina told her friend. "This is all surreal. I don't know what to make of it all."

"I'm here to help." There was rustling, and Trina heard Monica give a muffled, "Be right there."

"Look, I've got to go. I'll text you that number."

Trina hung up. A few moments later her phone pinged with a contact for a Blanche Grainger, Esq. The name sounded moneyed, and Trina thought of the dwindling account in her checking, and the nonexistent savings account she'd never started.

How was she going to afford a lawyer, with no money or connections? With Monica a low-level insurance agent, as her closest friend? God, she wished she had a rich uncle or even a gainfully-employed sister to fall back on. That she wasn't alone, almost on unpaid probation from work, hobbling along from one day to the next without anything to look forward to but the hot bite of cheap gin and the touch of a stranger's sweaty palms on her waist while the deejay blasted the extended version of "YMCA".

And of course that's when her mind went to Simon.

But Trina hated herself for it. Hated herself for even thinking it.

She went to her freezer and pulled out a fresh bottle of gin. A glass lay on the counter and Trina couldn't tell if it was clean or not. She poured a slug and swallowed it in one desperate movement.

Then she dialed his number. Because what else could she do?

———

She had papers to grade. And bills to pay. Men to fight. Police to avoid. Trina felt like a terrible country song, twangy and tuneless.

Simon didn't pick up when she called. After weeks of tracking her down, coming to her place of work and interrogating her students, now Simon was avoiding her.

Trina threw the phone on the counter. She was tempted to go online and read the news, but she couldn't risk the fear inside her chest swallowing her whole.

Broken glass glinted from the floor, and so she grabbed a dustpan and broom from the closet and swept up her mess, tipping it all into the trash can. She threw on her coat and headed out the door, not sure where she was going but needing to get out of the close air of her apartment. One of her neighbors was closing their door down the hallway, and Trina ducked her head inside her coat's hood to avoid catching their eye. She'd caught a glimpse of herself in her hallway mirror before leaving. Mascara streaked under her eyes like two bruises, hair scraggly and unbrushed, and her skin was dull from drink and stress and lack of happiness. But she couldn't stay inside. She needed to get out.

At the street she turned left and headed to the End Zone. The name suggested it was a sports bar, but it wasn't, except for the small TV in the corner that was always showing some sporting event on low volume. Otherwise, it was all dark wood and red curtains and good liquor with some sort of shipwreck theme that Trina could never really place. The bartenders were aloof yet friendly, and the other drinkers left Trina alone, which was the best kind of bar as far as she was concerned.

Tom never liked bars, and before he died Trina had never really spent time in one. After they started dating in college, it never became part of their routine with their social circle. They were more of the board games and dinner party crowd. They'd gone to a few bars when they were on vacation, mainly to check out the food flagged as really good on one of the apps Tom liked to read through when they traveled. But Trina never bellied up to a bar—she'd never felt the need to—until she lost Tom.

Trina didn't bother to glance at her watch when she stepped in. There was a quiet murmur inside, with a few groups of drinkers scattered around the small bar tables, and three lone men sat separately at the bar, wide spaces between them. Trina slid into the farthest stool on the corner and ordered a whiskey neat.

About to settle into her drink, Trina heard someone call her name as though they were happy to see her. She felt like garbage and would prefer to sink into some small slice of oblivion.

"I thought that was you!" Trina recognized Addy, her teaching assistant from last semester flagging her down. It had been a rough semester, in part because their work styles were decidedly different from each other. In other words, Addy was a woman in her late twenties unbruised by the world and on top of her shit, and Trina was a decade older and drowning underneath everything life had thrown at her so far. They hadn't gotten along very well, and in the end there was a formal reprimand threatened because of an email Trina sent where she *might* have implied Addy was purposefully trying to turn her students against her.

So why was Addy acting as though she was happy to see Trina in the middle of the afternoon at a crappy bar? Trina watched Addy stumble over to her, her high-heeled ankle boots catching on one of the seams in the floor. Addy fell over, catching herself on a bar table. There was a rip in her black tights that snaked its way up her thigh.

Addy was drunk. Very drunk.

"Oh my God it's *so good* to see you." Addy slouched onto the bar stool next to Trina. Looking around, Trina spotted a few other familiar faces gathered in a booth in the back corner. Graduate students in the department huddled together in their dark designer-knock-off coats and cheap beers.

Trina gave the group in the corner a nod, as they all watched the scene between her and Addy unfold. The bartender, a grey-haired man with a squinty eye, came over and set another shot down in front of Trina. "From the kids over there," he said, knocking his head back at an angle to indicate the grad student crowd.

"I didn't know people from campus came here," Trina said to Addy, because she wasn't sure what to say.

"You're from campus." Addy smiled and a hiccup burst out of her mouth. "And I am too."

"Fair point." Trina downed the shot and stood up to get the hell out of there. This was the last thing she needed right now.

"I defended my dissertation today." Addy threw her arms up in the air in triumph. "I passed!"

"Congratulations." Trina couldn't bring herself to give the standard response of calling Addy by her new title of "Dr. Simpson." She remembered when she passed her defense. How she thought that meant she'd achieved everything she could have ever dreamed of. She had Tom, she had her Ph.D., she had a great job lined up. Life was working out, one achievement racked up at a time.

Trina thought she might burst out in a sob. She threw some money on the counter and headed for the door.

"Wait!" Addy cried out. "I wanted to tell you something. That's why I came over here. It's important."

The last words smeared together in Addy's mouth.

When Trina passed her defense, Tom took her out to dinner at the burger joint across from their apartment. They ate fries and greasy cheeseburgers with chocolate shakes. It had been the perfect way to celebrate.

"I have to go." Trina pushed past Addy, but the young woman reached out and grabbed Trina's arm.

"You're in trouble," Addy said, her eyes steady and fixed on Trina. "There are lots of rumors going around the department."

Trina's brain was starting to cloud with the alcohol she'd drank so quickly. Was it the rumor that she was going to be fired? Or that the police were asking her questions down in the quadrangle at the center of campus?

"I know," Trina said. She reached over and gently moved Addy's hand.

"Dermot was a good guy," Addy told her. Trina's heart thudded against her chest.

"I didn't know his name," Trina said, before slipping out the door and into the cold air of the afternoon. The *was* of Addy's statement held firm in Trina's mind. Her head hummed from the whiskey and the stress and the knowledge that fucking Dr. Addy Simpson knew more than Trina realized.

CHAPTER EIGHT

JOYCE

"Should I make a fire?" Joyce asked her husband. Simon nodded, and the two of them sat down in the leather wingbacks in their library, a glass of Scotch in his hand and a fire poker in hers. Of course, that wasn't what Joyce was really asking. What she was really asking was whether they could draw a line, between the end of this day and the beginning of the next. Were they safe for now, nestled against the cold, dark night until morning came?

Joyce wanted confirmation that all that would be demanded of her now until sleep was a simple order of concrete tasks: place the fuel on the hearth, strike the match, rearrange the logs to keep the light and heat coming. That she could sit quietly with her love and know that—in this moment—he'd chosen her.

"Gary seemed a little off, don't you think?" Simon said.

They'd had the Worthers over for dinner. Joyce made roast duck with new potatoes and asparagus. Chocolate torte for dessert with raspberries and cream. Gary and Erica hadn't stayed for after-dinner drinks, begging off that the weather was turning and roads would be icy.

It occurred to Joyce that they were getting older, she and her husband and their friends, and that icy walkways were becoming more than just an inconvenience, but something to be accounted for and planned around.

"Their granddaughter has been sickly for some time. I know it's weighing on them," she replied.

"Of course." Simon took a sip of his drink, thoughtful. They both stared into the fire. Joyce loved the glow that it cast on the well-appointed room, with the tall shelves of books emerging from the shadows in the warm light of the fire. Simon looked younger by the fire, less worn. He was only in his shirtsleeves now, his jacket discarded somewhere between the dining room and their own after-dinner libations. She loved his hands, his long fingers so capable and strong. How many lives had they saved, she wondered? What magical precision had they been taught that could stop death in its tracks?

"What are you thinking about?" he asked her, and Joyce paused because they didn't speak to each other that way. Their thoughts were often their own. Just another reason their conversation at lunch was out of character for them.

Joyce should have stopped herself from asking.

Her mother's voice rang in her head. *Don't ask questions you don't want the answers to.*

She decided to be honest with him.

"I was thinking about your work. About all the people you've helped."

She looked up at Simon, allowing their eyes to meet. They hadn't spoken about their lunchtime disagreement, nor were they likely to.

His face shifted subtly in the firelight, and Joyce thought she spotted a flash of pleasure.

"I had a surgery this afternoon. Gall bladder."

"I know," Joyce replied. Simon took a long pull from his drink and rearranged himself in the chair, crossing his legs.

"I shouldn't have been in the operating room today."

"Of course you should have." The bite in Joyce's voice didn't surprise her or Simon. "Your patient is doing well, aren't they? They benefited from your care."

"Yes, but so many things could have gone wrong." Simon held out his hand, and both of them looked at the noticeable tremor. "It's getting worse."

Joyce remained silent. There wasn't much she could say that Simon didn't already know.

"I want to talk about what happened today," he said, standing up from his chair and turning his back to her as he faced the fire.

Something icy pulled at the back of Joyce's neck. "You want to talk about the fact that you were drinking at lunch, even though you had a surgery scheduled in the afternoon? What's there to say?"

Even Joyce hated herself as she said that. She was being cruel, poking at Simon in his weakest spots. Avoiding the intimacy he seemed to be seeking out in her tonight.

But that was the rub about letting someone see your soft underbelly—it made you vulnerable. And to expose herself to her husband was the worst vulnerability of all. Joyce had learned that the hard way.

She shouldn't have drunk wine at lunch, in lieu of eating her entrée. She'd started something that she wasn't ready to see through.

She waited for Simon to respond. The fire crackled, and Joyce reached for the poker to stir the logs into a deeper burn.

"You know that's not what I mean," Simon finally said, still not looking at her. "I want to talk about Trina. I want to talk about why you're so *obsessed* with how I feel about her."

The emphasis Simon placed on the word "obsessed" startled Joyce. Even though she couldn't see him, she could tell his teeth were clenched, the muscles of his jaw pulling the back of his neck tight.

She so desperately wanted to kiss that soft skin below his

hairline. Joyce wished she could use her body like she once had, to place her claim on her husband without the risk of rejection.

Right now, though, she couldn't bring herself to even reach out and touch his arm. Instead, she stared at the perfect seams of his exquisitely-made shirt. Money can buy so many things. Comfort, style, reputation.

And yet it was worthless where it really counted.

"I don't want to talk about that."

"Why?" Simon countered.

"Because it's irrelevant. I'm not obsessed with her. You're not obsessed with her. She's out of our life. Isn't she?" Joyce was testing him, and they both knew it.

"Then why bring up what you did at lunch today? Why storm off like some spurned lover, embarrassing me in front of all those people?"

"I'd had too much wine and not enough lunch. It didn't mean anything." She found herself shrugging her shoulders, even though Simon was still turned away from her.

Joyce moved to put the poker back on its hanger along the side of the hearth, but Simon's hand jutted out and snatched at her wrist. It had been months since she'd felt his skin on hers, and that was an accident when they'd brushed past each other in the kitchen, grabbing at cups and saucers while entertaining some other couple. Perhaps the Worthers. She couldn't remember. All she did remember was how her hand had brushed against Simon's, and the electricity it still struck deep inside her chest.

So much had changed, but Joyce still wanted her husband more than any other man. More than anything, if she were going to be honest with herself. Something which didn't come as naturally to her anymore.

"Let go," she told Simon now. Every piece of her wanted to scream the opposite.

"No." He moved to face her. "I won't let go. Not until you tell me that you'll stop this. That you'll stop letting Trina come between us."

"I can't promise that."

With his free hand, Simon yanked the poker from Joyce's hand. She couldn't get a purchase on the smooth metal of the handle, and it slid almost effortlessly from her grip.

He stood in front of her. The fire framed his broad shoulders and cast his face into shadow. Joyce had always loved the fact that her husband was so much larger than her, that he could consume her in his embrace if he wanted to.

Simon pulled Joyce closer to him, and their lips almost met. She felt his hot breath on her skin. He smelled of whiskey and the expensive cologne she'd bought him for their last anniversary, bergamot and sandalwood. She wondered what she smelled like to him.

Desire.

Fear.

Despair.

"Yes, you can." He kissed her, and at first she didn't respond to his insistent searching with his tongue. But then she felt the metal of the poker balanced against her thigh as it hung from Simon's other hand, and she decided she'd pushed him enough for one day.

She kissed her husband back. Hungry, unfamiliar and yet so ingrained in physical memory that their movements felt choreographed by some outside force.

They made love, there by the fire. Half-dressed and spent afterwards, Simon traced Joyce's chin with his hand. "Tell me you love me."

"I love you more than anything in this world."

He nestled into her body, wrapping his arms around her. "I love you, too."

It wasn't until the middle of the night, with the fire burned down and the air turned cold, that Joyce awoke to hear her husband crying softly by her side.

CHAPTER NINE

TRINA

One of her neighbors used to pound on Trina's door in the middle of the night. Trina knew he struggled with a psychotic disorder and if he forgot to take his medication while his mother was out working the swing shift at the hospital he'd often grow paranoid and violent. Trina'd talk him down, call his mother—Darlene—and try to get him back into bed without calling the cops. Sometimes Tom would have to carry him. It wasn't until a few months ago that Darlene asked Trina to give her spare key back. That one had smarted, but Trina understood Darlene's rationale. It had been raining outside and Trina was already a little drunk, but she was out of liquor somehow through faulty planning, and all she could picture as she slumped against the edge of the couch, propped up by her coffee table, was the gleaming liquor cart Darlene kept for an after-shift tipple. Trina was planning on buying more for them, it was just a borrowing, really, but the fact remained that she'd let herself into their apartment without invitation, stole from them, and managed to vomit on their front rug before making her exit.

Tuesday morning Trina awoke to banging on her apartment door, and although she knew in all likelihood it was the police and not Darlene's son, she still had a small hope her intuition was wrong.

Trina wrapped Tom's scruffy robe around her body, cinching it tight at her waist, and peered through the peephole. Two sets of scrutinous eyes peered back. Kirkpatrick sipped at a Styrofoam coffee cup and Bechdel stared back all sleek and rosy-cheeked from the cold.

Dammit.

"Professor Dell, can we come in?" Bechdel asked.

Trina glanced at herself in the hallway mirror. Her hair was wild, all random spikes and matted patches. She hadn't taken her makeup off last night before she passed out from cheap wine and too little Chinese take-out she'd ordered after leaving the End Zone. Mascara streaked across her face like a one-hit pop star. She wiped her face with the sleeve of her robe and opened the door a crack.

"It's early. I'm not even dressed yet." She cracked open the door and gestured to her robe, self-conscious now of the flimsy camisole and bed shorts she had on underneath. Her feet were bare, and a shiver ran up her legs from the damp floor.

"This will only take a moment of your time," Kirkpatrick said, moving fluidly through the crack in the door and settling himself on the couch. Bechdel followed, not making any effort to conceal her assessment of Trina's apartment.

Trina tried to see it from their eyes. Empty bottles askew on the coffee table, half-empty take-out containers open in a little sad tableau of her evening the night before. A spotless, unused kitchen, bare walls with patches that showed something important used to hang there. The smell of food left out too long and a bed slept in too many times without washing.

No one had been to her apartment in a long time, not even Monica. Trina pushed down the natural feeling of embarrassment, reminding herself that politeness would get her nothing in the end. How many people had incriminated themselves simply due to their unconscious desire to have people in authority *like* them?

And despite herself, Trina asked if they'd like some coffee or tea. Kirkpatrick wiggled the cup in his hand, and Bechdel declined with a curt nod.

Trina sat down on the lilac easy chair she'd inherited begrudgingly from her mother. The two detectives had already taken the couch, settling on opposite ends. Kirkpatrick took out his notebook, somehow balancing his coffee on his lap.

Trina thought about suggesting he set it on the table in front of him but caught herself.

She waited.

"We were wondering if you remembered anything further from last Sunday night?" Bechdel asked. The detective sat forward. She clasped her hands in front of her as she leaned her elbows on her knees.

"Anything further?" Trina asked. "I don't recall sharing much about my Sunday night with you in the first place."

Kirkpatrick spoke up. "You attended a wedding. You'd been drinking. You recognized the victim, Dermot Carine, although you stated you didn't know his name."

"Victim?" Trina asked.

"Dermot Carine is dead." Bechdel didn't shift a muscle.

Trina swallowed. Guilt rolled over her like a mist. She remembered thinking of him as desperate. His blubbery mouth and sweaty underarms.

"What does this have to do with me?"

"We think you might have been one of the last people to see Dermot alive." Kirkpatrick took a swig of his coffee. "You went to his hotel room with him, after leaving the wedding together. Witnesses state that the two of you kissed outside the banquet hall entrance."

A pounding started in Trina's neck and worked its way up to her temples. "What are you asking me?"

"When was the last time you saw Dermot Carine?"

Trina pictured Dermot spread out on the hotel bed, naked, his one leg askew in a way that looked uncomfortable. She'd cut herself on the edge of the broken champagne glass. Just a scratch, really, but had they found traces of her blood in the room? There were already traces of her all over him.

"In his hotel room. We'd... been together. We'd both been drinking. He passed out, and I gathered up my things and went home. He was asleep on the bed when I left."

"You had a good time together?" Bechdel leaned back.

"That's a strange question."

"Let me rephrase it. You and Dermot enjoyed each other's company? You didn't get into a disagreement at some point. You know, sometimes, when people have been drinking, a situation can turn very quickly from good to bad."

Trina felt like she was getting the elementary school public service announcement about the dangers of one-night stands.

"No, there was no arguing. We drank some more champagne, we had sex, and then I left. That was it."

"The champagne bottle wasn't broken, perhaps during a fight?"

"No."

"So, he was alive when you left?"

Trina nodded. "Yes."

The two detectives stood up, surprising Trina. "Thank you, Professor Dell. We'll be in touch if we need anything further."

They headed towards the door, Trina trailing behind them with a sense of whiplash. Something wasn't right about their coming here. This was too easy.

"Just one other thing." Bechdel paused at the threshold to the outer hallway. Trina caught sight of her neighbor, Darlene, walking by with her son's arm crooked through hers. They averted their eyes, but Trina was certain they knew her visitors weren't there on a social visit.

"Would you like us to tell you how Dermot died?"

"What?" Trina wasn't sure how to respond.

"Most people, they have us come by to talk with them about a murder, and the first piece of information they need to know is how it happened. 'How did he die?'"

"You didn't say anything about a murder before." The word slid off Trina's tongue like a slug. *Murder.*

"I suppose I didn't." Bechdel tipped her chin in a quick nod. "We'll be in touch."

The two detectives walked their way down the hallway, two black smudges against the beige anonymity of the apartment building.

Trina closed the door, counting the lies she'd told in her head.

Two. No, three.

It was getting hard to keep track.

CHAPTER TEN

LAURA

Laura cleaned the cheap fake wood of the dresser with a half-hearted swipe of her rag. The family who stayed in the room left her a heartfelt note, written in a child's makeshift handwriting, thanking her for cleaning their room and being such a special person to choose a career in cleaning up the messes of others, but then had forgotten to leave any sort of tip. The card was signed, "Love, The Peterson family", and Laura gave it only a brief glance before adding it to her accumulating bin of trash.

She couldn't afford the cost for a coffin and a burial plot. It was going to cost her two hundred and fifty dollars to cremate Dermot, and then another one hundred dollars for the cheapest urn they had available. A cardboard box was another option, but Laura felt like that wasn't fair to Dermot. He'd spent his life helping other people, especially kids who were struggling, and he deserved better than to end up in a thin paper box.

She hadn't decided where to bury him yet—or his ashes, rather. There was the creek by her trailer, where they'd liked to stand and talk about the future. The large oak tree buried deep on one of their favorite trails with their initials carved into the side, now stretched slightly as the tree had grown. Or maybe she'd just hang on to them for a while, although she'd have to keep it a secret from Terry. He'd be even nastier once he knew Dermot was inside their trailer, if only in carbon form.

She'd learned that from Mr. Kimble, before he'd died. All living organisms are made of carbon. It is the building block of life.

Laura scrubbed the toilet and folded the toilet paper into a tight triangle at the end. She wondered if some carbon was better than others. If what you learned in life was true in science.

Her boss, balding and pudgy-faced Joe, had told everyone at the morning meeting that Room 207 was still off-limits.

"The police haven't released it yet. It's still a…" He'd paused, wiping his forehead with one of the cheap tissues the hotel issued, leaving little bits of paper stuck to his skin. "It's still a *scene of interest* and we're not allowed in there. Do your normal routes, but leave that one alone."

"Who's going to clean it up eventually?" one of the new girls asked.

Laura shouldn't call her a girl, because she had the drawn face of a teen mom in middle-age and a barb-wire tattoo around her neck. Laura was a girl, or should have still been. Dead parents had a way of aging a person. Dermot liked to call her his "Girl Friday." She looked up the reference at the school library one day during lunch. It hadn't been quite what she'd hoped, but she still liked it.

She was always happy to help him with anything he needed. It's when he stopped needing her that things got tricky.

"They have special cleaners who come," Joe had answered, nodding solemnly.

Laura ran the vacuum, trying to find some spark of satisfaction in leaving clean lines on the carpet where animal cracker crumbs had been trampled in. Her back ached and her head throbbed. She'd kill for a moment to sit down and drink a cup of decent coffee.

But whenever she stopped moving or doing, her mind shifted back to that hotel room and what might need to be cleaned up. The parts of Dermot that might still be there, soaked into the sheets or the carpet. Were his fingerprints in dusty black flurries along the edges of a similar TV stand or the headboard of the bed? Had they brought in a black light to see if there was blood or other pieces of him cleaned up, but left behind?

Laura closed the door to the room. She was on the third floor, shuttling her cart between the few occupied rooms. Tuesdays weren't as busy as Mondays, with their turnover from banquets and parties held on the weekends. People didn't really travel to Summitville for the town itself. It was always for someone. Weddings, funerals. Family reunions and anniversary parties.

When Dermot called her Sunday morning to ask if she could slip him the key card for a room at the Marriott, Laura had thought that everything she'd wished for was about to come true. Of course she'd agreed, even though she'd never done it before. Cleaning staff didn't go behind the front desk normally, but there were plenty of opportunities to slip behind and snag a card when whoever was on the desk was hiding out in the back, watching funny videos on YouTube or trolling their ex on Instagram.

Laura met Dermot at the diner—*their* diner—slipping him the key card in a white envelope like they were on some TV show starring Jennifer Garner in disguises. He'd ordered a salad, already dressed up for the wedding. He'd told her it was a work colleague's friend who was trying to flesh out their side of the church, and Dermot had accepted the invite because he knew what it was like to not have family when you needed it. Laura was still in her work uniform, and as she sipped her chocolate milkshake she wished she'd thought ahead enough to bring a change of clothes.

"So why the room?" She'd leaned forward but avoided looking Dermot in the eye.

"I have some special plans for tonight," Dermot said, giving her a wide smile and taking a big bite of his Cobb salad.

"Oh," was all she'd replied.

God, did she regret that "Oh." Maybe things could have been different if she'd said something besides "Oh" when Dermot mentioned the room. Maybe they would have talked more about it, and she wouldn't have shown up that night in her best dress and the six-inch heels she'd borrowed from Rosie, only to see him with that other woman, devouring each other with sloppy mouths and hands as they headed into the room.

Maybe she wouldn't have made a second copy of the key card for herself.

Laura closed the door to the room she'd just cleaned. She pushed her cart forward, passing another woman whose name she didn't know working the other side. Tinny music played from a radio attached to the woman's cart, but the melody was lost on Laura.

She opened the door to the next room, ready to clean up another person's mistakes.

CHAPTER ELEVEN

SIMON

The couple sitting in front of him were not in a good place. After years of observation, Simon was skilled at reading the signs from his well-appointed office at the hospital. One member of the couple, usually the healthy one, would stare at the books lining the floor-to-ceiling shelves and make a comment on one or another title, usually saying they hadn't liked the book as much as the general public had. The other would hold their breath, trying to hide their irritation at their better half's pedantry. It was partly why Simon filled some of his shelves with popular novels and nonfiction, rather than just the standard medical references. At this point in his career, he rarely needed to use them anyway, and it was far more enjoyable for him to sit during his lunch break and page through Ann Patchett's latest contribution rather than review yet another poorly translated and proofread manuscript submitted to a top-tier medical journal hoping to slip through the editorial cracks.

It was an operable tumor, Simon told this couple. Just below the left breast, seated on top of her liver. Followed by chemotherapy, he anticipated she'd do incredibly well and would be back to her normal self in less than a year.

"A year?" her husband said. He was the one who had made the crack about the well-worn David Foster Wallace sitting on Simon's bookshelf. "Are you sure?"

Simon leaned forward in his chair, the satisfying creak of the wood against metal cutting through the air like an accent. He templed his fingers, and for a moment thought of Joyce. She'd kissed his hands last night, palm to tip, with her soft mouth. He didn't deserve her. He knew that, and he hoped she was still trying to convince herself that she didn't know it, too.

"Nothing in medicine, especially with cancer, is definite." He said the word—cancer—although many of his colleagues were superstitious in their own way, using euphemisms like "malignancy," "sickness," and "mutation." "But yes," he continued, "I'm very hopeful your wife will make a full recovery in a short period of time."

She gave a hesitant smile, and Simon felt a flash of joy as he saw her shoulders loosen, unburdened. He would help this woman. This is why he'd begun this work in the first place.

"But a year seems such a long time," the husband said, and then caught himself. "I mean, this is wonderful news." He gave a pleading look to his wife. "I just mean—she'll be needing help for most of that time, won't she? The chemo will make her sick, right? And the recovery from the surgery. I have a golf tournament I'm competing in in March. It was a very difficult spot to get. It's in Palm Springs. We're playing for charity..." He trailed off pathetically.

This wasn't the first time Simon had seen this type of reaction. "Perhaps there's someone that could come and help you?" He looked directly at his patient, not her husband, as he said this. "A parent or sibling?"

Because it's clear from the get-go that you're not going to get anything from this prick you married.

"My sister could come and stay for a little while," she offered.

Her lips pressed themselves into a thin line, and the slump of her shoulders returned.

Her husband leaned away, across the armrest of his chair. His eyes scanned the titles on Simon's shelves.

Simon considered asking him to leave, so he could have a private consult with his patient. "Leave him," he'd say. "Tell him that I was wrong, that you know in your heart you're dying and he deserves to live his life."

But then he saw her reach out her thin hand and grope for her husband's in his lap, and Simon knew it was a lost cause.

They scheduled the surgery for two weeks out. Her sister would come to stay, arriving a few days before. The husband confirmed his reservations at the golf resort, or so Simon assumed he would as soon as he arrived home. Perhaps he'd even do it on the car ride back, asking his wife to drive so he could dial the number.

This is why I drink, Simon thought as he closed his office door behind them.

Well, he corrected himself. *One* of the reasons.

He heard a knock, and Jackson popped his head around the door. "Your two o'clock had to reschedule. Something with a childcare issue."

"What does the rest of my afternoon look like?" Simon asked his assistant.

"A follow-up with Mr. Morris at 3. Consult with a new patient—a Ginny Whitcomb—at 3:30. And then open until tomorrow morning. Your first surgery is scheduled for 6:30am."

"Yes, Hazel Bloom. Pancreatic growth." Simon nodded.

Jackson asked if he needed anything, and Simon thanked him and said he'd be looking over charts in his office until his three o'clock.

Simon scrolled through his phone once the door was closed again and clicked on Trina's voicemail.

She needed money, which was something he could give readily. Joyce wouldn't even know, since he kept an account separate from their joint affairs. Hearing Trina's voice, and that she needed him, was a balm to his chafed sense of self. It had been a difficult trio of surgeries this morning, and he'd promised himself he'd only put cream in his coffee and nothing stronger beforehand. His hands were steady as he headed into the operating room, but his mind betrayed him as he slid his hands into the latex gloves.

Images of Tom, his mouth open and blood pouring down his chest, bloomed in Simon's thoughts and he found himself stumbling towards the patient. A nurse reached out and steadied him with a careful hand, which was humiliating beyond belief. And he hadn't even been drinking that morning.

Tom. Almost a year ago, come next week. It was hard to remember life before that afternoon. Before he'd seen Tom's body wrangled by metal and cement, and before he'd watched Trina's life spiral into a chasm of self-loathing.

Joyce and he couldn't have children. They'd convinced themselves a few decades ago that they in fact preferred it that way.

He reached into his desk, retrieved the flask Joyce had engraved tongue-in-cheek for their tenth anniversary: To sweet beginnings and smooth finishes. It was full of Lagavulin, and he took a hard pull before bringing up Trina's number to call her again.

As he was about to push the button, though, another call flashed across the screen. An unfamiliar number. He answered, as he was in the habit of answering unknowns. Sometimes patients passed around his personal number, which he gave out sparingly but with confidence it wouldn't be abused.

"Dr. Morgan?" The voice was female, clipped and authoritative.

Simon confirmed who he was, curiosity flaring in his chest.

"This is Detective Bechdel with the Summitville Police Department. We'd like to schedule an interview with you."

"Regarding what, exactly?" Simon took another swig.

"Your wife."

CHAPTER TWELVE

JOYCE

Joyce scheduled the appointment with Mamie Van Doren three weeks ago, in the hopes of recruiting her ample third-divorce reserves for the hospital's latest charity venture. Mamie lived on the top of a hill, in a Hitchcockian tower her second husband built as a temple to her fine Scandinavian-etched beauty, if not her aging hips and ankles. Approaching ninety, and only twenty years off her second marriage and letting the ink dry on her third, Mamie had the world come to her when making requests.

Joyce drove herself in the Jaguar, having learned stick as a sixteen-year-old romping around her small Ohio town in her father's old Ford F-150. The car drove like a dream, and Joyce loved the sensation of its purring engine bending to the smallest shift of her hands on the wheel. Inside the car was one of the few places she felt totally in control.

The irony of this position, compared to her husband's, was not lost on her.

Mamie welcomed Joyce at her own door, shooing the aged butler away like a middle-class housewife, which she had been once. Her first marriage began in love, ended in tragedy—a mill town accident too nasty to be described as more than a "gory tangle of blood and bone" (yes, Joyce had looked it up in the library archives)—and a huge payout to Mamie and the other widow involved. With only one child to provide for and a savvy head for investments, Mamie transformed herself from middle class into the elite. Which was exactly why Joyce was here today.

Not for Mamie's money, although that couldn't hurt. Hospitals always needed benefactors. But for information.

"Joyce, you look amazing." Mamie's voice had none of the wobbly tenderness of other nonagenarians. "Especially considering…" She let her insinuation dangle, and Joyce set her coat and purse aside on the gleaming end table and readied herself for the emotional gauntlet ahead.

Mamie led them into her formal drawing room, ensconced entirely in teal and cream like a child's candy.

"Thank you so much, Mamie. It has been an incredibly difficult time lately. This last year, in fact, has been more of a challenge than I could have ever anticipated." Joyce chose a round settee with bold stripes. The back was too far removed, and she shifted to keep her posture upright as she crossed her ankles and folded her hands in her lap.

Mamie nodded solemnly. "Julie Dreyfuss was just here yesterday afternoon—you know her, I believe. Tall, horse-faced, with an obscene sense of humor and too much money to be good at anything?"

Joyce had forgotten how sharp Mamie's bite could be.

"Yes, I know Julie."

"Well, she came over yesterday for a game of gin—and some gin as well, to be honest." Mamie leaned over the tea service the butler brought in moments ago and started to fuss with the tea things. "I'll play mother, yes?" she asked, without really asking. Her white hair sat in a soft cloud of well-managed curls around her head, diamond studs at her ear lobes and a creamy cashmere sweater and teal pedal pushers fit her petite figure well. Her shoes still had a slight heel, which clicked against the parquet floor as they walked from the entrance to their seats.

Joyce didn't have to tell Mamie how she took her tea—the woman remembered everything.

Handing Joyce her cup, Mamie settled into the back of her overstuffed armchair and examined Joyce with a gaze of unmitigated satisfaction.

"So, my dear. Tell me why you're here."

Joyce drank from her cup. The tea was still too hot and burned her tongue, but she fought not to show her gaucheness.

"As you know, the hospital fundraising committee has set a new goal this year, focusing on children's health…" Joyce began, anticipating Mamie's reaction.

"Oh, come now. You haven't come just to persuade me to donate to sick children, have you?" Mamie shook her head and added another cube of sugar to her tea. Catching Joyce's eye, she said, "At my age, what will a little extra sugar—or a little extra gossip—hurt?"

Joyce cleared her throat, hoping to seem uncomfortable with the turn of their conversation.

Mamie waved a hand dismissively. "Let's stop with the whole hand-wringing, 'I didn't come here to discuss these terrible things or ask for your help' nonsense and get down to it. I'm ninety years old. I haven't time left for all this decorum."

Joyce couldn't help but smile. So much of Mamie Van Doren's existence was decorum. Teal and white decorum.

"You're right," Joyce admitted. "I'm here to ask you about something more sensitive than giving money." She paused, and Mamie seemed to have her attention caught as she leaned forward in her chair. "As you know, my husband was involved in a tragic event around this time last year."

Mamie nodded gravely. "It was such a shame. So much awfulness that could have been avoided."

"Well, with the first anniversary approaching, it appears that we have yet to move beyond it as much as I had hoped. The woman whose fiancé died…"

"Catriona Dell. The professor. She isn't doing well, I've heard."

"No, and Simon seems to have taken her on as his own personal crusade. Calls, texts, money offered."

"I've heard nothing about an affair." Mamie offered a look of solidarity.

"But you have heard something?"

Mamie set her tea down. A loud jangle burst from the ancient-looking handset seated on the end table next to Mamie's chair. Holding up a finger to Joyce, she answered it, confirmed that she'd like the cucumber soup and some lightly toasted rye bread for lunch, and then hung up.

Joyce waited expectantly.

"I mentioned Julie Dreyfuss was here yesterday. Her husband is friends with the police commissioner, and when I told her you were coming by this morning, she made a not-so-delicate allusion to a recent police visit to your home."

"I wasn't there when they stopped by," Joyce said coolly.

"There's been a murder. A young, handsome social worker found dead in his hotel room after a wedding. Simply awful. Julie looked it up on her smartphone and showed me his photograph. Such potential, just lost."

Joyce hadn't allowed herself to read or watch the news related to the case yet. She knew once she saw him in the "before" pictures they always used in news reports on violent crimes, healthy and smiling, there'd be no turning back from the path she was on.

Mamie continued. "And it seems that this Catriona was the last person to see him alive. They'd met at the wedding. Apparently she's developed the habit of going to weddings to pick up men for the night. It's all rather sad."

Joyce had also forgotten Mamie's penchant for understatement.

"Why did they come to my home, then?" Joyce asked.

"Well, from my understanding, Julie said they're interviewing all of Catriona's recent contacts. They can access phone records remotely, check emails. Societal media accounts." Mamie corrected herself. "Social media, I mean. Such a strange phenomenon that is. Everyone putting their private lives online until they forget it isn't private anymore." She shook her head.

Joyce glanced at her watch, not really reading the time.

"Thank you so much for the tea, Mamie, but I really must be going."

"I remember the days of committee work." Mamie stood up. "From breakfast to brunch to lunch and barely home in time to change for dinner. It's a wonder I stayed so slim, isn't it?"

"You always look lovely." Joyce bent to kiss both of Mamie's cheeks. As she did, Mamie reached up and gently held Joyce's right wrist.

"Don't let them see you sweat," she told her, her blue eyes intense and clear. "Men only *think* they run the world." And with that, she let go. "Goodbye, Joyce. Come anytime."

Joyce showed herself out, giving a curt nod to the butler who offered her coat and bag.

As she got into the Jag, she tapped a new address into her phone and let the route snake its way along the screen. It would take thirty minutes to get to the Summitville police station. That gave her plenty of time to figure out what she was going to say.

CHAPTER THIRTEEN

LAURA

Terry was prowling around the kitchen when Laura got home from work.

"Why isn't there ever any creamer in this house?" He rummaged around the tin canisters on the counter, which were empty except for the very back one, where Laura kept an emergency pack of cigarettes, condoms, and a small roll of money hidden in an empty tampon box just in case.

Laura wearily pulled out a carton from the shopping bags in her hand. "I picked some up on my way home."

Her car was running on fumes, but they needed groceries. Payday wasn't until Friday, and it was only Tuesday. She'd had to drain her checking account to pay the funeral home a deposit to "care" for Dermot's body, and she didn't want to tell Terry. He'd always hated Dermot, jealous of his good looks and kind heart, Laura thought.

The TV blared out a mid-afternoon game show. The host looked overly tanned with bright white teeth. He was saying something about one of the contestant's love for dogs. Dermot had loved dogs, although he wasn't able to have one himself because he was gone from home too much.

"It wouldn't be fair to the dog," he'd told Laura. She'd thought about getting a dog herself. A big fluffy one with floppy ears and a tail that curled. Then Dermot could visit the pup at her trailer and stay for supper maybe. They wouldn't have to always go out, hiding on the trails in the dark or sitting across from each other at the diner. But Laura also knew Terry wouldn't be good around a dog. He'd love up on it until it was annoying or peed the floor or chewed one of his shoes, and then he'd kick it.

"Thanks," Terry mumbled, taking the carton, hesitating, and then motioning to take the other grocery bags Laura was carrying. Pasta and canned soup and some cereal. She'd heat up some vegetable soup later for dinner. Sometimes, if she was too tired, she'd just eat it cold from the can.

She hadn't had much appetite lately anyway. Everything tasted rotten. Today when she'd walked past the hotel room where Dermot died, she would've sworn she could smell the iron-rich tingle that meant blood.

Terry cracked eggs in a pan and fried up some bologna to go with them. Laura felt like she might throw up. She held a hand up to her mouth, trying to push down the nausea.

"I've got a job interview," her brother announced as the eggs crackled over the high heat. "R&S Market is looking for cashiers and shelf stockers."

Laura took off her coat and tried to make her way to the other side of the trailer, where her small room was sectioned off by another accordion door.

"That means I'll need the car this afternoon."

"That's fine," she said. But then Laura remembered. How could she have forgotten to stop on her way home? Now Terry was sure to find out.

"Can you drop me off in town when you go?" She forced her voice towards sounding careless. "I have a few errands to run. Still." She added the last word pathetically.

"Okay." She felt more than saw Terry shrug as he lifted his

eggs from the pan and slid them onto his waiting bread. The frying bologna was starting to shrink around its casing in the pan, bubbling up in the center like an ulcer.

Terry ate his sandwich while Laura sat on her bed, staring at the peeling pink flower wallpaper that covered the plastic vinyl.

It was starting to get dark outside already, and the dim light angled in. Laura closed her eyes, enjoying the bright fire-bursts of color on the back of her eyelids for a moment.

"Let's go," Terry yelled from the other end of the trailer. She heard plates clattering in the sink, and then the door close and the car start up on its third try. As she got up and passed through the kitchenette, she automatically checked the gas burner was turned off. It was, but sometimes Terry forgot. The thought kept her up at night, that her brother might blow them both up because he made himself a grilled cheese. Sometimes, she'd go outside and turn the propane cylinder off to avoid having to worry.

She could see Terry in the car, banging his hands on the wheel to what she assumed was the classic rock station on the radio—they only got a few stations this far out. She was about to hurry over and pull from her special cache in the canister when a car pulled up outside the trailer.

It had sleek lines like a jungle cat. Its paint coat was so shiny and black it seemed to flow over the frame, and Laura's first instinct was to go out and touch it. Her second instinct was to run.

A woman got out of the car, older than Laura but not old. Maybe in her early thirties? Trim blonde hair, slim, dressed in clothes that were simple but looked luscious under her thick winter coat.

"Hey!" Terry poked his head out of the car's window. "You're blocking me in here."

Her brother's tunnel-vision was forever reliable, Laura thought. If he were like some of the other guys who lived in trailers at the edge of the park, he'd have sized their visitor up as a mark, smoothed his hair, and tried to make her like him.

But not Terry. Terry was a man of principle, if not savvy. And he had an appointment to keep.

Laura opened the door as the woman climbed their cinder-block stairs. "Are you lost?" She tried to say it kindly, but Laura knew her voice had an edge. People like this lady didn't get lost out here.

"I don't think so." She was wearing too much makeup, with kohl-rimmed eyes and chalky foundation, but the woman's eyes were a deep brown and looked up with kindness at Laura. "I'm looking for Laura Taylor. Is that you?"

Laura bit back on the stock response of "Who wants to know?" Terry beat her to it anyway.

The woman turned and gave Terry an appraising look. "I'm sorry to have blocked you in. I can move my car if you need to get going."

Terry stood up out of the car, putting his hands in his pockets. "It's okay. I'll stay right here." He caught Laura's eye, and she gave him a slight nod.

"I'm Susan. I think you knew my brother, Dermot?" she said.

Laura's head spun for a moment.

"Dermot said he didn't have any family." Laura started to close the door.

"We'd been estranged. I was a lot older than him, and when my parents had him I was almost done with high school. I didn't realize what home life was like for him, being alone while my parents were already almost elderly." She paused and gave Laura a long stare. "I know he had a difficult childhood, and that he was trying to make the world better for other kids who were going through that."

"So why are you here?" Laura asked.

"Because a week before he died, I got a letter from him in the mail, telling me about you. After we got the news about his death, I knew that I had to come see you."

Laura paused. Then she extended her arm, waved Terry on, and opened the door wider for Susan. "You'd better come in."

She'd buy the pregnancy test tomorrow.

CHAPTER FOURTEEN

TRINA

Charley's was a dive bar around the corner from the insurance company Monica worked for. Trina's friend was meeting her there in a few minutes. They'd met at Charley's a few times for an after-work drink or a liquid lunch, but always more in a celebratory mood than anything else. Monica wasn't someone Trina went to for drowning her sorrows. She usually preferred to be alone for that, in the dark of her apartment with the curtains drawn and a bottle of wine propped up in her lap.

A brick square with no real charm, Charley's was a drinker's bar. Trina hoped there'd be some booths open in the back, away from the day-drinking crowd of nightshift cleaners, a few doctors and nurses from the MedExpress in the adjoining plaza, and the all-out alcoholics. When she stepped inside, the bar hummed with murmurs from a few groups gathered around the tall bar tables and the droning of a baseball game on the TV hung in the corner. She didn't see Monica yet, so Trina made a beeline for a booth in the deepest corner, away from the jukebox and pool tables.

She wasn't really sure why she was meeting Monica in the first place, except that her friend had insisted they meet in person. Whatever she had to tell Trina couldn't be said over the phone, apparently.

Trina ordered a gin and tonic from the waitress making the rounds. When it arrived, the drink was stronger than she'd anticipated and the large sip she took burned going down her throat, making her cough.

"Can't hold your liquor, huh?" Monica slid into the seat opposite Trina. "And what, you don't order anything for me?"

"I wasn't sure what you'd like." Monica wore a curve-hugging maroon sweater dress that cinched neatly at her waist, knee-high boots, dark stockings, and a fresh blowout of her chestnut hair. "You look gorgeous." Trina couldn't stop herself from rounding her shoulders in a bit, shrinking into herself.

"Thanks. I figured I needed to treat myself after the last few days I've had." Monica sat down and swept her hair over one shoulder. The waitress came over and Monica ordered a Scotch, neat. "Top shelf," she added. "None of that dishwater you keep lower."

"You, by the way, look kind of awful." Monica gave Trina a once-over. "When was the last time you slept?"

"I'm fine." Trina adjusted the neckline on her sweater and ran her fingers through her hair, which she couldn't remember if she'd brushed or not this morning.

Monica's gaze softened. "But maybe I can help." They paused while her drink came, and then Monica settled into her seat, sipping from the short glass.

"I have a friend who used to be a cop," she began. "She went into private security a few years ago, because the money is a lot— and I mean *a lot*—better. But she still keeps in touch with her PD pals and so she has connections. When I got the call from that detective on Monday, I got in touch with my friend to see if she had any information about what was going on with your guy. Want to know what I found out?"

"Of course I do. What the hell is going on?"

Trina leaned forward, keeping her voice low. No one seemed to be noticing them, but still she felt paranoid that perhaps one of the detectives had followed her there. She hadn't felt like her life was her own for so long.

"It looks like this Dermot guy was stabbed with a piece of champagne bottle."

Trina blanched. She remembered swilling from the bottle waiting in his hotel room. She'd thought at the time, through her fog of free wedding drinks, that it'd been a nice touch—the champagne bottle on ice in his room, waiting for her.

Now, looking back, she wasn't so sure.

"They haven't matched fingerprints from the pieces of the bottle they recovered to anyone yet, or from the shard that killed him."

Monica took another swig, draining the glass. She glanced at her watch. "I've got to get back soon. My boss will get snippy if I'm gone too long."

She reached over and took Trina's hand. "I wanted to meet you face to face because the cops are clearly keeping an eye on you, and they know that we're friends. I don't trust saying anything over the phone or through text, because they can get access to all of that stuff fairly easily now. At least, that's what my friend says."

Trina thought back to what she'd been doing on her phone and her laptop since this all happened. If the police were tracking her online movements, then they knew about Simon. But they more than likely already knew about him—and Tom—anyway.

She had an appointment with her lawyer later this afternoon. Simon was paying for it, because Trina didn't have any savings or money to handle such an expensive and unexpected cost. She barely had enough money to cover Monica's drink this afternoon.

"Dermot Carine was a social worker, and he had lots of troubled clients he worked with. He specialized in working with teenagers. And he had a few clients, *female* clients, that may have thought they were in love with him."

Trina let the information sink in.

"What are you saying?"

Monica started to put her coat on, slipping a few bills onto the table.

"These girls he worked with, they have brothers and fathers and sisters who may not be the best at taking care of them, but they're good at protecting certain things. This guy you were with, he had enemies."

"It was just the two of us that night in his hotel room," Trina said, replaying her evening at the wedding back through her mind. Were there people at the wedding who were angry with him? There was that one woman—almost a girl, Trina recalled—who'd watched Dermot and Trina. The one she couldn't bring herself to tell the police about.

"I know you feel like this is a terrible tragedy, and that you're caught in the middle of it," Monica said. "But you might have also been lucky that night that you didn't get mixed up in something that ended with you dead too."

Were they alone in that hotel room? Trina had to wonder, now. Was someone there, just waiting for Trina to leave?

"Be careful." Monica leaned in and gave Trina a quick but firm hug. "You can only get lucky so many times. You don't know who's still out there."

"Thank you for looking out for me," Trina said.

"What are friends for?" Monica swung her bag onto her shoulder, and as she headed across the room and out the door, several pairs of hungry, semi-drunk eyes following her shapely frame, Trina caught the waitress's attention and ordered another drink.

CHAPTER FIFTEEN

SIMON

He arrived at the station mid-afternoon, having cleared his appointments for the afternoon. Simon kept mints everywhere, in his desk and pockets and car, and he popped a few into his mouth now, hoping he didn't smell like whiskey and that he wouldn't crowd the small interview room with his breath.

A young detective who had the ruddy face of a pug took Simon to a room with the standard-issue metal chairs and table. Two dark-suited detectives sipped coffee from Styrofoam cups, the male one tugging at his shirtsleeves until they were the perfect length past his suit.

Seated on the other side of the table was his wife.

The detectives introduced themselves as Kirkpatrick and Bechdel. Joyce stood tentatively and kissed Simon on the cheek. As she did so, she whispered, "I know what I'm doing."

What Simon wished he could have told her was that he'd never doubted for a second, in all their years of marriage, that Joyce knew exactly what she was doing. What worried him was that he so rarely was able to guess what that was.

"Thank you for coming down to the station so quickly," Bechdel told him. She shuffled some paperwork in front of her, and Simon half-guessed it was random detritus she'd gathered up. He'd seen cop shows before. He'd watched *The Closer*. He was not about to be intimidated.

He saved people's lives, for God's sake.

"You made it sound like an emergency," Simon replied. "I canceled appointments with several patients in order to be here." He leaned back in his chair and glanced around the room, not meeting their eyes. Playing for advantage and feigning nonchalance. "So what is this all about?"

"Your wife was kind enough to stop by and offer information on a recent case we're investigating."

"I see."

"Darling, it was my civic duty to come forward and tell them what I know." Joyce reached out and took Simon's hand in hers. Her hands were so small. Simon felt the soft press of her wedding band on his knuckle.

"Your wife told us about Catriona Dell and your family's connection to her." Kirkpatrick read from a page in his notebook. "Which began a year ago, approximately."

"A year on Tuesday." Simon hoped she hadn't done it. Joyce couldn't have.

"Yes, when Catriona's partner, a Tom Hovisky, was struck by a car while crossing the street. The car left, not even stopping to check on Tom's status, but you saw the event and pulled over to provide assistance."

"That's correct," Simon confirmed. He wanted to take another mint, suddenly conscious of his breath again.

"Tom Hovisky was suffering from life-threatening injuries you determined, and as a trained surgeon you assessed him and began providing what you believed were life-sustaining measures."

Simon looked at Joyce, who stared back at him earnestly. *Go on*, her face told him. But how could he?

"Yes, that's correct."

Bechdel cleared her throat. "Which were ultimately unsuccessful."

"I'm sorry, but what does this have to do with your current investigation?"

"A young man was murdered." Joyce clasped her hands on the table. "It seems that he had connections to Catriona. I knew that it was important to tell the police what we'd been dealing with, having her harass us, asking for money, calling you at random hours of the day and night. It spoke to her instability, I thought. And I wanted to make sure she wasn't a threat to us."

"Has Catriona been in touch with you recently?" Kirkpatrick asked, pen poised above his notepad.

Simon felt Joyce's foot press on top of his underneath the table. "Yes, she has."

"In what way?"

He took a deep breath. "I'd tried to contact her, as the anniversary approached. I wanted to make sure she was all right, and ensure she wasn't spiraling out of control. It had been a difficult time for her, after the accident. We'd tried to help her as much as we could." An image of Joyce, standing at the top of the stairs in their home, holding a piece of paper and so furious her hands shook, the paper fluttering in the dark. "Recently, though, she's been in touch, asking for money."

Simon felt the shame press down on his shoulders. Joyce should never have done this. He wasn't perfect, but he didn't deserve this.

"Money for what?"

"A lawyer, for this case," Simon admitted.

"And have you provided this?"

"Yes, I helped her connect with Blanche Grainger. You might know her work. I've promised to pay the legal fees for her. She needs good representation."

"Is this the first time you've offered her money?"

Simon avoided looking at his wife, although he could feel her eyes on him. "No, it is not."

"When have you offered money to her before?" asked Kirkpatrick.

"After her fiancé died. She had issues with his life insurance. I stepped in to help with some of her bills."

"Mr. Morgan, are you involved at all romantically with Catriona Dell?" Bechdel asked, her look one of laser focus.

Simon swallowed and wished that he'd had a bit more to drink earlier.

"No, of course not," Joyce cut in.

"We would prefer that your husband answer the question, please." Bechdel leveled her gaze at him again.

"No, I am not romantically involved with her." And it was the truth.

Simon had never cheated on Joyce with another woman.

But it was also true that he was attracted to Trina. A mixture of shame and guilt and desire had merged together into a maelstrom he'd struggled with for the last year. He wanted to help the world, to heal those who were in pain.

And now all he could seem to do was cause more pain to those he cared about.

He'd had enough. "Are we being charged with anything?" Simon asked.

"No, no. You're free to go whenever you prefer."

"Then we're done here."

Simon stood and Joyce followed him out. Outside, at Simon's car, he turned and faced his wife.

"Do you really enjoy humiliating me that much?" he asked.

Joyce studied his face, and then leaned in to put a gloved hand on his cheek.

"I think we both love to punish each other." She kissed him boldly on the lips, and then walked away.

Simon glanced at his watch. He had paperwork to do, charts to finalize. He should go back to the office, but instead he got in the car, pulled out, and drove towards Trina's apartment.

CHAPTER SIXTEEN

LAURA

Laura offered Susan tea or coffee, like she was in a sitcom and Susan was a visiting PTA mom. Susan asked for coffee, and Laura brewed up a pot. While the machine bubbled and sputtered, Laura pretended to be busy around the kitchenette, gathering up spoons and creating a makeshift sugar bowl out of a chipped creamer jug hidden at the back of their cupboard. She put the milk in its carton on the table in front of Susan.

Part of Laura didn't want the coffee to finish brewing. She wanted to stay in the indefinite moment, where she knew that Dermot wrote about her—about her!—to his estranged sister. She could pretend that anything was in that letter. He could have told his sister he was in love with Laura, that he wanted to get married and have his family's blessing before he proposed. Another part of her realized he might have said things that weren't so kind. Maybe he talked about her struggles, and how they were affecting him. Maybe he talked about his problems at work, some that Laura had caused and others that she'd had nothing to do with. But why would he mention those to his sister, who he didn't talk to anymore?

Susan opened with, "He really cared about you," as Laura set down the two mugs.

A flame burned bright in Laura's chest. And then a nausea settled over her, hard and fast.

"Is that what you came to tell me? Because I already knew that." The harsh edge in her own voice surprised Laura, and she tried to remedy it with the next thing she said. "But I appreciate you coming all this way to tell me that."

"How long had you known each other?" Susan asked next. Laura knew what the question really meant. How old was Laura, and how long had she and Dermot been involved?

"I'm nineteen."

"Okay." Susan uncrossed and crossed her legs. "That's pretty young."

"How old are you?"

"I'm thirty-six." Susan pulled a lock of her perfect blowout off her face before tucking it behind her ear.

"You look younger," Laura said honestly.

"Thank you. So do you."

"I've been told that. Dermot called me *baby-face* sometimes."

Susan set her cup down on the table and clasped her hands. "What else did he call you?" Her face shifted from one of interest to something else.

A few weeks after Laura started working at the hotel, she'd walked in accidentally on a prostitute with a customer. The woman had been syrupy sweet, telling Laura it was an honest mistake and don't worry about it and let me walk you to the hallway so you don't get lost in this big suite—the guy had booked one of the suites on the top floor—and then when they were out of earshot of her customer, the prostitute whispered in Laura's ear that if she said anything to anyone she'd find her and stab her in the stomach.

That's what Susan's face reminded her of now.

So Laura was ready for something besides sweet nothings and love-letter reminiscences from Dermot's sister.

Laura shrugged. "Just Laura, I guess."

"When I called the police station, they told me you were the one taking care of his body."

"I didn't know he had a sister."

"That's very kind of you, but I can help from here." Susan pulled her wallet out of her bag. "How much have you spent so far?"

"I don't want your money." And it was true. Laura didn't want handouts from some long-lost sister. "Why were you and Dermot not speaking to each other? He made it seem like he didn't have any family."

Susan raised an eyebrow. "That's a long story."

"I have time." Laura settled into her seat opposite Susan on the sofa.

"Do you have anything stronger?" Susan wiggled the coffee cup in her hand.

"No." Laura kept a bottle of whiskey under her bed to sip from in case she had trouble sleeping at night, but she wasn't about to share that with anyone.

"Okay. Well, our parents were very religious growing up. The serious kind of Evangelicals who went to three-hour services every Sunday where people got up and spoke in tongues. Anyone who didn't follow their rules about living was going to burn in hell."

"I went to school with a few kids like that." One of them told Laura her parents died because they sinned and God was punishing them for it. His name was Pete Buckley, and after he'd told Laura her parents were dead because they were such terrible sinners, he'd added, "Or maybe it was your fault. Maybe you did something terrible, and God decided to take away your parents to teach you a lesson."

. . .

Laura had gone into the bathroom immediately afterward and thrown up.

"I was already married and living halfway across the country when Dermot was in high school. I'd been able to survive my parents by basically going along with whatever they said and then breaking from all of it once I was in college." Susan paused. "I didn't realize how bad it was for Dermot until afterwards. Things seemed to get worse after I left home. I came home to visit sometimes, but school kept me busy and it was hard to travel back. Our parents loved us, but they were incredibly strict. They wouldn't let Dermot date. He couldn't do most activities at school because our parents said they encouraged inappropriate behavior, and eventually they made him drop out to be home-schooled."

Laura didn't know anything about this part of Dermot's life. He'd just said he didn't have any family.

Susan continued. "He got his high school diploma by taking the GED and was able to get into a few different colleges. He went to the college furthest away from home. When he came back for Thanksgiving break that first year, I was home too for the holiday and we were all sitting around for dinner. Somehow while he was talking about his life at school he let it slip that one of his friends was gay. And that was it. My parents started screaming, calling him a heathen—just for having a friend who was gay—and Dermot wouldn't take it. Everything came out then, about our childhood and how he felt so trapped and how oppressive our parents were. Mom started crying, not because she was upset about the fight, but because she was certain that Dermot was going to hell. Dad just kept yelling.

"Dermot left, all the food for our Thanksgiving dinner still steaming on his plate, and he didn't come back. My parents wouldn't talk to him, Dermot wouldn't talk to them. And I was caught in the middle, but nothing I did seemed to help, until eventually I had to stop talking to my brother in order to keep a relationship with my parents."

"Was it worth it?" Laura asked.

Susan shook her head. "No, it wasn't."

She went on. "Both of our parents are dead now. Dermot wasn't lying about that." Susan started to blink and her eyes grew wet. Laura noticed the redness around them, which she guessed Susan had tried to expertly cover with makeup. Susan flicked a finger across her cheek and wiped the tears away. "And now Dermot is gone. I'm the only one left in my family."

"I'm sorry," Laura offered. And she was, although she still didn't trust what Susan was doing there.

"I'm sorry, too." Susan straightened her shoulders and took a deep breath. "You know, Dermot mentioned something else in his letter."

"Besides how much he cared about me?" There was that edge again. Laura forced herself to take a deep breath.

"He said he was in trouble. That if anything happened to him in the near future, I should get in touch with you."

"What?" Laura's mind raced from one possibility to another.

"Do you know what kind of trouble he was in?" Susan asked.

"It's not what everyone thinks." Laura unconsciously put a hand on her belly.

"He mentioned someone else, besides you."

"Who?"

"Someone named Tom."

"I don't know who Tom is." Laura tried to think, but she couldn't put anyone's face to that name. Maybe it was one of the kids Dermot had helped. "What did he say about him?"

"Laura," Susan's dark eyes locked on hers. "Dermot said he killed him."

CHAPTER SEVENTEEN

TRINA

The meeting with the lawyer wasn't for another two hours. Trina could stay at the bar, keep drinking, eat some of the party mix in the small wooden bowl, and go to the meeting slightly smoothed-over emotionally. But lately she'd spent too much time numbing out, to the point where she was now involved in a murder investigation as a prime suspect and her job was hanging on by a thread and her only friend had to meet her in a bar under some pretense to ensure she wasn't being followed.

She kept it to two drinks, which was an improvement for her. Instead, Trina got into her car, drove to a nearby park, and sat inside her warm seat while a class of preschoolers played in the winter light and she scrolled through her phone looking for Dermot's social media profiles. She started with Instagram, but she couldn't find anything close to him through a name search or her followers. She didn't have many—she lost a bunch after that one picture was posted, and gained a few that she blocked as a result, too. She imagined Dermot was probably the type of guy who had a handle that was descriptive of his lifestyle, rather than literally describing him by name. She tried a few other options that she'd gleaned from the headlines she caught online about the case, or learned from Monica. "Hotsocialworker" seemed crass, but she found a number of accounts came up, none of them Dermot. She tried "helpinghands" and "helpingprofdermot", but again there were too many and not enough. It was a mess, and Trina felt entirely out of her element.

She paused and looked out at the children. They all wore bright coats, pinks and lime-greens with a few neon-yellows and oranges thrown in. Like tiny gumballs tumbling around the patchy grass and blowing leaves.

Just before he died, Tom and Trina had started talking about having a baby. It seemed like the right time, both of them well out of school and settled into their jobs, stable in their love for each other, ready to put a down payment on a house—they'd also started looking at houses in neighborhoods with good schools. That's why they were there, walking down the sidewalk, that day. They had an appointment to view a house. Three bedroom, two and a half bathrooms, with a fenced-in yard and a huge oak tree that the kids could climb. They probably would have bought that house if everything hadn't fallen apart on the sidewalk that day.

Trina shifted over to Facebook and searched for Dermot by name. People seemed to prefer having their real names posted on Facebook instead of hipster handles. And sure enough, he popped up right away. A pit formed in Trina's stomach as Dermot's bright smile stared back at her. His profile was public, allowing Trina to click into his life instantly. Memories of their night together merged with what she saw on the screen as she moved through his posts and albums.

Dermot hiking, a waterfall in the background and droplets of water covering the bill of his cap and the bright-red poncho he was wearing. It was framed far enough away that someone else must have taken the picture.

Dermot's face, sweaty and bloated, pressed close to hers. Locks of wet hair dangling from his forehead onto her skin, and

Trina cringing as he tried to touch her, but letting him anyway because it was better than going home and being alone.

A photo of Dermot, clearly younger, with his arms around a group of young college-age men, all smiling in their soccer shorts and jerseys. Someone had gone through and tagged everyone in the picture. She could see Dermot commented on the photo. "Great times with great guys."

She was getting nowhere.

Dermot grabbing the champagne bottle, popping the cork and letting it spray over the room. Pressing the bottle to her lips and Trina pushing it away. Trina pulling at his pants, hungry to get it over with, but he'd drunk too much. His anger swirling with hers. The bottle falling to the floor, leaving a wet spot where the shards of glass lay like a ruined stained-glass window.

Trina wasn't even really sure what she was looking for. She just felt she needed to do something to understand who Dermot was. And if she could figure that out, then she could make a plan for how to get herself out of this situation without getting hurt or going to prison.

Most of Dermot's pictures were of nature scenes. He wasn't even in them. Snowy fields shifted to sun-drenched trees. Fall leaves scattered on the ground in the shape of a heart. Trina would have appreciated some of the photos and their composition if her viewing of them was under different circumstances. As it stood, she wasn't finding anything that could remotely help her.

Until she did.

It was a photo hidden in an album titled, "Wanderings," which Trina instinctively balked at. But inside, amidst pictures of fields and rivers and other trails, she found a photo of a young woman, staring back at the camera. Her eyes were slightly farther apart than would be considered conventionally beautiful, which made her face even more interesting. Short, blunt bangs and a rosebud mouth. She might be sixteen, she might be twenty-three. The girl or woman seemed almost ageless, her skin glowing in the light that Dermot captured as he took the picture.

Trina recognized her from somewhere. Those strange eyes.

Where had she seen her before?

The car was getting cold now that the engine was off. The children went inside a while ago, probably for snacks and a nap. The cold air would help tire them out.

Trina turned the car on, wondering what this connection was that she'd found. She scanned through her memories of the women at the wedding. Her students. Friends of friends.

Nobody matched that face. But the tight grip of certainty in her chest remained. She knew this woman.

Trina clicked through a few other photos on Dermot's Facebook profile. Next, she searched his list of friends, and then went to the link for the social service agency he worked for. And that's when it finally hit her.

Seeing Dermot, all suited up in front of the squat gray building he worked in, posing with a rigid smile with his colleagues at the agency, triggered another memory for Trina.

Dermot, pulling out his key card outside his hotel room door, his suit jacket slung over his shoulder and his tie loosened at the neck.

"Shall we?" he said, swinging the door open and sweeping his arm in a wide arc to welcome Trina inside.

As she stepped into the room, something caught Trina's eye in the gloom of the hotel hallway. A cleaning cart squeaked, and behind it was the woman—the girl, really—in Dermot's photo. The dim light of the hallway and Trina's muddled brain wouldn't make for perfect recognition, but those eyes looked back at Trina long enough to make an imprint on her mind.

She'd watched Trina go into Dermot's hotel room.

Dermot hadn't given her a second glance. He may not have even known she was there.

And yet he had an intimate photo of her buried in his Facebook profile.

Trina needed to go back to that hotel. The woman was pushing a cleaning cart, but she hadn't worn a uniform. From what Trina could recall, she'd worn a tight red dress.

Trina started the engine and reached to shift the car into gear when something tapped at her driver side window.

Trina flinched and automatically reached to lock her door. Looking out, another familiar face stared back at her, his expression one of desperate concern.

Dammit, it was Simon.

CHAPTER EIGHTEEN

SIMON

"How did you know I was here?" Trina's face had looked frightened, and then annoyed once she recognized Simon. There was a dip in Simon's chest as he worked to push down the anger that bubbled up automatically.

"I was driving by on the way to Blanche Grainger's law offices and happened to see you parked here." Which was partially true. There was no need to mention he'd been heading to Trina's apartment when he spotted her car in the park.

Trina pursed her lips.

Simon didn't mention that he was coming from the police station, or that he'd been on his way to her apartment when he spotted her. He didn't mention that his wife had scheduled a special meeting with the detectives, implying that Trina was unstable and stalking them.

"I didn't know you were planning on coming to my appointment," Trina finally said.

A biting wind kicked up and Simon grimaced against the cold that scraped at his face. "It's freezing out here," he said, stating the obvious.

"The appointment's not for another hour," Trina told him. He clutched at the lapels of his coat and pulled them tighter around his body, trying to stand up straight and lean towards the window to talk to Trina at the same time.

"I'll leave you to it then," Simon said and made to head back to his car, which was parked in the overflow lot off to the left.

Trina's face softened just slightly. "Thank you for helping me," she said, and then added something else that the wind snatched and whisked away before Simon could hear.

He approached her car again, aware that they must look like a clandestine couple meeting in the open privacy of a public park. A small blush crept up his neck, despite the below-freezing temperatures.

Simon wondered if Joyce followed him.

"What was that?"

"I said, I know it's not your fault."

Something gripped tight at Simon's heart, and for a moment he considered turning again and just walking away. He wasn't prepared for this type of discussion.

He didn't say anything. He'd been waiting for this conversation for an entire year, in hospital rooms and lawyers' conferences, on voicemails and unanswered calls and "chance" meetings at her apartment. A few meetings at his home, when Trina had shown up drunk and screaming his name so loud that Joyce threatened to call the police.

Joyce said it was humiliating.

"I know you were only trying to help." Trina paused for a second, looked at him, and then turned back and moved to put the car in reverse as she rolled the window up.

"No!" Simon wasn't trying to yell, but Trina was startled nonetheless.

He continued. "You can't say something like that, giving me an opening to finally *talk* about what happened with Tom, and then just leave."

· · ·

The shift over Trina was immediate. "I was the one who loved him." Any hint of understanding in her was gone, and Simon couldn't blame her. What he said was selfish, almost cruel. And yet, it was exactly how he felt. Like parched soil just promised the rain, only to have it replaced by more dust.

"Please, Trina. We need to talk about this."

"No, *you* need to talk about this."

"Fair enough. But tell me." Simon leaned his arm on the top of the car and bent down awkwardly. It felt wrong hovering over Trina the way that he was. He cast a sidewards glance to the empty center of the park. A leaf danced in the wind. "How often do you drink yourself to sleep each night? How often do you go out looking to pick up random guys just to numb yourself? The police think you had something to do with that young man's death. Why were you even with him?"

Something flickered across Trina's face. She got out of the car, pushing Simon back with her door as she opened and then slammed it shut.

Her beautiful face was so close to Simon's that he could see the gold flecks in her irises. From a distance, they looked green, but standing near to each other, they appeared almost metallic.

"Why was I with him? With Dermot Carine?" Trina threw her hands up in the air.

Simon stumbled as Trina tossed the young man's name into the wind. No one, not even the police, had said the victim's name yet. Hearing it, especially from Trina's mouth, made it all too real for him.

Trina continued. "Why am I with any of the men I go home with?" Trina clenched her teeth. "Because Tom, my would-be husband, was walking with me because I wanted to go get ice cream after looking at the house we were going to buy. It was a beautiful evening. Do you remember?"

Simon nodded, pathetic in the knowledge of where she was

about to go. Why did he think having this conversation would help?

"And then a car on the street lost control, and rammed up onto the sidewalk, and Tom threw himself in front of me so that I would be protected." Tears welled in Trina's eyes, beginning to stream down her face as she continued. "Which meant he was crushed by the impact."

She took a deep, shuddering breath, and although Simon reached out to comfort her, she moved away quickly and he let his arm fall.

"The car backs up and drives away. I don't see the driver, or if there were any passengers. Everything is just chaos, and all I can focus on is Tom, crying out in pain. I don't even see the color or make of the car, although at the hospital when the police collect Tom's clothes they'll find flecks of blue paint on his shirt.

"And then, it's a miracle! A doctor—even better, a surgeon—is on the same road and sees it all happen. He pulls over, runs to help Tom, and starts performing life-saving measures. I follow his instructions, trying to help where I can, but my hands are shaking and I can barely hear what's happening because the blood in my ears is pounding so hard."

"Stop," Simon's voice was taut, strung like a bowstring about to snap. "Please, just stop." He raised his hands up in surrender.

"No, you wanted to talk about it. So, I'm talking about it."

Another slash of wind whipped through the space between them. A lone dog walker approached from the opposite end of the park before turning and heading back in the direction they came.

"But it turns out this savior of ours was a drunk—*is* a drunk—and he starts making mistakes. He actually cuts into Tom with a penknife, supposedly to relieve the pressure from the internal bleeding, but he misses and punctures Tom's spleen, and worsens the bleeding. It also turns out that this doctor was driving after downing a fifth of whiskey, so he was terribly drunk and shouldn't have been helping anyone, let along cutting them open on the side of the road."

The weight of his guilt sunk onto Simon's shoulders, holding him in place while Trina listed out his sins.

"They said he would have survived if you hadn't been there." Trina was quieter now, her voice barely audible over the wind. "And nothing happened to you. You're still practicing, you didn't even get charged because of Good Samaritan Laws. And now you want to follow up with me, *check in on me*, give me money. As though I owe you something."

"You don't owe me anything," Simon said, and instantly regretted it.

"Of course I don't," Trina replied. "And you owe me everything."

She stopped and stared at him. A few strands of hair blew across her face, and Simon was reminded strangely of being with Joyce on a vacation to Switzerland, when they were first married. It had been winter, and the skiing conditions were perfect. They were at the top of a mountain slope, the sun shining across the snow, and he'd looked at his wife and realized just how lucky he was to have her.

The energy vibrated off Trina so intensely it was almost visible. She clenched her fists, reached up with a jagged hand and pulled the hair off her face, and then silently walked back to her car, turned it on, and pulled away. Simon was left standing there in the empty park, watching her leave, willing her to go.

CHAPTER NINETEEN

LAURA

Laura thought Dermot's sister would never leave, but Susan finally stood up after another half hour of going round and round about the letter Dermot wrote and made her way out, pausing at the door to put a hand on Laura's shoulder and remind her she was there for Laura if she needed anything. And then Susan got in her fancy car and drove off, leaving in her wake more questions for Laura than she'd been able to answer.

Laura's phone beeped. It was a text from Rosie, wanting to get together for drinks or something a little later in the day. By drinks, Laura knew it meant holding court on the sunken couch in the apartment Rosie shared with her cousins, slugging back shots of cheap vodka and shouting at reality TV shows. Laura didn't really like going, but Rosie was one of her few friends and she didn't want to be here when Terry got back.

It was just a two mile walk into town, even though it seemed like their trailer was parked in the middle of a vast forest, so it didn't matter that Terry had the car. Laura could be over to Rosie's in twenty minutes if she walked fast, thirty if she was tired. And she was always tired now.

She texted Rosie back, telling her she would be over soon,

bundled herself into her hand-me-down men's coat, hat, and gloves but then decided at the last minute she needed to change her outfit. She still had on her work clothes, and she didn't need to be seeing friends in the dingy polo and polyester pants issued by the Marriott. Laura rummaged around in her closet and eventually found what she was looking for. Dermot took her shopping a few weeks back, insisting she get whatever she wanted, and so she'd asked to go to one of the little boutique stores in town with mannequins that always featured tiny black dresses with strappy heels and chunky necklaces.

"I'd thought something more like a sweater," he'd teased, moving over to the storefront next door that sold hiking gear and their window display of colorful fisherman's sweaters.

"You don't need to buy me anything," Laura told him.

"I know." Dermot smiled, running his hand through his dark hair. "But I want to say thank you, for everything you've done to help me these last few months. Being with you." He paused, and in that pause Laura heard more than anything Dermot could have said to her.

Dermot went on. "Being with you has been one of the few things in my life that have made me happy. Truly happy."

Laura stared at her closet, remembering those words. She pulled out the dress he'd bought for her, not too short or tight— Dermot had insisted—but a beautiful fabric and cut. Body conscious without being sleazy. There was a word for the type of dress, but she couldn't remember it. It was higher end than anything else Laura owned. She'd come out of the dressing room and she swore she saw Dermot's face light up with desire when he first saw her. He'd shifted his features quickly into one that was more brotherly, but Laura knew what she saw.

That had been the beginning of the end, she thought now.

Laura pulled off her clothes and slipped the dress over her skin. The fabric felt rich and clung in all the right places. Looking in the mirror, she expected to see a beautiful woman staring back at her. Instead, she saw her gaunt face and pale skin. The dark circles under her eyes and sunken hollows around her collarbones. She was a ghoul, not a princess.

She ripped off the dress, let it crumple into a pile on the floor, and grabbed whatever she found first in her closet to wear. A chunky sweater, paired with clean but beaten-down jeans, and she walked quickly back to the front of the trailer, rushing out the door while still pulling her coat and hat on.

Snow and a crust of ice crunched under her boots as she walked. She ran her fingers over the roll of bills coiled in her pocket. The pharmacy should still be open in town.

Susan's voice rolled around in her head as she walked. "He said he'd killed him."

Tom.

But neither Susan nor Laura knew who Tom was. Dermot's sister said she couldn't think of anyone from his childhood or high school years that she knew of, and Laura had no memory of a Tom coming up from Dermot's catalogue of clients he worked with. She'd told Susan Dermot didn't seem to have too many friends. He was always working, meeting with clients all over town.

Except when he was with her, Laura silently added.

None of it made any sense.

Laura kept walking, trying to think through everything that had happened in the last few weeks. Losing Dermot, his sister showing up—claiming that Dermot confessed to killing someone. Laura missing her period. Terry getting angrier and angrier each day, and Laura never sure what was going to upset him.

Chickadees played in the bushes along the road, and their mechanical call cut through the riot of Laura's thoughts.

A car drove past, going too fast down the icy country road, and almost clipped Laura on her elbow before she could safely get to the side berm. Once the car passed, she promptly bent over and threw up the small bit of food she'd managed to eat today. She put her hand against a tree to brace herself and tried to steady her vision, which was spinning.

A bit of vomit landed on the top of her boots, and she rubbed them in the leaf litter scattered on the ground. Laura was thankful she hadn't worn the dress.

A trail opened up to her right, marked with a painted blaze of red and orange. Laura had forgotten the Midwest Appalachian Trail cut through her road. She and Dermot had never hiked this one. He always preferred to take her further afield, to see new spots and visit lookouts that weren't familiar.

She stopped, trying to decide whether she should turn back home and rest or keep going towards town, her friend, and some more answers to where her life was about to head. Her fingers on the tree trunk rubbed against something smooth, and Laura looked up to see initials carved into the bark. Cut fresh enough to still be seeping sap from the gouges, she brought her fingers to her nose and smelled the bright spark of pine.

Laura took a step further to the right, where the initials faced the inner part of the trail. D.C. + J.L., with a heart drawn around them.

Dermot had done something similar when they were on the waterfall trail, taking out his pocketknife and marking a tree with D.C. + L.T. *Dermot Carine loves Laura Taylor.*

That's what she assumed it'd meant, anyway.

Laura knew there was a chance of another D.C. carving their initials into this tree, but her instincts told her it was Dermot. After all, he'd done the same thing with her.

Which left her wondering: *Who the hell was J.L.?* And riding right behind that question, like an avalanche about to crack, was another one. *How many secrets could one man have?*

CHAPTER TWENTY

JOYCE

She followed Simon to where he met up with Trina at the park. Joyce was constantly surprised by her husband's failure to recognize that she was in fact the jealous type, although she hated to admit to even herself how she fit such a familiar mold.

Her mother had also been a jealous wife, folding her tired children into the back of the family Buick and following her husband when he returned to the office after dinner, supposedly to catch up on paperwork. As Joyce remembered it, most of these reconnaissance missions were unproductive. Joyce and her brother would sit in the car, taking up a distant place in the parking lot, for what felt like ages, until their mother decided she'd seen enough and it was time to go home. They always made it back before their father, who Joyce realized now must have been working long hours as a way of avoiding his home life. She'd seen Simon do it, too.

This was the way her childhood weekday evenings went, until one night. Her mother was dozing off in the car, her head bobbing onto her chest, but Joyce was wide awake and terribly bored, blowing her breath onto the cool glass of the back window and writing messages in the steam. Joyce saw a woman, perfectly done up with her sleek black coat pulled tight around her shoulders and red lipstick outlining a pouty mouth. She remembered the woman had curly blonde hair piled on top of her head, like a poodle. She was very pretty, and Joyce found herself waking up her mother to point her out.

"Who's that pretty lady?" Joyce had asked.

Her mother woke with a start, took a look at the back of the woman as she went through the entrance to her father's office building, and then instructed the children to stay there. Joyce remembered her mother paused a moment before getting out, like she was making a decision. Then she leapt out from the car, through the glass double doors of the building, and disappeared into the darkness of the foyer. She returned what must have been only a few minutes later, her eyes red and bulging and wiping at her nose, started the car without a word to Joyce or her brother, and drove them home.

Her father never came home that night, and a few months later Joyce found herself living in a run-down apartment with her mother during the week and sharing her old home with her father and the poodle-woman, whose name turned out to be Marla, on the weekends.

But so far Simon had proved to be faithful to Joyce when it came to Trina, as far as the physical aspect of intimacy was concerned. But just like Joyce learned in one of her archaeology courses when she was at university, "absence of evidence is not evidence of absence."

Simon didn't touch Trina the entire time he was with her at the park, but Joyce knew her husband. Even from a distance, she could read his face. He'd somehow convinced himself that he was in love with this woman, through some special alchemy of guilt and attraction and—if she were honest with herself—neglect.

She followed Trina now, driving behind her car at a distance. Simon was still in the park. The appointment with the lawyer was coming up soon though. Joyce saw it scheduled on Simon's calendar when she checked it this morning. But after seeing Trina's reaction to him, Joyce assumed Simon was giving her space before they joined up for the meeting with the lawyer Simon arranged for Trina.

The thought made Joyce feel sick to her stomach. Yet another of Trina's tentacles grasping at Joyce's life.

As she drove along, they passed the center of town with its patch of green and welcoming gazebo. They headed out of town a distance, through the strip mall with the nail place that Joyce liked to go to for a quick manicure when she was in a hurry, and finally pulled into a lawyer's office mimicking an old colonial building with its candles in the windows and brick façade.

Joyce didn't pull in after Trina. She didn't want Simon to see her there, too, when he joined Trina for the meeting.

Joyce decided to turn around and get a manicure at the nail place. Her nails were bitten down to the quick, and it would soothe her to have the ritual of it all. There was only one other car in the parking lot during the odd midday time. It was the expensive kind of shiny and black and almost as out-of-place in the strip mall as Joyce's Jaguar.

The tinkle of the bell soothed Joyce immensely as she stepped through the door, but upon entering the salon she saw the young woman who she usually worked with was busy with another client. Middle-aged, with a blunt blonde bob and expensive clothes. Her voice rang through the small space.

"I'm here just visiting for a bit," the blonde said as the nail technician scrubbed her nail beds. "It's all rather tragic, and I don't really want to talk about it."

Joyce sat down at the next station, her ears pricked at the woman's declaration. When people make the point of saying they don't want to talk about something, they usually really do.

"I'm so sorry to hear that," Joyce offered. And she was. She knew how tragedy could hang around your neck—your family's neck—like a millstone.

The woman looked up at her, her blue eyes wide and searching. "Thank you. It's been difficult."

Joyce held her hands out across the table, and another young woman took them in hers and started to remove the chipping polish Joyce chose last time, and will choose again, because it's her color. Cherry Bomb Red.

"We don't want to pry," the blonde's nail technician said, keeping her eyes lowered and looking up through her lashes.

"Well, it's just all so upsetting." The blonde woman made to tuck her hair behind her ear, but stopped herself, realizing her polish would smear. Joyce noticed she'd chosen a dark purple. "You see, my brother and I were estranged. And then he sent this letter to me, totally out of the blue, telling me all about his life and certain—mistakes—he'd made."

"And then, oh God, it was awful. I get a call from the police a few days later, before I even had a chance to reach out to him, and they tell me he's dead."

There's an audible gasp across the nail salon, as though everyone stopped breathing at the same time.

"Oh, my dear," one of the older nail techs said. "That's terrible."

The blonde woman rubbed her wrist under her eyes. "You don't need to call me 'dear'. Susan is fine."

She sniffed, and a shudder went through her shoulders. "But it's not just that he died before I could make amends with him." She looked up and made eye contact with each of the women in the room, including Joyce.

And Joyce, as nasty as it sounds, had to stop and ask herself if perhaps this was some sort of performance. If perhaps this Susan had done this before. She'd seen it, in Simon's practice. People who clung to tragedy, and fed off it in their own, maladjusted way.

Susan took a deep breath, as though to steady herself, and went on. "He didn't just die. My brother was murdered."

Joyce flinched at that word and accidentally knocked the bottle of nail polish over on her table, the creamy red spilling over the white surface like blood.

"I'm so sorry," Joyce said, but this time she wasn't sure she meant it.

CHAPTER TWENTY-ONE

TRINA

The meeting with the lawyer was pretty much the same as all the others Trina'd had in the past—too long and too expensive. Trina couldn't decide if she liked the lawyer, this Blanche Grainger. She was all hairspray and shoulder pads, sat serenely at the head of the table with her arms crossed and a knowing look on her face.

She recommended Trina not talk to the police without her present. She had a few friends on the force, Blanche told Trina and Simon—because of course Simon was there, since he was paying for the meeting and keeping Blanche on retainer for Trina, and honestly that's the least he could do for Trina after what he did to her life—and Blanche could put pressure for them to back off a little.

"I can't influence an investigation, obviously." Blanche looked solemnly at her two clients. "But, I *can* help maintain a quality of life for my client while the investigation is ongoing."

Trina wasn't sure what she meant by quality of life, but assumed it had something to do with keeping the police from showing up at her classes on campus or coming around for questions at her apartment in the middle of the night. Blanche could keep it all "respectable", as Simon would say.

As they wrapped up, Blanche's assistant came in with a questioning face and Trina swore she saw Blanche mouth the word "two" with her hot-pink lipstick as she held up two fingers. Trina checked her watch. They'd been there an hour and fifteen minutes, but it seemed Blanche rounded up when it came to fees. Trina just hoped Blanche wouldn't have the same fuzzy math if she had to negotiate sentencing for Trina.

But that won't happen. Trina won't let herself even consider it. This all just needed to go away. Simon should just make it go away. He owed her that.

After the meeting, Simon settled the bill and they all dispersed to their separate channels of life. Outside in the parking lot, Simon moved as though to comfort Trina, and she shifted deftly away from him, climbed into her car, and drove off. They'd spoken enough for one day. He could go home, grab a snifter of whiskey, and feel good about himself for helping Trina.

Trina had other plans.

Monica's warning from their conversation earlier kept ringing in her head. "He had enemies." If Trina was going to get out of this mess, she needed to figure out who those enemies were. And to do that, she needed to learn more about Dermot.

She had a class tomorrow she needed to prepare for, because even though she was under investigation for murder the academic calendar does not stop turning and Trina couldn't risk losing her job. Not now.

She headed back to campus, and by the time she walked the stairs to her office it was too late for her to turn onto another floor when she recognized a familiar voice.

"Oh, it's you." Addy Simpson looked just as uncomfortable to see Trina as Trina felt.

Just move on, Trina thought. She gave Addy a curt nod and kept walking up the stairs. Her side satchel felt heavier than usual, weighing down her shoulder so that she was lopsided and curvy-spined as she passed Addy.

The two hadn't seen each other since the night in the bar, when Addy was drunkenly celebrating passing her dissertation defense and Trina had been doing her usual routine of trying to forget.

"Hang on, would you?" Addy held out a hand towards Trina. "Can I talk to you for a second?"

"Okay." Trina turned and waited for Addy.

Addy looked around. A door opened and closed upstairs, and footsteps echoed in the stairwell. "Somewhere private?"

Trina glanced at her watch. She did not have time for this. "I have class in thirty minutes." She didn't add that she hadn't reviewed her material for class yet.

"It won't take long." Addy went ahead of Trina, the two women walking in unspoken agreement up the stairs, into the third-floor hallway, and arrived at Trina's office door.

Trina set her bag down and gave Addy a questioning look.

Addy's dark hair was in braids today, with bright gold bands wrapped around a few of them. Her sweater flaunted a Fair Isle print, and paired with the slim jeans and knee-high boots she was wearing she could easily have been mistaken for an undergraduate rather than a freshly minted Ph.D.

"I wanted to apologize for what I said the last night." Addy stared at a brown stain on the carpet. Trina couldn't remember if it was coffee or whiskey. A blush rose on Addy's cheeks as she continued. "I was celebrating a little too much."

"We've all been there."

Addy made a noncommittal noise.

And that's when Trina remembered what Addy said to her.

"I knew Dermot," Addy said, as if reading Trina's thoughts. Addy twisted her hands in front of her like a nervous child. "He was a really good person."

Trina looked at the young woman in front of her, not sure how to proceed. Eventually, she decided on just being honest.

"I didn't know him that well, but I'm really sorry for what happened to him."

Addy nodded, taking that in. Then she seemed to feel the need to explain herself. "We met through friends. I was doing some research with foster kids, and my friend put me in touch with Dermot. He was a social worker, and really nice and friendly. We got along great, and sort of became friends."

Maybe that's also why Addy was drinking so much that night, Trina thought.

She repeated, "I'm sorry about your friend."

Addy locked eyes with her. "They're saying that you were with him, that night."

"Who's they?" Trina asked.

"Everybody. People saw the police talking with you on campus, and so word just started spreading around."

Trina wondered how much of that was due to Addy herself. A memory flashed up from that night in the bar, Addy saying she knew Trina was in trouble. That rumors were spreading around the department.

"We met at a wedding. He was just a guy who I thought was cute and…" Trina paused, and then just got on with it. "And I slept with him. He had a room at the hotel where the wedding was held. I didn't know him well, at all."

"The police think you're the one who hurt him?" Addy's face was unreadable.

"I think so. But too many pieces of this situation don't fit. There are people who say Dermot was such a great guy, but I think he had problems."

"What kind of problems?"

"The kind of problems that would get him killed," Trina said simply.

Addy paused for a second. "I think I can help you," she told Trina.

"How?"

Addy pulled out a ring of keys from the pocket of her jeans. "I have a key to his apartment." And then she began to cry, shaking so violently that Trina reached out and wrapped her arms around her slight shoulders, telling her that everything would be okay.

Trina had always been a good liar.

CHAPTER TWENTY-TWO

LAURA

Everything in Rosie's apartment was slumped and disheveled, which was exactly the opposite of Laura's friend. Rosie opened the door, crisp white shirt, short jean skirt, and her dark hair pulled back in a tight bun with two perfectly coiled curls framing either side of her forehead like a makeshift crown.

"It looks like you need a drink," Rosie said as soon as she saw Laura.

Laura stepped across the threshold and wiped her snowy boots on the mat in the outside hallway, although the carpet was already stained with slush and debris. Rosie lived with two brothers and two other boy cousins, and it was a constant fight for her to keep the apartment livable, let alone pristine.

Laura caught her reflection in the hallway's bronze-framed mirror and barely recognized herself. A pale, gaunt face stared back, her eyes sunken and her cheeks chafed from the wind on her walk to Rosie's apartment. The plastic bag from the pharmacy she stopped at on her way over to Rosie's crinkled in her pocket, the pregnancy test shrouded just barely by the thin material. Handing over fifteen dollars to the judgmental cashier had been awful.

Who was J.L.? Jennifer. Judy. Jolene. Julie. It was like an itch that Laura's mind couldn't scratch. She was certain the woman Dermot was with at the wedding wasn't someone he'd met before. They'd acted like strangers at first. And then as not-so-strangers, she reminded herself.

Laura watched her leave, in the early morning hours. Someone who carved your initials with theirs into a tree wanted you to stay the night, right? Although, Laura thought, Dermot had carved his with hers, and yet he hadn't asked her to go with him to the wedding. He'd just wanted a free room. She'd worn the dress he'd bought for her, the one she almost wore over to Rosie's today. When Laura walked across the hotel lobby, the heels she'd borrowed from Rosie had clicked in that satisfying and classy way they do in movies. They were six inches high, with sparkling rhinestones set into the straps, and they cut into her feet as she'd moved over to the carpet and climbed the stairs, her footsteps silenced then by the rich nap she hated vacuuming but loved walking on.

"Come on, honey," Rosie said, cutting into Laura's thoughts. She smiled. "I've got the apartment to myself tonight, which means we can make popcorn and watch whatever we want on Netflix. I've lined up three or four Hugh Grant movies. Oh!" She threw her hands up in the air, as though she just remembered. "And I made signature drinks!"

Rosie passed her a martini glass full of a vibrant pink liquid, and Laura slugged it down in one gulp. It tasted sickly sweet with a burn afterwards, like fake strawberries and cheap vodka.

Rosie followed suit, and the two women gave a little cheer as they refilled their glasses and headed to the couch. On previous visits, the couch had smelled of cigarettes and boy—that was the best way Laura could explain it. Today, though, she noticed Rosie had tucked a clean polka-dot sheet over the couch as a slipcover.

A scented candle burned on the coffee table, giving off the smell of clean linen.

"When did you have time for all of this?" Laura wanted to slip into the bathroom and find out what she was going to have to do next, but she couldn't ignore her friend's kindness.

"It's amazing what you can get done when you're not picking up after three boys." Rosie settled herself onto the couch and patted the cushion next to her.

"I'll be right back," Laura said. "I just need to use the bathroom."

"Well, here, let me take your coat." Rosie reached out as she stood up.

"No, I'm fine." Laura kept walking towards the bathroom, which was down the hall past the three bedrooms. "I'll be right back."

She locked the door behind her, turned on the overhead fan and ran the faucet, hoping to conceal the crinkle of plastic as she unwrapped the test. Laura knew Rosie would be suspicious of all the noise, but she couldn't wait any longer.

J.L. J.L. J.L. Why had she ever trusted Dermot in the first place?

Laura read the instructions for the test, holding it underneath her over the toilet, her muscles so tense she had to try for what felt like an eternity before she could pee on the stupid stick, and then sat and waited to see what it would tell her.

Her stomach twisted from the alcohol and sugar sitting like an unexploded bomb inside her. She hadn't eaten since this morning, which was only a burnt piece of toast and a massive cup of black coffee.

Laura checked her watch.

One more minute.

There was a knock at the door. Rosie's voice came through, an edge of concern coloring it. "Are you okay, honey? Do you need help?"

Why did Laura drink that alcohol? That would be bad for the baby. If there was a baby.

She checked the stick, but still no answer. She looked at her watch. Still thirty more seconds.

"Why don't you come out and we can talk about it?" Rosie twisted the handle on the door, but the lock held fast.

"I'm fine. Just not feeling so good."

Laura looked at the stick. Something had changed, and she compared it now to the instruction packet that trembled in her hands.

"Do you want me to call Terry?" Rosie's voice had turned pleading, and Laura felt awful because she knew she was about to ruin the relaxing evening Rosie had planned out so carefully for the two of them.

She opened the door. Rosie was there, a look of concern on her face. "What can I do?"

"Don't call Terry," Laura said. The last thing she needed was her brother, strutting around and making everything worse with his hot head and skewed moral compass.

"I won't. I didn't want to in the first place." Rosie took Laura's hand. "You're so cold. Do you want some tea? Something stronger?"

Laura looked at her friend wide-eyed. "I'm pregnant." Saying the words out loud made everything seem all too real. She stumbled a bit, and Rosie—dear Rosie—held on to her and guided her back to the couch.

"I've been so stupid."

"Haven't we all at some point." Rosie sat next to her and held her hand. The apartment was silent, except for a drip splashing into the sink in the kitchen.

Finally, Rosie broke the silence. "What are you going to do?"

"I don't know," Laura said honestly.

"It's going to be okay," Rosie said again, less convincingly this time, and the two women fell into an uncomfortable silence.

CHAPTER TWENTY-THREE

SIMON

The drinking started when Simon first suspected Joyce was having an affair. They'd been married for a while at that point, with him moving right along the path of promotion at the hospital and Joyce working at the accounting firm. They'd been younger than they were now, of course, but not quite young. Both of them felt the pressure of starting a family.

Medical school pulled some of the last reserves Simon had out of him, and then residency left him drained and exhausted every night to the point where he'd stumble into bed some days just as Joyce was getting up to go to work. There were weeks where they barely saw each other, passing ships in their rigid schedules, and the thought of ripping each other's clothes off or even just touching each other in a way that required attention and focus was beyond him. Making a baby seemed such a long-off goal when all he wanted to do was sleep and sleep and sleep.

It took Simon crumpling in on himself in one of the hospital breakrooms filled with cots, crying and mumbling that life wasn't worth the pain, for someone to realize that what he was going through was more than just the effects of the grinding fatigue of medical training. It was a colleague of his, Renée Baxter, who was just at the cusp of her brilliant career as a neurosurgeon, who found Simon, promptly called a friend who was a clinical psychologist, and got him booked in for a therapeutic assessment that afternoon.

Simon was prescribed three weeks' rest, plus medication to manage his serotonin levels in his brain, and a rigorous self-care program of walks outside, nutritious meals, and daily journal entries. He was clinically depressed, it seemed, but from what all of his expert colleagues were telling him, he didn't need to be if he just stuck with the program.

Joyce took the first week off work, allowing herself to nurture him in a way that she'd never been like before. After three or four days of sleeping with gaps of breakfast in bed or a favorite television show watched with Joyce stroking his hair, he felt more human. The brittleness that had settled into his bones seemed to take on greater flexibility. He found himself wanting to touch Joyce again, to cup her breast in his hands and make her moan his name. Not that he did any of that just then, but he could feel the spark returning to his life.

One night after Joyce decided it was safe to return to work with her accounting firm, he had enough energy to cook a simple dinner of roast chicken, light candles on the table, and pour two glasses of wine. He put on slacks rather than his drawstring pajama pants, combed his hair, and shaved with precision. He was getting better, and neither of them were getting any younger.

When she came home, a takeaway from the Chinese restaurant down the block slung over her arm and an air of distraction pervading her, Simon realized his mistake in keeping his effort a surprise. They sat down to dinner, nonetheless, and Joyce told him about her client who was making terrible decisions because he'd just left his wife and fell in love with someone younger.

"He can't think clearly," she said. "The poor guy has himself convinced he's in love and that she deserves half his money.

Meanwhile, his wife, who he's been married to for fifteen years and they have three kids, is left to fend for herself because he says he doesn't love her anymore. The whole thing is ridiculous."

Joyce took a sip of wine and ate a bit of the chicken Simon made. He'd cooked it perfectly and was proud of how juicy the meat was.

It was then Simon asked the question he wished he could take back. Not that it would have changed anything in the course of his life. Not really. But it would have delayed him knowing what was happening, and in that fact perhaps things could have been different.

"What strikes you as ridiculous?" Simon asked, mainly just wanting to hear his wife's voice as he ate the meal he'd prepared for them and his chest relaxed from the grip that had made it hard for him to breathe these last several months. His brain felt like it was humming again, taking in all the information from his surroundings. Simon was alive, and in love, and even the drops of rain clinging to the window next to their dining-room table were beautiful.

"Oh, well, isn't it obvious?" Joyce took another bite of her meal. Simon reached over, hoping to take her hand as she spoke, but she shifted it ever so slightly away, and then tucked it into her lap to grab her napkin and wipe at her mouth.

She explained, "He should have stayed with his wife. Keep their family together, let her have some of the funds without all the mess, and enjoy his love affair on the side. There's no reason he should have to rip apart his family for this new woman. I mean," she waved her hand in the air to emphasize the point, "he's already shown his love doesn't last, so why assume the next one will be any different?"

A chill went up Simon's spine. He'd never heard Joyce talk that way.

"But maybe this new woman is the love of his life?" Simon smiled. Joyce remained focused on the flame of one of the candles while Simon tried to meet her gaze. Joyce's mouth curled at the edges, but her eyes were glassy. She wasn't reacting to him.

"If you believe in that sort of thing," she said.

They didn't make love that night, or the next night. When Simon finally brought up hope that they'd start their family, now that he was feeling more like himself, Joyce brushed off the idea with a deftly aimed barb.

"Soon you'll be back to work, dear. Let's see how you do once you have those pressures put back on you."

It stifled Simon's hopes, and his loneliness grew.

Two weeks later, Simon was back to work, with medication and a journal and daily walks outside on his breaks. It wasn't until three months later, when he happened to be organizing the paper recycling and found, shoved in a large, crumpled envelope, a receipt from a clinic an hour away for a D&C. Joyce had gone alone. She hadn't told him she was pregnant, or that she was getting an abortion.

Of course it wasn't his. They hadn't been intimate in months.

But Simon stayed, because he equally loved and feared his wife.

He started to drink in his office.

Years passed.

One small snifter of whiskey that grew into two and then more until he felt that welcoming numb wrap around his brain. Simon found he was happiest then, in the quiet moments after his last patient, before he headed home to play at being happy in his big house with his beautiful wife.

CHAPTER TWENTY-FOUR

JOYCE

Joyce offered to buy Susan—which she found out was the woman's name—a coffee once their nails were dry, and they set off for a café Joyce knew in the middle of town. Café Leo featured red-and-white awnings, flower boxes that held bright-red geraniums in the summer, and excellent lattes.

Joyce chose a table in the back corner and waited for Susan to arrive. A small glass vase with a red rose sat in the center of the table, and the daily menus were printed in sweeping script on creamy cardstock.

She glanced at her watch, considering that perhaps she was being stood up, but then the bell on the door jingled and Susan stepped in. She shook the cold from her beautiful black coat, ran a hand through her hair, and searched the restaurant until her eyes fell on Joyce. The dark nail polish added an edge to her very proper look, Joyce noted. While Susan walked over to the table, Joyce looked down at her own nails, and the bright red she chose suddenly seemed tacky.

She felt old.

"How are you feeling?" Joyce asked Susan as she sat down. She reached out a hand and patted Susan's forearm, giving it a friendly squeeze. "It sounds like you're dealing with a lot right now."

Susan took a sip from the glass of water sitting on the table. "This place is nice," she said, looking around. It wasn't lost on Joyce that she was avoiding her question.

"They just renovated." Joyce made a noncommittal noise and waited, because she was certain Susan would not have come here if she didn't want to talk about her brother.

Silence settled over the table, and a waitress stopped by to get their orders. Cobb salad and sparkling water for Susan, a green salad and skinny latte for Joyce. Throw in some pearls and a binder with fundraising raffle items and she could be at a regular committee meeting.

Joyce took a sip of her latte once it arrived, working to hide the tremor in her hand. Susan scrolled through her phone.

The two women were still sitting in an awkward non-conversation when their salads were delivered by their waitress. Joyce wondered if she'd made a big mistake inviting Susan out. Neither of them had touched their salads, and the café was starting to fill with the murmur of conversations around them as more couples and friend groups arrived to get a treat in the middle of the day.

Joyce decided to give it one more chance before asking for the check and calling it a wash.

"I invited you here in case you wanted to talk about your brother." She said it quietly, with respect.

"That's very kind of you. I just couldn't seem to hold it together at the nail salon. I was feeling awful and thought I'd go and do something for myself that usually calmed me down, but clearly—" She gave Joyce a rueful grin. "Clearly that didn't work."

"Losing someone close to you is its own special kind of pain, I think. Until I lost my parents, I didn't know what real sorrow was." Joyce's parents died just a few months apart. For all her toughness, her mother didn't seem to want to live in a world where she couldn't actively hate her ex-husband. Joyce missed them both terribly, in her own way.

A shadow passed over Susan's face. "My brother and I weren't close. I hadn't spoken to him in years."

"I can see how that would make this all the more difficult."

"I feel like a fake." Susan folded her hands delicately in her lap and straightened her back. "I don't know how to handle any of this."

"Death is always a challenge to cope with. We don't give anyone the tools to deal with it properly, even though it touches everyone's life." Joyce had certainly heard enough stories from Simon to know that, even when a loved one was heading into a risky surgery, nobody was ever truly expecting their mother or cousin or child to die. Until it happened to you, death was something that affected *other* people. Of course, Joyce was at the point in her life where she knew death well.

Susan snapped her head up and looked Joyce straight in the eye. "What about murder? What kind of tools are there to deal with your baby brother being murdered?"

Joyce couldn't hold Susan's gaze and blinked several times before reaching for her latte. "I don't know," she finally answered.

"He was naked, in a hotel room, apparently. It's all so sordid. I mean, I just remember him as my little brother, gawky and sweet. Dermot was a good person. He helped people, especially children who were having problems at home. That's why he went into social work to begin with."

"It sounds like you knew him fairly well," Joyce observed.

"I knew the basic facts of his life. You can get those off Facebook or Instagram. I mean, we were connected through those. We weren't cut off from each other or anything." Susan twisted a strand of hair around her finger, and then seemed to think twice and folded her hands into her lap again. "But we didn't talk, you know? I didn't *know him*, as a person."

"I understand."

"And there's also this piece that I can't fit into everything else. I'm not sure if I should tell the police or keep it to myself." Susan's eyes roamed around the room, looking for somewhere to safely focus. She settled on the rose in the center of their table.

Joyce sat perfectly still, as though she might startle a fragile creature. She felt as though Susan was about to unfurl something that could never be put back inside once it was let out.

She listened.

"Dermot wrote a letter to me, just a few weeks before he died."

"Yes, you mentioned that at the salon. He reached out to you." Joyce said it as a statement, hoping that it would help Susan find some comfort in the belief that she and her brother weren't so disconnected.

And that it would encourage Susan to keep talking.

"At first, as I was reading it, I thought it was a letter about his life. He told me about his work, and his friends. He talked about falling in love with a woman, and how happy he was with her. That was really wonderful to read, although he said that there were some obstacles to the two of them being together."

She paused. Joyce waited.

"He asked about my children, his niece and nephew. And then," Susan closed her eyes and a tear slipped out and down her cheek. "Well, he confessed to something."

"Oh, I see," was all that Joyce could think to say. "What had he done?"

Susan swallowed, and then looked around at their fellow café customers, who all seemed to be engrossed in their own conversations. "He confessed to killing someone."

Something cracked inside Joyce, and she felt tears welling up inside her. Whatever Joyce may have been expecting, it was not this. She hadn't cried since she lost the baby, almost twenty years ago.

"Well, we all make mistakes," Joyce offered, and then reached out to hold Susan's hand.

She didn't ask Susan if she thought the two were connected—Dermot's death and this other loss he apparently felt responsible for. She didn't ask Susan about the love affair Dermot mentioned in his letter. There would be time for that later, she was certain of it.

For now, she just waited while Susan composed herself, and then she asked, "Did the police ask you about a woman named Catriona Dell yet?"

Susan sniffed and wiped her eyes and nose with the café's cloth napkin she'd draped over her lap.

"No. I haven't been interviewed by them yet. I'm supposed to go to the station later this afternoon. Why?"

Joyce took in a deep breath. Was she really going to do this?

"Because Trina Dell was the last person to see your brother alive."

CHAPTER TWENTY-FIVE

TRINA

Addy drove to Dermot's apartment. Her green VW bug was pristine on the inside, to the point that Trina felt self-conscious climbing inside with the slush and salt sticking to her boots. They didn't talk during the drive, and Addy left the radio off. Trina stared out the window, watching the neighborhoods pass by as Addy navigated to the high-rise apartment complex seated towards the edge of town.

When they arrived, Addy pulled a ring of keys out of her purse and Trina followed her up the staircase to Apartment C20. A wreath hung on the outside of the door, made of sprigs and berries in bright blues and purples. A quick stab of pain shot through Trina's chest. It was such a homey touch for a young guy living on his own to have. She felt certain it was a gift from someone who cared about him.

Trina looked over at Addy. Her face was tense as she slipped the key into the lock and opened the door further into Dermot's life.

"The police haven't closed this off to people?" Trina asked, a little late on the realization.

Addy ignored the question and stepped inside the apartment,

Trina following behind her. Apparently not, Trina thought. There were no barriers, or signs that anyone had been in the apartment, looking for clues as to what happened to Dermot in that hotel room.

The apartment was a one-bedroom, with a living area and galley kitchen and a bathroom leading off from the side of the hallway to the bedroom. Trina could see the light-blue sink through the cracked door. The bedroom door, or what she assumed was the bedroom door, was closed. Everything in the apartment was neat and organized. The kitchen counters were immaculate, with a toaster and red dish towel the only items taking up space. A beige couch with black-and-white cushions sat in front of a television hung from the wall. There were a few plants—Trina didn't know what kind—scattered in bright clay pots around the apartment.

There were no pictures hung on the walls or decorating the shelves.

Looking around, Trina's first thought was that the wreath on the front door was the most personal piece of the apartment. Otherwise, it looked like a rental someone staged for a real estate viewing. Stylish but without any personality.

Which was kind of how Dermot struck Trina when they met at the wedding. She tried to dismiss the unkind thought, but it stuck to the side of her mind like an unwelcome visitor.

Addy fidgeted with the keys in her hand. "I'm not sure what we're looking for."

"Neither am I." Trina thought about how she could really use a drink right about then, to steady her nerves and blunt the hard-edged feelings that kept rising when she was unprepared to handle them, which was essentially any time.

Trina took her boots off on the small patch of tile by the apartment door and laid her coat over the back of the couch. She had no clue what she was looking for or where to start, so she headed to the bedroom at the back of the hall. The walls of the apartment were thin, and she could hear someone talking in the apartment next door. Footsteps creaked above them as Dermot's upstairs neighbor moved around.

At first Addy stayed on the tile patch by the front door, her coat on and her wish to leave as soon as possible clear. But then she took off her own shoes and placed her coat next to Trina's, joining Trina at the threshold to the bedroom. The door opened easily. Trina noticed the carpet was worn but clean below their feet.

The bedroom had a twin bed, a small end table with what looked like a second-hand lamp poised beside it, and a bookcase partially full of old paperbacks. Trina was immediately drawn to the books and had to get close to read the spines in the dusky light of the bedroom. They were each well-loved, with cracked spines disguising some of the text, but Trina noted the majority of the books were crime and mystery novels. New and classic: Gillian Flynn, Ruth Ware, Dorothy Sayers, and Agatha Christie.

"Was Dermot a big reader?" The question came out before Trina could filter herself.

"Does it matter?" Addy replied, moving towards the bed and smoothing her hand over the bedspread, which was a plain-blue cotton.

Trina opened the closet to find a typical array of shirts and pants, mostly grey and black. To the right side were several fleeces and a few neon-orange sweatshirts, the kind Trina recognized were popular with hunters or hikers.

She pictured that young woman's face—practically a girl— smiling back from the photo on Dermot's Facebook page, the forest alive in color behind her. The one she saw looking at her and Dermot as they slipped into his hotel room the night he died.

"Are you almost done here?" Addy's voice had taken on an edge. Trina looked up and saw her standing by the bedroom door, inching out into the hallway.

"You were the one who offered to bring me here," Trina

reminded her. "Why do you have a key to his apartment, anyway?"

"I watered his plants for him a while back, when he needed to go out of town. He gave me a key, I came and watered a few of his plants, and then I sort of forgot about it until all of this happened, and I saw you in the stairwell." Addy crossed her arms over her chest and leaned against the doorframe as she spoke.

"What was he going out of town for?" Trina opened the drawers on the bedside table.

Some pens, a few pads of paper that were blank, and a random mix of headphones coiled into each other in a tangled mess. The white kind, that came with certain laptops.

"I don't know. He said for a work thing. Look, I'm not really comfortable with this anymore. Can we just go?" Addy glanced over her shoulder, as though she was worried someone might come in. Trina realized Addy might be right.

"Just another minute, I promise. I really appreciate you helping me with this, even if we don't find anything that might clue me in to what's going on." Trina moved over to the bed and bent down to look underneath it. "What was the work thing?"

"I don't know. And, honestly, I'm not sure if it really was for work."

Trina looked up. "Why do you say that?"

Addy shrugged. "I don't know. Just a feeling. When I came over to water the plants, there were a bunch of clothes scattered all over his bed, and they were the kind of things you'd wear on a date, you know? Not business casual. And there was a receipt on the kitchen counter—it was right by the note he'd left me about which plants to water, that's why I saw it. I wasn't snooping—for two bottles of really expensive champagne that he'd bought on Friday just before he left. So, I figured he was going away with someone."

"How expensive?"

"What?" Addy looked even more uncomfortable.

"How expensive was the champagne?" There was nothing under the bed. Trina lifted the mattress slightly and slid her fingers between the mattress and box spring.

"Like, three hundred dollars for two bottles."

The upstairs neighbor must have been doing an indoor workout, because the ceiling started to bounce slightly and the bedroom filled with the percussive noise of someone jumping.

Trina's fingers felt something sleek and hard shoved between the mattress and the box spring. She pulled it out, and sure enough it was a laptop. Dermot had felt the need to hide it underneath his bed, which made Trina think it was probably not his normal day-to-day computer. Trina could only assume the police had missed it because Dermot's main laptop was easily found somewhere else in the apartment.

Addy had been looking down the hallway, and when she turned and saw what Trina found, she blanched. "Where'd you find that?"

"Underneath the mattress. Let's go." Trina stood up, placing the laptop neatly underneath her arm. She'd check through it from the safety of her apartment.

"Are you allowed to take it?" Addy asked.

"As much as we're allowed to come into an apartment that isn't ours." Trina moved by Addy and headed down the hallway.

"I told you…" Addy started to cut in, but Trina stopped her.

"Hey, I'm sorry. I didn't mean to be rude. You've been really kind." Trina forced herself to look Addy in the eye. "Thank you."

Addy uncrossed her arms and started to say something, her face softening, but a sound interrupted her.

Keys jangled in the door, and from their position in the hallway they heard the front door open as heavy footsteps sounded against the tiles. Somebody else had keys to Dermot's apartment.

CHAPTER TWENTY-SIX

LAURA

Two women stood in Dermot's apartment. The younger one looked terrified to see Laura and Rosie step through the door, her arms wrapped around her chest with fingerless gloves that Laura remembered the artsy kids at high school used to wear. The other was older, and Laura decided she would be pretty if she didn't look like she hadn't slept or eaten a real meal all month. Rosie put her hand on the small of Laura's back and scooted around to stand in front of her.

"Who the hell are you?" Rosie asked, standing with her legs slightly apart and her shoulders squared. For such a tiny woman, she looked tough as nails. She balled her hands into fists, and for a second Laura thought that she might actually punch someone, just to prove her point.

"I know you," the older woman said, looking at Laura.

"Let's get *out of here*." The frightened one moved towards the door. "I'm sorry about all this. Dermot gave me a key to his place to water his plants. I was just trying to help."

She held out the key in the palm of her hand, extended towards Rosie.

"Nobody's going anywhere," Rosie said. "Answer the question. Who are you?"

"Are we making introductions now? Fine, I'll go first. I'm Trina, this is Addy." The strung-out woman gestured to the younger one. Laura noticed Trina's other hand held a silver laptop.

"I know you, too," Laura replied coolly. "You're the woman who was with Dermot the night he died. I saw the two of you together." As soon as she said it, she wished she'd just kept her mouth shut.

Trina's eyes narrowed. "Seems like we have something in common. We were both there the night Dermot was killed."

Laura hadn't realized she'd been seen. She'd been watching, hoping the signs she read were wrong, and that Dermot wasn't going to go through with it. Laura followed the two of them from the wedding party up to the room he'd asked for, wishing he'd turn around at any point to say he couldn't do it. In fact, Laura was certain he would. He was drunk that night, but he wasn't cruel. Deep inside, he knew he loved Laura and that they should be together. That he'd never want to do anything to hurt her. She had to believe that.

And then Dermot and Trina disappeared behind the hotel-room door, and Laura was left alone in the hallway she'd vacuumed just a few hours ago for minimum wage, with nothing waiting for her at home but a pile of dirty laundry and her brother barking orders to make him a sandwich.

"Whoa, what are you talking about?" Rosie took a step further into the apartment. "Are you implying that my pregnant friend had anything to do with what happened to Dermot?"

That word—pregnant—sucked the air out of the room. Everyone went quiet, Trina and Addy still pushed together at the end of the hallway and Rosie standing guard in front of Laura like a pit bull ready to pounce.

Laura should have waited, done the test at home and hid the

garbage in her purse. Or done it at the bathroom at the McDonald's, maybe. But she had to know, and Rosie was there, ready to be such a nice friend, and Laura had forgotten that Rosie, like most of the people in Laura's life, had problems thinking through the consequences of her actions.

Trina wouldn't look at Laura. Addy seemed less nervous, at least.

"I think we have some things to talk about." Addy moved from her spot by Trina and sat on the couch, adjusting a pillow behind her back and then leaning forward, her hands in between her knees. She took a deep breath, sucking it in through her nose and blowing it out through her mouth.

Rosie, Laura, and Trina all watched her.

"I get panic attacks sometimes," Addy explained. "I have to think through the situation, focus my thoughts, and breathe deep. I can usually make it go away."

"I'm sorry we made you panic," Laura told Addy. "We just didn't know what was going on."

"Still don't," Rosie cut in. After Laura told Rosie she wasn't sure who the father of her baby was, Laura also told her about Dermot. How she'd loved him. How much she missed him. How she didn't have anything to remember him by, not really.

Rosie had raised an eyebrow at that. "Except for maybe a really big thing," she'd said, looking pointedly at Laura's still-flat stomach.

Rosie convinced her that the two of them should go over to Dermot's apartment. Laura made a key for Dermot's place a while ago.

"What are your names?" Trina asked.

"I thought you knew who I was." Laura couldn't help it. She didn't like this woman. Not one bit.

"Yeah, but I don't know your name."

"Maybe we should keep it that way." Laura snatched a glance

at Addy, who was breathing deep again. She didn't like hurting people. "It's Laura. And this is my friend, Rosie."

"Okay, so we have that cleared up. How about you tell us why you have a key to Dermot's apartment?" Trina looked pointedly at Laura.

Again, Rosie decided to fix the situation herself. "She was Dermot's girlfriend. Of course she has a key."

Laura doesn't correct her. What would be the point?

Trina moved over to the couch and sat down. She looked very, very tired all of a sudden, her eyes pinched at the corners and her skin pale. "Oh," was all she said.

"Yeah, so like I said, we have some stuff to talk about." Rosie pulled up a kitchen chair and angled it across from the couch. "You sit here, *Trina*." She gestured to the hard chair. "Let my pregnant friend sit down on the soft couch."

Laura took a seat, and after Rosie grabbed a chair for herself, she started their little discussion group.

"So why are you taking my dead boyfriend's laptop?" she asked Trina.

CHAPTER TWENTY-SEVEN

TRINA

So much of this situation is surreal to Trina. She'd slept with so many men over the last several months, remembering few if any of their names, and then this one—this Dermot—stuck to her like a burr in the forest, rotting away as he clung to her. She couldn't help hating Simon even more than she already did, because none of this would be happening if he had never stumbled his way into her life with his God complex and his drunken hubris.

Trina looked at Laura, and not for the first time she thought about just how very young she was. Her skin had the creamy, plump texture that only came with youth and that nobody appreciated until they were too old to have it anymore, although there were thin lines already forming around her mouth, probably from smoking.

That won't be good for the baby, Trina thought automatically.

"They think I killed him," Trina told the makeshift collection of women touched by Dermot's life and death who'd gathered in his apartment. The guy must have passed out apartment keys like phone numbers. Something tracked as desperate to Trina in his willingness to open himself up so easily, but then again she wasn't the best judge of vulnerability lately. Maybe that was just what people did now—normal people, that is.

"Did you?" Rosie stared her down. If it were any other circumstance, Trina would like her. As it stood, she found herself annoyed at the fresh bravado the petite brunette kept pushing out into the world.

"No, but somebody did," Trina replied. "That's why I need his laptop. I think he might have gotten himself in trouble with some bad people."

"So what? You're going to hack into his email and see if he was messaging criminals about stuff? What's the likelihood of that? I mean, come on." Rosie stood up and started doing something in the kitchen. She ran water from the sink, opened and shut a few drawers, and soon Trina heard the familiar sounds and smells of coffee brewing.

Rosie was right. Trina didn't know how to hack an email account. She wasn't sure what she was looking for, or even if finding something could actually help get her out from under police suspicion. If they learned she broke into Dermot's apartment, it might make them more focused on her.

She had an impulse to call Simon, and tell him to figure out what was wrong, which was pathetic. Trina hated herself a little bit for even considering it.

The laptop sat as dead weight on Trina's thighs. She moved it to the coffee table, leaving it closed.

She met Rosie's eyes over the kitchen counter. "I need coffee if we're going to get into all of this kind of tradecraft bullshit," Rosie told the group. "Who else needs some?"

She brought over four mugs and set them on the coffee table, but then snatched up the one in front of Laura. "I'll make you some tea. Coffee is bad for the baby."

Laura fidgeted in her position on the couch. Trina noticed her hand go over her stomach for a moment, and then move back onto her leg.

Sipping the warm drinks seemed to settle all of them, and the tension that'd been in the air since they discovered each other dissolved into an almost-friendly quiet.

"He and I carved our initials into a tree, at the start of one of the trails by my house." Laura avoided looking at anyone while she spoke. "And then, walking into town today, I saw another carving, with his initials, and someone else's, at the trailhead that links onto the main road. We didn't do that hike together, but Dermot said one time that he loved the way it opened up at the top, by the vista." Her voice trailed off.

"It could have been anyone." Rosie reached out and put a hand on Laura's knee reassuringly.

Laura shook her head. "No, it wasn't. I'm sure it was Dermot. And the carvings were fresh, fresher than it would look if I went back and found our initials."

Addy had been sitting, staring at her feet. Now, she spoke up. "What were the initials?" Trina sat closest to Addy, picking at the corners of her nails while her thighs pressed her hands together.

"What does it matter?" Laura asked solemnly. "They weren't mine."

Addy turned suddenly to Trina. "Did you sleep with him that night?"

Trina didn't even try to stall. "Yes. That's the only reason I went up to his room. He was a one-night stand, not a boyfriend. I'm certain he didn't carve my initials into that tree."

"Were they mine?" Addy asked Laura.

"What are you saying?" Rosie narrowed her eyes. "Were you sleeping with him too?"

Addy remained silent again.

"Oh good Lord." Rosie let out a long sigh. She reached up and took a sip of her coffee before responding. "Don't tell me one of you is pregnant, too."

"No." Addy looked around worriedly. "It was just a few times. We were both lonely. It wasn't a relationship."

"No, the initials weren't yours," Laura chimed in. She surveyed the room with her light-blue eyes, something like pain pulling at the corners of her mouth. "I knew he had other women he was with. I just thought…" She ran her hand through her hair, scraping it back from her face. "I just thought he'd stopped once he knew I wanted to be with him."

"I'm sorry," Trina and Addy said simultaneously. Trina continued. "I didn't know. He was just a guy I was using to try and forget about my life for a little bit."

"It was awful, seeing you there with him," Laura said. Trina tipped her chin up defensively, and then stopped herself. There was something different in Laura's voice.

"I'm so sorry," Trina offered again. And she meant it, not just for Laura, but for herself.

"I had to call, every chance I had, to try and get them to release his body to me from the morgue," Laura continued. "He didn't have any family. Not that I knew of, at least. And I couldn't even afford to bury him, so I was going to cremate him instead. But then his sister showed up, and she's the one who's going to bury him now. I thought he was faithful to me, and he wasn't. I thought he didn't have any family left, and he did. What else did he lie to me about? Every day, it's like there's another stone I have to turn over, and underneath is only ugliness. Maggots and huge black beetles with pincers. And death. And now I'm supposed to have a baby? None of it is right. None of it is fair or makes sense."

Laura finished and stared into the middle distance. Her face was ashen, but her eyes flashed as they started to sweep from one corner of the room to the other. "There's no sign that I was ever here. That I was a part of his life."

And that's when Trina accepted what her gut had been telling her this entire time they'd been sitting and talking.

She could have done it. This small, foolish girl could have killed Dermot.

What Trina was going to do about that, she had no idea. The only thing she was certain of was that Dermot Carine wasn't afraid to hurt people to get what he wanted, and that was probably why he was dead.

CHAPTER TWENTY-EIGHT

SIMON

Trina's apartment was dark when he arrived. He didn't know why he was there, except that he didn't want to go home. Simon didn't have a key to her apartment, of course, so he sat in the car, considering whether Joyce was home yet and if he should stop by the liquor store on his way back to her. He hadn't driven drunk in his car since the accident last year, but if there was ever a time to start it seemed like now, with that young man and all his potential dead, the police homing in on the woman whose fiancé Simon killed as their main suspect, and his wife encouraging the process like a twisted sort of ringmaster.

He stayed for another ten minutes, and then decided to run to the store on the corner, buy a cheap bottle of whiskey—anything would do—and then drive back to his office and get horribly drunk, eventually slumping over in his office chair to sleep it off. No one would be at the office now, all the appointments were cleared for the day. He could be alone with his thoughts.

Trina's neighborhood was fine, but it wasn't the posh area that Simon lived with Joyce. A few teenage boys hung out on the corner in puffy down jackets, their breath misting in the cold air.

A siren cut through from somewhere in the distance. Simon turned up the collar on his coat and walked towards the neon sign flashing "R&S Convenience" above the corner store.

A bell rang out as he stepped into the store. An older man in a turban sat behind the counter. He gave Simon a nod, his eyes turning back to a television screen propped up in the corner of the front counter. Passionate dialogue in a language Simon didn't recognize buzzed in the background from the TV.

The liquor was in the back aisle, and Simon snatched a bottle of Seagram's off the shelf, thought twice, and then grabbed a second. He passed through the chip aisle and tucked one bottle under his arm in order to grab a bag of pork rinds. His stomach rumbled just thinking of their salty, crackly taste. He'd eaten them often as an undergrad, chugging through the day on little to no sleep, copious amounts of coffee, and junk food he could grab from the vending machines in the lobby of the library. He'd had a scholarship to keep, and his dormmate was a philosophy major who smoked pot and espoused wisdom to his little gaggle of friends into the small hours.

The bell above the door dinged again as Simon started to walk up to the counter and pay. Two of the boys from the corner had come inside, along with a new guy Simon didn't see before. This man was tall and rangy, with sunken cheeks and hair that could use a wash. The two teenage boys moved over to the snack aisle, clocked Simon standing there with the whiskey and chips, and moved swiftly to the door and out back into the cold, their hands empty. Simon looked from their exit to the other man, who was clearly not here with the boys, but had simply walked in with them.

The rangy man seemed startled that the boys left so suddenly. His eyes scanned around the store, eventually catching on Simon. The man moved towards Simon, and the way that he carried his shoulders told Simon that he didn't need chips. He grabbed

Simon by his upturned collar, slammed his forehead into him, and pulled a long knife from the waistband of his jeans. He held on to Simon, his forearm tight against his throat with the knife tucked underneath his chin. The man turned Simon so they were both facing the storeowner, whose eyes were so wide Simon could see the whites of them from where they were standing.

Simon didn't struggle at first. He'd never been in a fight, and having another man put his hands on him felt almost absurd. After a few seconds, though, Simon reached up with his hands and tried to twist out of the man's grip, but his knife pricked at the skin of his throat and Simon had trouble breathing.

"Give me all the money, or I'll kill him and then I'll kill you!" Spit from the man's mouth flew out as he shouted at the storeowner and it landed on Simon's cheek.

"It's okay," the storeowner said, holding his hands up. "I'll give you the money. Just let him go."

A memory flashed through Simon's mind of the first time he was in surgery, the clean lines of the incision masking the blood and gore of it all, and how his own blood pounded in his ears when blood swamped the open cavity unexpectedly and his patient's blood pressure dropped. In that moment, Simon felt like he would die along with this patient.

He didn't feel that way when he ran over to Tom and Trina that day on the street, after he realized that what he was doing was worsening the situation rather than helping. He knew he wouldn't die if Tom did, he would just wish that he had.

"What's your name?" Simon's voice came out clearer than he thought it would.

"Arvind." Fear stretched the storeowner's reply across the space of the store.

"I'm Simon. What about you?" He tilted his head towards the man holding him.

"I'm not giving you my fucking name! Just give me the

money." The man shifted his hold on Simon, and a waft of body odor rose through the folds of his thin coat. Simon thought he smelled the acrid scent of urine, and silently moved his hand to his pants to check if he'd wet himself.

He hadn't.

The storeowner started to reach down, but the man pressed the knife further into Simon's throat. A sharp pain shot through Simon's skin as the knife's edge dug in.

"Hey, hey! What are you doing?" the man shouted at the storeowner.

"I'm getting the money."

"Slower. Go slower." The man moved Simon forward as he stepped towards the cash register. "Easy now."

"I feel like I should know your name."

The storeowner kept moving his hands below the counter.

"I said slower." He took the knife from Simon's throat and jabbed it towards Arvind.

But it was too late. The storeowner brought a shotgun from under the counter, braced it against his shoulder, and pulled the trigger. Simon moved out of the man's grasp and fell to the floor just in time. He ducked below as the sound of the gun's report threatened to burst his ear drums, and then wetness sprinkled onto his face.

The man who held him at knifepoint didn't have a chest anymore. It was a bright red mass, and even though Simon was a trained surgeon, he couldn't make sense of the pieces that tore apart from each other.

"Help me! Help me," the man begged. Simon knew he should go over, assess his wounds, start to provide first aid. But he couldn't make himself move from the ground. Simon's body felt like a hard plank of metal come loose from its fittings. Unmovable.

"Simon!" the man called out.

At the sound of his name, Simon looked up and locked eyes

with his would-be captor. He saw his pain. He saw his desperation. "My name's Terry. Please, help me."

But Simon didn't move. He remained where he was, waiting for the police to arrive and for someone else to take on this burden.

CHAPTER TWENTY-NINE

TRINA

There were police cars parked at her corner when Trina returned to her apartment. An ambulance was parked near the R&S Convenience market, but no lights flashed as she watched two EMS workers roll a stretcher into the back of the vehicle and close the doors. A sheet was pulled over the top of the stretcher, but two heavy boots peeked out from below on the other end. She figured heart attack, but knew it could be something much worse. There had been several robberies at the store already this winter. Trina went there to buy liquor when she was desperate, otherwise she went to the ritzier Wegman's across town, where she could pretend that she was going to buy groceries and just happened to buy a few bottles of wine. Although the storeowner was always friendly to her and made a point of looking away when she showed up with smeared mascara and bed creases on her face, desperate for a Red Bull.

Her hallway was empty, and Trina let herself into her apartment with a quick swish of her keys. She'd dropped Addy off back on campus, where she had to do some revisions on her dissertation. Trina didn't know where Laura and Rosie went, although they exchanged numbers and made tentative plans to text each other for another meet-up. Trina had promised to update everyone with what she found on Dermot's laptop.

It sat heavy on her shoulder and Trina set her bag down on the counter. She still couldn't believe the other women had let her take it home without much protest. Trina expected them to fight her for it, or to demand that they review the contents all together. But after Laura's confession about Dermot's lying, the energy of the room shifted and everyone seemed to want to get the hell out of his apartment. Like something of his own problems might taint each of them if they stayed there too long.

Trina poured herself a huge glass of Chardonnay from the fridge and settled into the couch. She hadn't eaten much of anything for the last several days, which meant she'd be feeling a buzz sooner rather than later. She'd need it to give her the edge necessary to poke around a dead one-night-stand's computer. On her way home, she considered for a second it might be wise to drop the laptop off at the police station, but she dismissed the notion almost as soon as she recognized it. What she needed more than anything was to get as far away from the police as possible, not to give them more reasons to suspect she was involved in all of this. And if she showed up with Dermot's laptop, which she magically found somewhere, she'd have to explain how she was able to get into his apartment and discover it when the police had been unable to—which still struck her as ridiculous, given that hiding things under a mattress was something every thirteen-year-old knew to do. Trina didn't want to get Addy, or Laura, or anyone else caught up in this mess any more than they already were.

She was betting, too, that there wouldn't be much on Dermot's laptop, or that it'd be password protected and no one would be able to get into it. In other words, she wasn't expecting much joy from her little foray into cyber-crime. Still, she had to try, just in case there was something on it that could help her show picking up women at weddings and cheating on his teenage pregnant girlfriend weren't the worst things Dermot had gotten up to.

It was a small, neat laptop with an icon of a soccer ball positioned over Dermot's name. Trina clicked on it, expecting a password to pop up, but instead it took her directly to the home screen. The background Dermot had set revealed nothing—a generic sunny field that came pre-canned with the laptop. There were a few folders on the desktop. One labeled Bills. Another listed as Photos. The last folder was called *Misc*. Miscellaneous.

She'd look at those in a moment. First, she opened up the web browser and examined Dermot's email saved in the recent history. He seemed to use a Gmail account, like a billion other people, with his username being Derm5028, which sounded like a skin condition to Trina. She clicked into his account's login and it opened straight up to his inbox, but even after going through the Trash and Junk folders, Trina didn't see any messages. The entire email was empty.This struck her as odd, because Dermot died on Sunday, and he hadn't been able to check into the account for several days. There were no junk emails or spam. It was completely blank.

Which meant that Dermot was using this email for a select set of correspondence. Not to sign up for free accounts to get discounts or free shipping. And whoever he was writing back and forth with didn't communicate often. Or they were the ones who killed him, and knew he wouldn't be able to reply anyway.

A noise came from the hallway outside her door. Trina listened for a moment, thinking it was Darlene or her son coming home, but there was no sound of keys jangling in the lock or of doors opening.

Delivery, probably. Trina took another sip of wine.

She clicked on the small green box in the bottom corner, opening up Dermot's text messages linked to that laptop. Very few conversations were listed, and none of the numbers had names identified with them. Instead, there were four or five different conversations with different numbers, each coming from local area codes. The numbers listed addresses, and then Dermot would reply with a C or NC.

"Coming" or "Not coming", Trina figured.

Trina skimmed through the addresses. She didn't recognize any of them at first, but then she saw one number at the very end of the list. There was only one text exchange from the number, whereas the others had several different back and forths with addresses and confirmations. Trina recognized the location. She put the same address listed in the text into her phone last Saturday night, looking for the Marriott after taking a wrong turn down Delaney. Someone texted Dermot the address for the hotel, and he had replied C.

She looked at the date on the text. It was sent Saturday morning, and Dermot replied that Saturday afternoon.

Who had wanted him to go to the Marriott?

Suddenly, Trina felt a cold draft blowing in across her living room. She got up, following the chill into her bedroom. Her bedroom window was cracked slightly, and icy air streamed in from the open top. Sometimes her windows shifted size, growing and shrinking with the humidity of summer and the freezing temperatures of winter, and could open on their own.

Trina shoved the window closed, grabbed a blanket from the end of her bed, and wrapped it around her shoulders as she walked back to the living room.

She started to put in the other addresses that Dermot had texted with. Each one came up as a hotel or motel in the area. What was Dermot doing, and who was he meeting? There were no pictures attached to the messages, no emojis or other indicators that there might be some sort of affection between Dermot and whoever he was messaging with. All different numbers, with four or five exchanges before it'd switch to the next number.

Trina clicked over into Dermot's photos. These were

organized into folders labeled "Hiking" and "Work". Trina clicked through them and found little else besides some group birthday photos of who she assumed were Dermot's coworkers, and lots of photos of trees and other pretty landscapes. She didn't see the photo of Laura that Dermot posted on Facebook.

Scrolling through the "Hiking" folder, Trina found another folder, seemingly randomly labeled with numbers and letters. It looked like the kind of folder your phone would sometimes create when it connected to your computer, downloading photo items without you realizing. It would stay on your computer, even after you deleted it from your phone.

Trina clicked on the folder to open it and saw a small thumbnail of one picture. She could tell just from the miniature preview that it was a photo of a naked woman. Holding her breath, Trina opened the file, waiting for it to load onto the screen of the laptop.

As the image came into resolution, a deep pit of fear and anger formed in her stomach. Or course it was her. *Her.*

Trina finally opened the Misc. folder. There was only one document stored there. The details for the file showed that it was created and last updated nine months ago.

Trina opened the file, read it, and immediately thought she'd be sick. Her stomach heaved.

Two competing desires pulsed in Trina's chest. She needed to show everyone what she'd just read. And no one could ever see what Dermot had written.

A rage-filled scream rose from her lungs. But she'd never get the chance to let her despair out.

From behind Trina, a voice broke into the quiet that had settled over the apartment. "So now you know our dirty little secret."

The rope slipped around Trina's neck smooth and supple, like a lover's hands. She couldn't work fast enough to move her fingers underneath the garrote before it tightened.

Trina realized she was cying.

It didn't take long, Trina thought, her brain flooded with Tom's brown eyes as he lay there with Simon bent over him, pain streaking across h s face in short, intense bursts. *At least it didn't take long this time.*

CHAPTER THIRTY

LAURA

It was the second time Laura had been called by the police in under a week. Her brain buzzed with adrenaline as the uniformed officer guided her down the hallway and into the room, where the same two detectives who interviewed her about Dermot sat across the table. Bechdel had her hair down and tucked behind one ear. Kirkpatrick was flipping through paperwork, but he looked up with a kind turn of his mouth when Laura came into the room.

"I'm so sorry," Bechdel said, reaching her hand out to pat Laura on the forearm. Laura was surprised by how good it felt to be touched in a kind way by a stranger.

"They wouldn't tell me what happened," Laura said. She'd been at Rosie's, trying to process everything she'd learned at Dermot's apartment. Rosie made scrambled eggs, even though it was dinnertime. She said her grandmother always made scrambled eggs when someone needed comforting. Extra butter, a dash of salt, and you don't break the yolks until the whites are slightly cooked.

Laura had been surprisingly hungry, eating the entire plate before Rosie could sit down and join her. Then Laura's phone rang, and even though she should have just let it go to voicemail she picked it up, thinking it might be Trina or Addy, calling to confirm they had her number entered right into their phones. She hadn't had a chance to put them into her contacts yet, although she'd do it as soon as she could.

But it wasn't one of them. It was the police, calling to say her brother was dead. That he had been shot, in a violent exchange he started. Just like when she found out about Dermot, Laura promptly threw up.

It was such a shame, Laura thought now as she looked across the table at the two detectives. *She'd never want to eat scrambled eggs again.*

The male detective was saying something, but Laura felt like she was underwater. She couldn't understand the words coming out of his mouth. She reached underneath the table and pinched her thigh, but she couldn't feel anything.

"Are you okay?" Kirkpatrick asked, waving his hand in front of Laura and snapping his fingers. He still had that kind look on his face, but Laura realized it was more like he was talking to a dog than a person. She tried to picture herself from the outside and see what the detectives saw.

Her hair was shoved into a low ponytail, and the shirt she'd worn to Rosie's had speckles of vomit down the front. She couldn't remember putting makeup on this afternoon, but she must have because when she wiped her hand over her face her fingers came back streaked with gooey black from her mascara.

"Tell me what happened, please," she managed to say. Getting the words out winded her, like she'd just run a few miles. She tried to take a deep breath, but the pressure on her head clamped down on her throat, cutting it off.

"Your brother tried to rob a convenience store. He had a knife." Bechdel gave her a steady look, as if she were trying to will Laura to just hang on.

"And he's dead now?" That same fatigue settled into Laura's chest as she breathed the words out.

"Yes." Kirkpatrick cleared his throat. "There are witnesses to the entire incident. Your brother tried to take one hostage."

"Oh," was all Laura had to say to that. Sharp edges tore at her brain. She was totally alone in this world now. Her family was gone. Dermot was gone.

She touched her belly, like she had a stomachache. Not totally alone, she reminded herself. At least not for now.

Laura didn't know what she was going to do about the baby.

"Do you know why your brother was robbing a store?" Kirkpatrick asked.

"No."

"Did he need money?" Bechdel gave her a searching look. "Drugs. Booze. Maybe he got caught up in something he shouldn't have?"

"We all need money," Laura told them, which was true. "And Terry had been sober for six months. He was going to meetings, talking to his sponsor."

"It sounds like he was getting his life on track." Kirkpatrick leaned back in his chair and then seemed to realize he was being insensitive and pushed himself forward, elbows on the table.

"Yeah, he was." Laura didn't want to be here anymore. "Look, I really just want to go home. I can't really handle much more today."

"What else happened today?" Bechdel asked. She tried to hide it, but the detective's voice had perked up.

Laura fought the urge to scream. Her throat burned from the eggs mixing with her stomach acid.

"Nothing." Laura slouched in her chair. As far as Laura was concerned, this conversation was over.

"Do you think this is connected to what happened to Dermot?" Kirkpatrick asked Laura, which sparked a flame of anger to replace her weariness.

"Do I think my brother getting shot trying to rob a grubby corner store has anything to do with the love of my life being murdered in his hotel room while he was cheating on me?" She sucked in a breath of air. "No, I don't."

There's a subtle shift in the atmosphere of the room, and the two detectives sat up taller and leaned in towards each other slightly.

"You and Dermot Carine were romantically involved?" Kirkpatrick asked.

"I told you that already," Laura replied.

Bechdel shifted closer to Laura. "We're just trying to get everything straight. Can you tell us again, about you and Dermot?"

"Can I get a glass of water?" Laura wanted to focus on Bechdel's face, but things blurred in front of her.

"Sure, no problem." Something silent passed between Kirkpatrick and Bechdel, and he eventually got up and left the room. There was a couch over in the corner.

"Can I lie down?" she asked, already moving towards the soft cushions. If she could just lie down, maybe all of this would be over. She'd wake up, and everyone would be alive again.

Dermot. Terry.

Her parents.

"Tell me more about Dermot," Bechdel said, helping to pick Laura's feet up and resting them on the other end of the sofa.

And so Laura did, until she drifted off, dark and dreamless.

CHAPTER THIRTY-ONE

JOYCE

Joyce had spent too much time in hospitals over the last twenty years. Surgeon's wife. Fundraising guru. More recently she'd been the supportive spouse to a broken man, and potential criminal, while Simon sat covered in blood that wasn't his own, not a scratch on him. And now, victim's spouse, but with the same touchstone of a stranger's blood marking her husband's features.

Simon called her from the back of the ambulance. He'd sounded fractured, like he was drunk but without the ease that smoothed his edges when he drank. He explained there had been a crime, and a killing. He'd been taken hostage. A man, almost a boy, Simon said, had died.

The words tumbled into Joyce's ear, and she couldn't stop the first response that came out of her mouth. "Did you do it again?"

She always knew there was a vile streak in her, but she was usually so good at hiding it from the important people in her life. Especially her husband. But this was too much. It felt as though they'd just finished hobbling through the past year. And just when she thought she'd ensured Trina would finally be out of their life, here came another disaster Simon was in the center of, one that Joyce needed to clean up—literally and figuratively.

Perhaps she should have left him, back when he was in medical school and he had his breakdown. She knew he was weak, but she stayed with him anyway. Because the poor, bald fact was that she loved her husband, however pitiable and problematic joining her life to his might have been.

She dabbed a damp piece of gauze on Simon's forehead now, wiping away the other man's blood. Simon stared off, seemingly focused on a yellowed stain in the middle of the linoleum floor. Nurses and doctors in their various scrubs passed by the window of their room, but for now Joyce and Simon were alone.

"I'm sorry," she said, moving the cloth down to his temple and wiping as gently as possible. She reached to grip Simon's hands, which sat in his lap, but he held them firmly together and wouldn't let her pull one of them free. *Always his hands*, she thought. They could bring her back to him or push her away. Or kill them both.

Joyce went back to cleaning up his face, moving gradually down his neck. She'd thought to bring a clean shirt for him from home, and like a mother caring for a young child she undid the buttons of his shirt and helped him slip off the bloody one, wiping away at any gore that made it through the fabric of his shirt, and then eased his arms through each of the shirtsleeves. She felt the tremor in Simon's hand as she helped him dress, and wondered if he was going to cry, or apologize for not letting her touch him a moment ago.

Joyce could always count on Simon to do the right thing, in the end, and she preferred to think of that as his ultimate strength. In their marriage, she was the one who brought the other forms of strength to their life together. She took care of the problems Simon couldn't.

"I wasn't going to let it happen again," Simon said. He wouldn't look at Joyce. She sat on the hospital bed next to him and wordlessly pulled his left and then his right wrist into her lap, buttoning his cuffs. He didn't resist, and when she was finished he leaned into her just the slightest bit, and Joyce felt a rush of compassion for Simon that threatened to overwhelm her.

Where would he be without her? She didn't dare to consider.

"Will the police be interviewing you again?" Joyce asked. Joyce had a full morning to coordinate tomorrow. She'd texted earlier to confirm plans, but hadn't yet received a reply. She had to consider whether spending the morning at the police station would be helpful or a hindrance.

"I don't know. Everything at the store was a jumble. I talked to a few officers, but I don't know if anything official happened." Simon leaned into her further, and she put an arm around his waist. "I couldn't do it."

"Couldn't do what?" she asked, although she already knew the answer.

"I couldn't help him. The man—the boy who was shot."

"The man who held you at knifepoint, you mean?" There was no sarcasm in her voice. She stated the facts. Simon had a tendency to get lost in the emotion of situations, and Joyce often brought him back to the realness of the circumstances they found themselves in.

Simon was silent again for a beat, and then, "Yes."

"Why should you have helped him?"

"Because I'm a doctor, that's what I was sworn to do."

"You were in shock. You'd been held at knifepoint and seen a man shot. Nobody expected you to leap up and start performing surgery on the man."

"His face was so young." Simon's voice hovered soft and quiet. "Just a kid, really. But hardened, somehow. He stunk, while he held me close to him. And that's all I could focus on. That he smelled terrible."

"That's only human," Joyce assured him. She squeezed her arm around him.

Joyce continued. "I'm glad you didn't help him."

Simon shifted away from her slightly. "Why?"

"Because he didn't deserve your kindness."

"But you didn't know him. You didn't know his story, or why he was in the store today. You don't know why he needed the money."

Joyce stood up quickly. Simon lost his balance as she moved away and threw a hand onto the bed to brace himself.

"That's true." She peered out the window into the hallway. People rushed around, faces focused or worried or blissfully unaware. "But there are lots of people who need things, and only a small portion of them will actually go to the point of killing another person to get them."

Simon and Joyce looked at each other, and it was as though they were seeing each other—really seeing the other person—for the first time in years. Not just the hard or soft shell that formed when you lived with someone, day in and day out. But underneath, into the core that pulsed out their decisions, that determined their perception of the world.

They held each other's gaze, neither willing to let go just yet.

Until there was a knock on the door, and Joyce turned to see who the next intruder into her marriage would be.

CHAPTER THIRTY-TWO

ADDY

The guy said Addy's name several times before he got her attention. Her cappuccino sloshed over the side of the cup when she grabbed it from him, making a slick pool of foam on the wooden countertop of the café. She didn't know why she ordered it. Habit, Addy supposed. When she was writing her dissertation, going to the café was one of her major splurges twice a week. She'd take herself out to the café, plug in her laptop, sip on a cappuccino that wasn't made from cheap Trader Joe's espresso, and write and analyze and read far too many but never really enough research studies, and then write some more. It was a comfort to her, to know that she could go to the small wire table in the corner and just be alone amongst people for a few hours.

Now, she took a seat and set her drink down in front of her, not sure what to do. Certain only that the pit in her stomach kept growing.

She couldn't get the girl's face out of her thoughts. The way she looked in Dermot's apartment, so young and broken, made Addy want to chuck all of her achievements over the last several years and explain that she was sorry the world was shit and that people hurt each other and that, if she'd known Dermot was making promises to Laura, Addy would have never slept with him.

Addy's phone buzzed in her pocket and she pulled it out. It was a message from her mother, asking how her day was going. Addy shoved her phone back into her jeans. Her mother would have to wait, because there was no way to explain over text to your mother that you'd somehow found yourself in the middle of a murder investigation because of your poor choice in men, just a few days after you became Dr. Simpson and your parents sent you flowers and a huge teddy bear that barely fit in your studio apartment.

She had revisions to do. The deadline for filing them was next Friday, and although she didn't have many, Addy needed to start on them soon. Her mind wouldn't focus, and instead of writing she stared out the window, her hands wrapped around her coffee.

A young mother went by her table, jostling Addy's elbow with the edge of her stroller and offering a harried "sorry" as she continued on her way, a toddler protesting angrily in the stroller seat. Addy decided it was time to go and made for the door as well.

Her phone buzzed again, and she expected it to be her mother's message repeating itself, but instead it was a new message from Laura. The three women swapped phone numbers yesterday before leaving. Trina was going to send updates about what she'd found on Dermot's laptop.

Have you heard from Trina yet? Laura wanted to know.

Which is when Addy realized she'd been so focused on her own mistakes that she'd missed the obvious concern of Trina not sending any follow-ups of what she'd found, if anything. It was Wednesday morning. She'd assumed they'd hear from Trina sometime last night.

No, she replied.

I'm worried, Laura wrote back.

Addy called Trina's number, but it went straight to voicemail. She tried again, but nothing. She knew where Trina lived, and over the group text she offered to go over to Trina's apartment and check on her. Laura didn't protest, just responded with an *Ok.*

I'll let you know what I find out, Addy wrote back. Trina didn't live far from the university, and Addy decided she could walk there. The cold air would help clear her head.

Addy met Dermot at one of those graduate student dinners celebrating someone's birthday where everyone only pays for their own meal and the poor waitstaff are forced to make twenty separate checks for ten or twelve dollars each. Addy went with her friend Gina, who knew the English program grad student whose birthday it was. Gina's friend was studying Hemingway's letters and had spent most of the evening being just drunk enough to wax poetic on why Ernie was a genius and Virginia Woolf was a hack, but not drunk enough to offer to buy a round for everyone. Addy thought he was a douchebag, and she'd excused herself to go to the bathroom, instead heading to the bar to hopefully soften some of her irritation before having to go back.

She'd ordered a whiskey neat, and as she waited for her drink a handsome guy with dark hair and the healthy kind of glow you get from spending a lot of time outdoors sat down on the stool next to hers.

"Anyone who reads Hemingway is just trying to prove how deep they are," he said.

Addy smiled. "People who point that out are just trying to prove how smart they are."

"Fair point," he replied, smiling back. The bartender brought Addy her drink, which she slung back in one deep pull.

"I'm Dermot. Can I get you a drink?"

Addy glanced back at the table, where the birthday boy was now waving a glass around and talking about Keats.

"Yes, please," she'd said. She'd gone home with him that night, and the sex had been intense. Addy hadn't slept with anyone since she was an undergraduate and being with Dermot and having him touch her in such an expert way made her feel alive more than she had for a long time.

The next morning, she left before Dermot woke up, leaving her number on a notepad by the bed in case he'd wanted to get in touch with her. And he had, but only to ask her to watch his apartment for him while he went away for the weekend.

She felt like it was some sort of sick joke he was playing, giving her a key to his apartment and a chance to poke around his things without him there, and at the same time rejecting her unspoken offer to be together again.

As she walked to Trina's apartment, Addy passed by a convenience store on the corner, the R&S, and thought about stopping in to get something to bring with her. What do you bring when you're going to someone's apartment hoping they've found the evidence to clear them of a murder charge?

Cake? Entenmann's?

She kept walking. Trina's apartment was just another block down, in a building resembling a brick frown.

Addy didn't pass anyone when she went up the stairs to Trina's second-floor apartment. She called Trina when she got to her door, and the chimes of Trina's phone were loud enough that Addy could hear them through the thin material of the walls. Addy knocked, banging on the door as hard as she could.

She realized Trina might be drunk, even though it was only 10am. It had been a rough time for Trina over the past year—Addy knew that.

Addy heard movement behind her, and a scrawny teenager with lanky hair and a face that seemed to wiggle too much stood in the hallway behind her.

"I have a key," he said. "She helps my mom sometimes."

"Oh," was all Addy could think to say. The boy opened his apartment door, called something in a language she didn't recognize to whoever was inside, and reappeared with a key in his hand.

"Do you think she's okay?" the boy asked. "Ms. Trina is always really nice to me."

"I don't know," she said.

But when he opened the door, the answer to the boy's question was obvious.

Trina wasn't okay. Trina was dead.

CHAPTER THIRTY-THREE

SIMON

Detective Kirkpatrick had a bright pink sprinkle dangling from his upper lip. Simon couldn't stop staring at it while the detective spoke.

"Where were you last night, Dr. Morgan?" The sprinkle fell onto the papers scattered over the interview table. The detective took another bite of donut, followed by a sip of his coffee.

Simon had been in the shower at home, washing off his own sweat and the blood of that dead boy. Terry. They'd spent most of the night in the hospital, with Simon protesting he was fine and the EMTs demanding he wait to be looked over by an ER doctor. A different set of police officers took his statement, twice. The knock on the bathroom door had made him jump, even though Simon knew it could only be Joyce, coming to check on him.

She'd told him to hurry up because the police were there waiting for him.

Again.

Trina was dead, Joyce told him. A young woman—one of Trina's students—had found Trina this morning in her apartment. Joyce said the student's name was Addy. *Did he know anyone named Addy?* Joyce had asked.

"Did they question you too?" he asked Joyce. He didn't know why the police had shared so much with her.

Joyce shook her head. "No, they want to talk to you." She seemed to understand his confusion. "The reporters are here already." They must have asked the same question of Joyce when she let the police in. *Do you know the woman who found Trina? Do you know Addy?*

Simon had never heard that name before in his life.

Maybe he would have if he'd followed Trina even more, kept better tabs on her. Then she would have never been with Dermot on the night he died and none of this would have happened. She'd still be alive, which meant there'd still be a chance for Simon to make things right.

"I was the victim of kidnapping and armed robbery," Simon answered Det. Kirkpatrick's question. Simon rubbed his hands over his face. The weariness of his life sank in between his shoulder blades like a knife. "I was at the hospital, there were several witnesses."

"Yes, we've read the statements." The other detective, Bechdel, nodded and held her pen poised over a fat little notebook. Simon thought law enforcement must be the only career that still encouraged the use of actual written notes. Even the journalists who had hounded Simon and Joyce after the accident last year used their phones to tap out notes rather than be hindered by paper.

Which reminded Simon that they would surely be getting visitors camped outside their door again soon once the connection between their shared past and Trina's death was made. Joyce wouldn't tolerate much more, he thought. Last year nearly broke them.

"You were attacked at a store not far from Trina Dell's apartment."

"I had stopped to buy wine for dinner that evening."

"Why were you in Ms. Dell's neighborhood?"

"What does it matter?" Simon was losing his self-control. His hands shook despite him trying to hold them folded in his lap. He needed a drink, or a nap, or another life. Maybe all three.

"Because the robbery took place at 6:10pm, according to the security videos at the store." The sprinkle fell from Kirkpatrick's mouth, and Bechdel flicked it off the table with a small moue of distaste. Kirkpatrick didn't notice, instead picking up the line of questioning.

"And based on what the coroner can initially tell us, Trina Dell died anywhere between 4:30 and 8:30pm."

"Ah, I see." Simon couldn't seem to swallow. He coughed in a series of raspy blows after some of his own spit caught in his throat. "You want to know if I killed her."

"We'd like to know where you were during that window of time."

"I've already told you. I was at the police station—*this* police station—then I was at the park to clear my head, followed by Trina's meeting with the lawyer I'd arranged. Afterwards I headed home and decided to stop at the R&S and get some wine for my dinner that evening."

"You don't have any wine at home?" Kirkpatrick looked back at Simon innocently. "Most people usually have a bottle or two on hand?"

"And it's not like the R&S is a place anyone would go to get a special bottle, you know what I mean?" Bechdel offered a conspiratorial smile. "I mean, you seem to be a man of some taste."

Simon sighed. *What was the point?* Trina was dead. Someone murdered her. What did it matter for him to keep up appearances? "I planned to buy some whiskey and drink it back at my office."

"Why?" Kirkpatrick asked.

"I'd come from the police station, where my wife accused

Trina Dell of being responsible for that young man's murder. My connection to Trina Dell is complicated—"

"You contributed to the death of her fiancé as a result of your drunken attempts to save him—" Bechdel offered.

"Yes, thank you for the clarification." A fist gripped the inside of Simon's chest and squeezed tight. He flinched as Kirkpatrick leaned forward in his chair, his survival instincts triggered. Simon's brain sensed danger, not realizing that it was the threat of his life changing irrevocably rather than merely ending.

"So you're a drinker," Bechdel stated.

"Yes, I am."

"Had you been drinking that afternoon already?"

Simon thought about the snifter he kept in his office. "Yes, I had." He stopped himself from saying he wished he had some right now.

"When did it start?"

"The drinking?"

"Yes, the drinking." Kirkpatrick was being droll.

"It got worse after the accident."

"But that wasn't when it started," Bechdel amended.

"What do you want me to say? Yes, I've been a drinker for a long time."

"We're just trying to get a sense of what happened last night."

"I spent the night in the hospital, covered in another man's blood. I saw him shot, just moments after he held me close to him as his prisoner. All this, and then when I am finally able to go home, I'm accosted again by the police because a woman whose life I ruined is dead. Murdered. Just a week after her supposed lover was found dead. Do I have that right?"

Bechdel and Kirkpatrick remained still. In the brief silence, Simon realized he was doing exactly what they wanted him to do. Talking and talking, streaming out anger and, with it, information.

"Were you in love with Trina Dell?" Bechdel's voice sounded

kind. She gave Simon a knowing look. Simon wanted to smack it right off Bechdel's face.

"What does it matter?" Simon was cold in the thin T-shirt he slipped on from the shower. His hair was still wet in places.

Where was Joyce? Why hadn't she come to the station with him? Suddenly he desperately needed her there with him.

"Because the opposite of love isn't hate," Kirkpatrick said. "It's indifference. And it seems clear from your actions—calling regularly, lending money, hiring a lawyer for her, visiting her classes on campus—that you were anything but indifferent to Catriona Dell."

"And if I hated her?" Simon asked.

"We both know you didn't hate her," Bechdel replied. "You don't really hate anyone—it's not your style."

"Except one person," Kirkpatrick tossed in, like it was an afterthought.

Myself, Simon silently finished for him.

CHAPTER THIRTY-FOUR

LAURA

The vacuum was clogged. Laura tried to open the compartment with the sweeper bag, but the tab kept sticking and she couldn't slip her thumb around it. She considered throwing the entire machine out the window, except none of the windows in the hotel opened.

She'd wanted to call off sick today, but without Terry's income she would have serious trouble making rent and paying the electric bill when it came. They'd need another propane tank soon, it'd been so cold lately. So she was at work, the day after her brother died in a botched armed robbery and a week after the man she thought was her boyfriend was killed in the same hotel she was now considering relieving of one of their vacuums. And she'd woken up with morning sickness, except now it was well past two o'clock and she still felt nauseous.

She couldn't believe she'd essentially passed out in the interview room with the two detectives yesterday. If they hadn't known she was pregnant yet, they sure as hell did now. It had been nice talking about Dermot though. About all the good things he'd done, for Laura and for others. They'd only asked her once about the complaint Terry filed with the social service office against Dermot, and Laura had told them the truth. It was a year and a half ago. Terry was just being an asshole, complaining that Dermot was spending too much time checking up on Laura. This was before Terry had gotten clean, and Dermot hadn't wanted Laura to be living on her own with a drunk and a druggie. It'd all blown over in the end, but not without Dermot having to go to sensitivity training and having a tense meeting with his boss.

Laura also told the police officers that Dermot had never done anything romantic with her until after she was eighteen and no longer under his supervision through social services.

That'd been true too.

Laura walked back into the room to switch the pillowcases and fluff them up for the next customer. A twenty-dollar bill was shoved underneath the television remote from the previous occupant and she grabbed at it greedily, shoving it into the pocket of her uniform pants and doing calculations in her head about whether she might be able to stop at the grocery store on her way home from work.

She looked at the clock on the bedside table and decided she had time to sit down for a minute. Her mind swam with thoughts, each one moving around in her head like a tadpole, and she couldn't make sense of much beyond the fact that she needed to figure out how to fix the damn vacuum so she didn't get fired.

Laura closed her eyes for a second and her hand went instinctively to her stomach, even though it looked flatter than usual. She needed to eat something.

Her phone buzzed with a message in her pocket. She knew it wouldn't be Trina. Laura texted and called her several times yesterday, but Trina ignored each one. It was hard for Laura to admit she didn't know Dermot well, but she remained certain she knew him better than Trina.

Her phone buzzed again, and Laura decided she might just have to look at it, but when she sat up to pull the phone out of her pocket there was a knock on the door behind her. She turned from the window overlooking the parking lot to see a man standing in the propped-open doorway of the room. His blond hair was slicked back in a stylish way, and he wore a suit. The nice kind, that fit him just so in the shoulders. Laura could almost smell the money coming off him—maybe it was the pregnancy—and she wondered why he was standing there, in this mediocre hotel in the middle of nowhere.

"Sorry, I didn't mean to scare you." He stepped into the room. His voice was deep and had the smallest trace of an accent Laura didn't recognize.

"I'm not scared." Laura stood up, but her head swam and she had to reach out to the arm of the chair to steady herself. She prayed she wouldn't be sick in front of this stranger. She really needed to eat something.

The hallway outside had gone quiet. Laura couldn't hear any of the other cleaning women working. No radio on, no feet rustling on the carpet.

"Be careful." The man came over and placed his hands gently on Laura's arms and guided her back to the chair. "Are you all right?"

"Do you need help with something?" Laura asked, ignoring his question. She'd prefer to be alone right now. She closed her eyes for a minute, hoping the room would stay still.

"I stayed here last night," he explained. "I think I left something in the bathroom."

"I didn't see anything when I cleaned in there," Laura lied. She hadn't cleaned the bathroom yet, but she was getting a strange feeling from the man and she wanted to encourage him to leave as quickly as possible. The stairwell door scraped open and closed somewhere down the hallway, but the footsteps disappeared into another wing of the hotel.

She was alone with him.

"It's very tiny. You might have missed it." He stood so close to her that she smelled his cologne, which, unlike his suit, was cheap. Laura didn't wear perfume. Dermot always smelled like dryer sheets and ivory soap.

"Like I said, I didn't see it. Maybe someone else turned it in at the front desk."

"I'll just go check."

He went into the bathroom while Laura stood there. She heard him pull back the shower curtain and the dull plastic thud of moving the wastebasket and setting it back down. The noise stopped, and from the bathroom he called, "I found it!"

He reappeared from the bathroom holding a small silver tube. "My lucky lighter. I can't make a sale without it." He smiled.

Laura gave a wobbly smile back. Maybe the guy was just some salesman, traveling from one town to the next.

She felt so awful lately, and her life had basically imploded, that this small glimmer of happiness from a stranger made Laura want to be kind and normal, if only for a few seconds.

"What do you sell?" she asked.

"Oh, you know. Stuff." He waved the question off with his hand, like he was saying no to the offer of more bread at a restaurant. "It's boring. Not nearly as interesting as you."

Laura gave an automatic smile, but then his response made its way through her foggy brain and his words registered. The smile stayed on her face like a mask. "What do you mean?"

He moved towards her, and the friendly swagger he had a second ago shifted into something venomous. "I know all about you, Laura."

"How do you know my name?"

"I know everything about you. I know you live in a trailer out off Rockland Road, I know your brother was a recovering addict, I know that your boyfriend died and then your brother died." He glanced over at the door of the room, which was still open. There were voices, somewhere in the distance.

"Get away from me." Laura took a step back.

"It seems like people who are close to you keep ending up dead."

Her heart pounded. Laura thought her chest might burst into a thousand pieces. She couldn't believe what a complete nightmare her life had become. Her mind couldn't make sense of any of it.

"I haven't hurt anyone."

"Are you sure of that?" He was very close to her now. Close enough that he reached out and twirled a lock of her hair between his fingers. Laura's entire body started to shake.

"Yes." The word barely came out.

The man leaned in. As his cheap cologne wafted over her, nausea rose up Laura's throat again. His breath warmed the outside of her ear, and Laura secretly hoped she might vomit on his shiny shoes. And then she hoped that she wouldn't, because she was certain he might kill her just for that.

"Be careful, Laura. Stop looking in places where you don't belong."

He let go of her hair, and before Laura could do anything he was out the door and gone.

Laura stood in the same place for what felt like an hour but was probably only a few seconds. She reminded herself to breathe.

She pulled out her phone, not sure who she would even call.

The message that arrived earlier glowed on her screen.

It was from Addy.

Trina is dead, it said.

CHAPTER THIRTY-FIVE

JOYCE

It's strange what a person can get used to, Joyce thought as she dialed the number for their lawyer once again. Simon was at the police station, being questioned about another young person's death, but this didn't give Joyce much pause. Not like it did a year ago. A lot can happen in twelve months.

A lot can happen in twenty-four hours.

She'd thought about accompanying Simon to the station, but she was finding herself at her breaking point for compassion towards her husband. She had other important matters to attend to. At the rate things were going, she'd be spending all her time in hospitals, police interrogation rooms, or morgues if Simon didn't get a handle on their life.

Joyce was glad Trina was dead, although she wasn't glad for the extra hassle she and Simon would need to go through to prove he was innocent. God, she needed a vacation.

Another call came through on her other phone while Joyce was talking with the lawyer. Which was a joke unto itself—as if the two of them could be considered a family.

When she clicked to see who it was she read the name and sighed, because there was no way she wanted to have this conversation any time soon. The message she was waiting for hadn't come through yet—plans had changed, been updated. She needed to know everything was in order, but she also needed to be patient. Joyce sent a text in reply to the caller.

She set the kettle to boil on the stove and listened for where Clara was inside their house. The vacuum hummed from somewhere upstairs. Joyce sat down to a little privacy in her kitchen. She retrieved another cup before she settled, anticipating Clara coming down for a chat soon.

Her secret phone pinged with a text. It was all righteous indignation, because she put the guy's name into her other phone wrong. She called him Ralph, but his name was really Randy. Oh well, she thought. Close enough. But still, she'd have to work on his bruised ego, and that was effort and time she didn't have.

Joyce really should be more careful, although she didn't think Simon suspected anything. Over the years her affairs ranged from passionate indiscretions to almost bleak, frozen meetings where she came away more closed and dispassionate than when she arrived.

There was one time, where a man she'd met in the grocery store earlier that week had come to the house—it was Clara's day off—and they'd ravaged each other like two wild animals on the floor of the formal dining room, until Joyce heard the distinct sound of Simon's keys in the lock and she'd had to rush her gentleman caller out the back door, pull her pantyhose up, and smooth her skirt before Simon made his way further into the house. She'd worried he could smell the musky odor of sex on her, but he'd been distracted by a situation with a patient and had headed straight for the drink cart in the study once he found her to say hello and tell her he was home early.

Another time she'd met a man—a boy, really, God he must have been only nineteen or twenty—at the Motel 6 outside the edge of town and he'd been so nervous she finally had to ask him what was wrong. He confessed that he didn't really want to sleep with her, he was just trying to make his wife jealous.

"Wife?" she said. They'd met online, a dating site for older women to find younger men. It had an awful name—Cougar Hunting or something like that—but this boy messaged her first, and so she thought it would be a good fit for a time.

"We got married after high school because she was pregnant, and then she lost the baby and we were just married." The poor kid sobbed on the stiff polyester bed cover and Joyce tried to muster something that was kind or maternal, but she just found herself annoyed she'd wasted a perfectly good afternoon not getting laid.

That time she'd just rolled up her clothes, patted him on the shoulder, and then driven home to wait for Simon to be done with his last appointment.

Another call came in, on her normal phone this time.

She didn't recognize the number. She picked up for the banal thrill of not knowing what would happen when she did.

"Joyce?" The voice quavered on the other line. "It's Susan. Can we meet?"

A feeling grew in Joyce's chest, like a stone dropping into a deep pool.

"Of course we can." Joyce pulled the kettle off the stove as it started to whistle. "What's wrong? You sound upset."

"I'll tell you when we're together. I don't want to mention it over the phone."

"All right." Joyce suggested a small café near her house, different from the one they went to yesterday. "Do you need me to pick you up?"

"No, no. I can drive. I just need to talk to someone, you know? Who isn't a police officer."

"You had your interview with the detectives? Is that what you're so upset about? What did they say?"

Susan paused. Joyce heard traffic in the background. Snippets of a conversation leached down the line, something about school lunches and a PTA meeting that was abruptly canceled.

"Where are you?" Joyce asked.

"I don't know. In a park somewhere in the center of town."

"Does it have a little climbing wall and an orange slide?" Joyce asked.

It did.

"Hold on, I'll come to you. We can walk through the park and talk. It might be easier for you than sitting at the café."

"All right," Susan acquiesced.

Joyce told her she'd be there in five minutes. She knew the park well from walks she'd taken with Simon. There was also a public bathroom made of red brick, where she'd met a few men over the years for fun in the dark. Most of the time it had actually been nice, despite the dampness of the concrete floor.

"Just stay put. I'm coming."

Clara walked in as Joyce hung up. "Can I help you, Mrs. M?"

"Where'd you put my gun the last time you cleaned it?"

Clara gave her a knowing smile. "Exactly where you prefer me to put it." Clara walked to the wedding photo of Joyce and Simon hanging in the front hallway, only to swing it aside and reveal the safe behind it.

The code, of course, was Joyce's wedding anniversary.

CHAPTER THIRTY-SIX

ADDY

She didn't want to be here. The psychology department office felt abandoned after 5pm, with most of the faculty clearing out and the staff gone as of 4:30. The days were short and the building had few windows to begin with, so most of the hallways and communal areas were almost blacked out by the time Addy made it to the office after waiting at Trina's apartment for the police to arrive and for them to interview her.

Everything felt surreal, like she was moving through a fine and suffocating mist. When she passed a fellow grad student who was leaving for the day Addy could barely keep herself from screaming out "Trina is dead!" instead of the passive smile and head nod she managed to eke out. While she'd stood at the scene, wrapped in a metal emergency blanket from the EMS who'd arrived with really nothing to do except comfort her and offer condolences before taking a smoke break out back, she'd succumbed to the habit of checking her email and noted two from her advisor, with increasing urgency asking for results prior to her revisions being posted to the committee.

In academia, not even death could slow the cogs of bureaucracy. Addy turned the key in her shared grad student office and flipped on the light. The department packed twenty students into a windowless office built comfortably for four. Dividers and shared desk space where you signed out time was supposedly the answer. Usually someone was cranking away at one of the old desktops in the office, but no one was there, sitting in the dark coding data or polishing citations.

Addy wished she wasn't alone.

She could have gone back to her apartment, but she wasn't ready to face seeing her excessively chipper roommate, Eve, who would likely be making a vegan stir-fry in their kitchen and want to know how Addy's day was. She'd been avoiding Eve as much as possible since everything with Dermot went down, but Addy couldn't hold out forever, and she didn't feel emotionally or physically capable of watching Eve's smiling face deteriorate into genuine pain as Addy told her about today. Eve would want to hold her hand and sit on the couch together while she asked Addy gentle questions and assessed whether she was okay or needed further support. Eve might suggest Addy text a crisis helpline.

Addy couldn't handle any of it. Focusing on her data, on crossing the finish line of her graduate program, would be a welcome distraction. This is what she needed to get through the next twenty-four hours—science, determination, grit. She kept telling herself that on the way over to campus. And one day she could tell her children how she'd finished her dissertation despite her recent lover being murdered and finding her would-be friend and faculty member dead in her apartment.

On second thought, perhaps she'd never tell anyone about this.

Addy settled into her shared desk, brushed crumbs from someone's granola bar off the fake wood surface and into a garbage basket, and clicked into her account. She needed to do some analyses, and the department wouldn't pay for her to get a personal license on her laptop for the program she used.

It was cold in the office, as though the heat had been turned down at the end of the day, and Addy pulled her coat around her shoulders. It didn't register to Addy that her weary body might simply be in shock.

A half hour passed without her mind cracking open at the horror of it all, and she managed to work through two of the points on her revision checklist. The data appeared to be behaving itself, and she remembered to click the right boxes in the analysis to manage to keep the results printing the way she needed to without having to resize everything for her dissertation. The world might be digital, but the graduate school still measured margins with a ruler to ensure doctoral candidates followed their designated minutiae.

Addy's desk sat at the back of the room, and she couldn't see the front door of the office from where she was sitting. She heard the door open. Footsteps moved along the spaces created within the warren of little office cubicles. It wasn't until after she called out "Hello" and no one answered that she realized she should have locked the door behind her. Anyone who was supposed to be there would have a key to get inside.

"Hello," she called out again.

A scrape sounded against one of the desks, but not as though a bag or purse was being set down. More like something heavy had been pulled over the surface.

Addy's anxious mind flashed to what she'd seen earlier when she entered Trina's apartment: Trina's neck, covered in a necklace of bruises, and Trina's vacant eyes staring out at nothing. For a second, Addy tried to convince herself the sound could be another graduate student stumbling around while lost in thought, but her body wouldn't listen. Instead, Addy's heart slammed against her ribs, demanding she do something besides sit and wait to be attacked.

Adrenaline raced underneath her skin, energizing her weary

body. Her mind screamed inside her head. *This office is a coffin*, it said. *You need to get out.*

Addy craned her neck to see above the cubicle dividers, but she was too petite and would need to move her chair back and stand in order to see above them.

She carefully began to push the legs of her chair away from the desk, her hands trembling. She tried not to make a sound. The scrape came again, this time deeper in pitch.

And closer to Addy's desk.

Addy froze, her legs cramped in a half-crouch inches above the chair seat. Her knees made a hollow crack as they knocked against each other. Fear threatened to overcome her.

She caught a glimpse of either dark hair or a sweatshirt hood poking above her sight line. She couldn't tell which.

Addy assessed the pathway to the office's secondary door leading her out of the office and into the main corridors of the building. The door was almost directly opposite to the main entrance, and much closer to Addy's side of the office. It opened directly into the outer hallway shared with other departments. The English department, which shared the floor with the Psychology department, always ran on a later schedule, and she'd be bound to find some people milling around.

If she could just get to the door.

Based on the scraping sounds, the intruder was coming in from her right, so this was her one chance to break away and escape.

Addy shoved back her chair fully, not caring this time about any sound it made, and fell to her knees, thinking if she got down they wouldn't be able to see her as easily. She crawled along the ground, the coarse industrial carpet digging into her knees and tearing at the tights she had on underneath her denim skirt. Her palms sweated damp handprints into the carpet.

When Addy was halfway to the door, she realized she'd forgotten her purse. She still had her coat wrapped around her shoulders. At least she could go outside and make it home without freezing. What she wouldn't give to have Eve's kind face looking back at her now, instead of this terror lodged inside her.

The scraping sound had stopped. Addy didn't dare look up or stand to see where the person was within the office. She kept crawling towards the door. A slim shaft of bright light came from the outer office somewhere, shining through the frosted-glass partition next to the doorframe.

And then she was there, at the door. No one was near her. Addy was going to get out. She'd head straight to the English department, where she'd have safety in numbers.

Addy felt a disorienting relief as she reached for the knob. What if no one was actually chasing her? It was probably just some other graduate student, zombified from reading their advisor's research articles for too long. She hadn't really seen them, and no one had threatened her. A brittleness settled over her body. How did children grow up in war zones? How did human beings cope with seeing their friends shot on the battlefield or next to them on their way to school? People coped with so much, and yet here Addy was suffocating from the stress of the last few days. All the trauma of the last week was getting to her, making her paranoid.

Addy resolved to go home to Eve, have her listen to what she'd been through, and let her make her a cup of sweet tea and tuck her in with a blanket. Oh, how Addy wished she could call her mother right now.

She turned the knob to open the secondary door, but it wouldn't move. Quickly, Addy checked the lock on the door and found it wasn't engaged. Addy tried again, but nothing happened.

Someone must have jammed the second door before entering through the main entrance to the office.

The realization hit Addy like a punch to her chest.

None of this was an accident. It wasn't a misunderstanding. She wasn't paranoid.

She was in danger.

"Where are you going?" a voice said. A fragrance assaulted Addy's nostrils. Pungent. Cheap.

The lights in the office went out. Only the soft glow through the frosted glass of the door illuminated the space around Addy. Everything else was pitch black.

The scraping sound came again, so close it was difficult for Addy to tell if it came from in front or behind her.

Addy felt breath on her cheek. She was trapped.

CHAPTER THIRTY-SEVEN

JOYCE

The text Joyce was waiting for arrived just as she was about to leave for her meeting with Susan. It was from another "friend," but at least this one was truly a man with benefits. Unlike Ralph. Or Randy. Whatever his name was.

Joyce read the message, which confirmed what she'd been hoping. She had one errand to run, but it wouldn't take long and would make her life easier in the end.

Afterwards, finally at the park, Joyce felt the weight of the gun in her bag like a phantom child she carried; dense, familiar, and needy. She hadn't shot the gun in a very long time, and even then it was just at the firing range, but it was a talisman for this meeting with Susan that she couldn't go without. Joyce hoped she wouldn't have to use it, but simply knowing it was there, snug in her purse, was a comfort.

Clara was the one who'd bought it for Joyce, years and years ago now, after she'd discovered in her housekeeping that Joyce was in the habit of meeting with sometimes less than savory men. She'd been surprisingly accepting of Joyce's indiscretions, not appealing to Joyce's sense of loyalty or fidelity, but Clara remained insistent that Joyce have some form of protection.

'Not all men are as kind as your husband,' she'd told Joyce, and although Joyce's initial reaction had been to respond with a sarcastic comment, she'd recognized the truth of Clara's words and kept her mouth shut while Clara explained. It so happened Clara had a cousin who traded guns out of the back of his van, and for two hundred dollars she could get Joyce an unmarked handgun.

Joyce met the cousin, with Clara in tow, in the alley behind the diner in the center of town, and although the price point was good, Joyce decided to go the legal route. The cousin had a squirrelly look to him, his eyes shifting right to left even though nothing was moving around in the alley. Instead, Joyce applied for a conceal/carry license at the gun shop on the freeway outside town. Being an upper-class white woman in America with no criminal record, Joyce was carrying a loaded Smith and Wesson pistol in her purse before the end of the week—with the safety on, of course.

"Is your cousin one of the men who isn't as nice as my husband?" Joyce had asked Clara after the alleyway meeting.

"Oh, yes," Clara replied.

Joyce spotted Susan almost a block away. Her shiny blonde hair fell in a sharp line along her chin, and she wore a bright-pink coat for their meeting. It struck Joyce as rather strange, that a sister would think to pack multiple coats when traveling to sort out her murdered brother's affairs.

Although Joyce might have been inclined towards the same sort of sartorial planning. When life hurtles out of control, what you put on (or in) your own body is sometimes the only bit you can take hold of.

Joyce joined Susan and slipped her arm through the younger woman's. "How are you?" she asked.

Despite her sleek exterior, Susan's face looked ravaged. Her eyes were bloodshot, and her foundation had seeped into the cracks around her eyes and mouth, aging her. Some of her makeup was smeared onto the white neckline of her silk blouse.

She looked like a woman in the throes of grief.

"I've been better." Susan gave a small conciliatory laugh and wiped at her eyes with a handkerchief. "It's all just so much, you know."

"I don't think I can imagine what you're going through right now," Joyce replied. The two of them started walking around the perimeter trail of the park. The sun was out, and despite the chill of winter it was pleasant in the sunshine.

"The police contacted me earlier this morning, just before I called you. They had a suspect in Dermot's murder, the woman you told me about yesterday—"

"Trina?" Joyce's throat tightened. The past tense of Susan's statement pricked at her composure. She knew Trina was dead, but Susan didn't know that. Simon was already being questioned at the police station about it. The meaning of Trina's death was more slippery than Joyce had anticipated.

The gun's weight offered a welcome pressure to her left side as she and Susan continued their walk, balancing Joyce's momentary wave of dizziness.

"Yes, Catriona Dell. The professor at the university. They said she'd had a history of imbalance, recently, just like you told me."

"Had?" Joyce caught the word and threw it back at Susan this time.

"Well, that's why I wanted to meet with you. That's why the police were calling me. This suspect of theirs was found dead in her apartment yesterday."

"Was it suicide? How dreadful." Joyce paused, appearing to think. "But at least it will bring you some closure."

"No, no, nothing that..." Susan appeared to struggle for the word. "That *simple*. She was murdered." Susan stopped walking and turned to face Joyce. "And they want to know where I was yesterday. I need to account for my whereabouts."

Joyce played dumb. "But why would they need that?"

"They need to rule me out as a suspect for this woman's murder! They think it might have been a revenge killing, for what she did to Dermot. And that's just it. I met with you, after getting my nails done at the salon. And then I went to the police station, gave my statement, and headed back to my hotel room. After that I was alone for the rest of the day."

"Did you talk to your family? Your husband or children?"

"Yes, we had a call to say goodnight around 8:30pm."

"Any room service? Did you go down to the front desk for anything?" They'd begun walking again.

"No, I wasn't very hungry." Susan turned her head as a flock of starlings spilled off a nearby tree and into the sky. "Look, I appreciate your help in trying to poke holes in the police's questions for me, but what I really need is something else."

"Of course." Joyce didn't dare look at her in the moment. "You need an alibi."

"And I don't know anyone in this town, besides the nail-salon ladies and the police."

"What will you say? We need to get our story straight."

"It's not so much what I *will* say, as what I've already told them."

Joyce felt a sharp bristling in her chest. "All right." She fought hard to unclench her jaw.

"Can you take me back to your house? I told them we were together, talking for most of the afternoon and then had dinner together at your place."

"Well, that might work. There's just one thing," Joyce replied.

"Please, Joyce. I don't have any other options."

Joyce led them to a park bench and Susan obligingly sat down, turning to face Joyce. Susan looked at her as though she were falling down a long, dark hole.

Joyce reached out and held her hand. Her fingers were cold.

"There's just one problem. I was talking to the police yesterday."

"Why?" It wasn't clear if Susan was talking to Joyce or asking the universe.

"Because my husband was nearly killed yesterday afternoon."

Susan let out a heavy sigh. "Death seems to follow you, Joyce."

CHAPTER THIRTY-EIGHT

SIMON

The police ended their interrogation of him after an officer arrived in their interview room, whispering something in Bechdel's ear that she nodded solemnly to. He drove home, each turn and traffic light happening as if in slow motion.

He'd forgotten about the numbness, how it came over you like a fog. He knew, intellectually, that this was simply the body's way of surviving trauma. Shut down the thinking part of the brain, then reduce the feeling part to only the emotions which will help you stay alive. Fear, anger, defensiveness. But sadness, horror, terror—those were all blunted. Which is why he was able to stand in front of the stove at his home, just hours after watching a man die violently, learning that a woman dear to him was murdered, and make an omelet. And not just make it, but make it perfectly, with a lovely browning and perfectly fluffy interior. He'd shredded some Gruyère before cracking the eggs, and now he sprinkled the cheese over the midline of the omelet to melt before he plated it.

Joyce was not home. A small kindness, he felt. He could eat in peace, thinking through his next steps.

He'd set the table with a napkin, plate, silverware, and the small crystal salt and pepper shakers they'd been gifted for their wedding. Simon placed a tumbler of Scotch next to his plate at the head of the table.

The omelet finished cooking and Simon settled himself at his seat. The scent of cheese floated up into the air, mixed with the slight buttery hint of the eggs. Simon's stomach growled, all the physical systems of the body working in spite of the maelstrom he'd found himself in.

It only took him a few minutes to eat. He tried to savor the flavors and textures, as it would be the last decent meal he'd have in his home. He dabbed the napkin at the corners of his mouth, took the dirty plates into the sink, and put them away after washing them. He left the kitchen as though he'd never been there.

The house was quiet, no Clara moving through the house, straightening and cleaning. Simon sat down by the fireplace, which was empty and cold, in one of the large wingback chairs. It'd started to rain a wintry mix outside, and the thrum of the weather on the roof lulled Simon into a desperate sleep, his body clawing towards respite from the fatigue it was managing.

He woke perhaps an hour later, disoriented and with a dry mouth. His shoulders ached straight down to his core, like a string pulling through his body until it was tight.

The sleet had stopped and darkness filled the windows, such that he could only see his reflection in the glass. He looked at his hands, not able to tolerate even a blurry version of his face.

It was time, and he knew it. It took him just a few minutes to drive out to the station. He had to take a parking ticket in order to park in the lot, and he thought about how he should really get a sort of frequent visitor parking pass, given how much he had been spending time there.

Although now it wouldn't matter.

He sat in the parking lot, thinking about what he was about to do but not questioning it. Just working it through his mind, like water flowing over a stone, already smoothed from the passage of time.

This remained the best option. He was certain of it. If he kept choosing himself, just like he had his entire life, and especially this last year, then those he loved would be hurt even more. Joyce had suffered enough, and yet stuck by him.

The long days and even longer nights, his episodes that left him derelict to the world, and the drinking that helped him manage the difficulties of life. The obsessions and transgressions, his heart opening up when she wasn't around and closing itself off whenever she tried to get closer to him.

She deserved better. She deserved a second chance. This is what he repeated to himself when that part of his brain—the thinking part—threatened to turn on again.

He'd hidden his true self long enough.

The station was empty, except for a single officer at the main desk, sitting behind a guard of clear plastic.

"You're back," she announced, not unkindly.

"I need to speak to Detective Kirkpatrick or Detective Bechdel," he told the uniformed officer. She wore her hair in a tight braid, and when Simon glanced down he noticed she was doing a crossword puzzle.

The mundanity of her afternoon slammed into him, and he thought he might vomit his perfectly made omelet onto the laminate surface of the processing desk. He pulled his hand to his mouth and turned his back, swallowing down the bile that had risen in his throat.

"Let me see if they're available," she said to his back.

Simon took a seat in the formed plastic chairs lining the room. His eye automatically skimmed the titles of the magazines strewn over the end table. *Guns & Ammo. Family Circle. Newsweek.*

It was Detective Bechdel who appeared at the swinging wooden door separating the waiting area from the working police officers behind the plastic partition.

"Dr. Morgan." She nodded and turned, expecting Simon to follow.

They walked through the station, down the right hallway to the interview room Simon was getting to know rather intimately.

"I'm very glad you're here, despite everything you've been through recently." Bechdel looked at him with a curious expression on her face, as though she wasn't certain whether to pity him or antagonize him. "We were going to call you, but you've preceded us."

"We?" Simon asked, looking around for Detective Kirkpatrick.

Bechdel swung the door of the interview room open. Her partner sat inside, sipping a Styrofoam cup of coffee. The two seats across from him were already filled.

Joyce sat in the left-hand chair, her hands folded meekly on her lap and a lilac cardigan slung over her shoulders, as though she were in a drafty restaurant waiting for her meal to arrive.

Next to her was a woman Simon had only seen in a photograph, younger and less polished. Her face was pained, her eyes rimmed red. She clutched a lace handkerchief in her palm. Like a Southern Belle, Simon thought.

His mind skirted along the edges of reason.

"Did you call our lawyer?" Joyce asked Simon, as though she were asking if he'd picked up milk on the way home.

He was too late. His wife had beaten him to it.

CHAPTER THIRTY-NINE

JOYCE

She wasn't quite sure how they'd ended up at the police station. She was only certain this was exactly where they both needed to be—she and Susan. Having Simon show up was a happy coincidence, one she could work with. Joyce just needed to think it through.

But before that, she needed to get through this interview and ensure Susan was safely handled.

Joyce left her gun in the car, tucked away in the folds of her glove compartment like a 1970s crime boss. She'd sent Susan in ahead, while she parked, and Susan was more than happy to sneak out the door and secretly smoke a cigarette before they went inside together. Joyce didn't know why people felt the need to hide their true natures so poorly. Either let them out in full color or bury them deep—but you should choose one or the other.

"Have a seat." Detective Bechdel gestured to Simon while Kirkpatrick pulled up a chair.

Joyce assessed her husband. He did not look well. His shirt was partially untucked, his eyes sunken into his face, and his hands and neck chaffed, she assumed, from scrubbing at the blood splattered onto him from the robbery. Kirkpatrick was placing an additional chair on the side of Susan, but Joyce stood up as though to help and moved it to her side. Simon sat down in her chair, and she took her spot beside him. Underneath the table, her hand sought his.

"I don't think you've met," Joyce told Simon. "This is Susan. Her brother was that young man killed in the hotel last week. We met by chance at the nail salon yesterday."

Joyce purposefully placed her left hand on the table, so everyone could see her fresh manicure. So often a story was in the details. She glanced over at Susan, and luckily she wasn't a nail biter—her coat of dark polish was still immaculate.

"Why are you here?" Simon's voice was still resonant, but Joyce caught the warning at its edge.

She locked her eyes on him, not wanting to bring Simon more pain but also relishing the moment. "They need to rule out suspects for Trina's death, and Susan reached out to me because we were together yesterday. I'm her alibi."

"And she's yours," Simon replied.

"Not that I need one." Joyce allowed herself to bristle at Simon's unfurling nastiness. It would help the detectives believe what she needed them to think.

"Of course you don't." Simon turned to the detectives, who were sitting back and watching the show.

And that's when Joyce's husband finally, and truly, surprised her.

"I'd like to make a confession," he said. "There's no need to look for witnesses or alibis. I did it. I killed them both."

Joyce's heart thudded against the cave of her chest. Why was he doing this?

"You couldn't have hurt either of them," Joyce said crisply, willing her body and her mind to behave. "You and I were together."

"Well, hang on." Detective Kirkpatrick pretended to reference his notes in a small notepad he pulled up from the table. "You said you were with Susan yesterday afternoon at the time Ms. Dell was murdered."

Simon stood up, pushing his chair back from the table. The aluminum legs made a terrible screech against the cement floor. "Get them both out of here! You don't need either of them anymore. It was me. I confess!" He held up his hands and threw his head back. "Just let them leave."

"Stop it!" Joyce wanted to smack Simon like a misbehaving child. "What are you doing?"

The two detectives had perked up, both sitting forward in their chairs.

Simon looked at Joyce, and in his gaze she saw the ugliness that was their life now, what it had been for the last year when she discovered the truth that night, after the blood and the recriminations and the fumes of whiskey echoing off her husband's breath.

She took his hand, everyone else in the room dropping away, and said, "Don't do this." So soft and gentle, as though she were kissing away his bad dream.

He raised her hand to his mouth, kissed it, and let it go. "Get them out of here," he said to Bechdel and Kirkpatrick.

The detectives silently communicated with each other, Bechdel lifting her chin eventually in a signal of affirmation. "Would you like a lawyer present?" she asked Simon.

Joyce's husband shook his head.

Joyce and Susan were escorted from the room by two uniformed officers. She called out, demanding to stay with Simon, but the officers who moved her down the hallway explained she wasn't the one to make the decision. If Simon didn't want her there, there was nothing she could do about it.

"But I'm his wife!" she cried out.

"It doesn't matter," the officer explained calmly, depositing her and Susan at the plastic chairs in the front lobby and disappearing back into the labyrinth of the station.

Susan wouldn't meet Joyce's eyes. "Thank you for your help, but I should probably be going." She started to button her coat, heading towards the front door. "I'll have an Uber pick me up and take me back to my car."

"Wait," Joyce said. "I'll come with you." Her mind moved fast, ideas ticking through the possibilities of what she could make of this situation.

Once they were outside, Joyce asked her question. "How well did you know your brother?"

"I already told you, we were estranged for several years." Susan crossed her arms over her chest and let out a breath. "It's been a hell of a long day. I want to go back to my hotel and talk to my family." She turned away, her cell phone poised in her hand.

"They'll be back."

Susan kept walking.

"The police. My husband's confession won't stick."

"Why's that?" Joyce knew Susan couldn't help but ask. Curiosity has a way of pushing people towards endpoints they'd otherwise avoid.

"Before I explain, there's something you need to know about my husband."

"All right." Susan put her phone in her pocket.

"He's been cheating on me for years."

"That's not noteworthy. Lots of guys cheat."

"It wasn't much of an issue until we both ended up sleeping with the same man."

"Oh." Susan's mouth made a wide circle, her eyebrows raised. "I thought you were..."

"Happy? In a way, I suppose we are. But you see, the reason I know my husband didn't kill anyone is because he can't hurt anything that he loves."

"You might think that," Susan began.

"No, I know. He loved Trina, almost as a daughter. And he loved Dermot."

"Dermot. My brother?"

"Yes. Simon and I were both seeing him." Joyce watched the information settle on Susan.

"And your husband was in love with him." Susan sounded circumspect.

"I believe so, yes." Joyce shrugged. She'd never expected Dermot to be faithful. He was one of those pretty boys, although his sleek edges were blurring as some of his bad habits caught up with him. Dermot wanted to find a way to be everything to everyone, including himself.

Susan shook her head. "But Simon hurt you, by having his affair. It doesn't add up. You can't assume people you know well, even people you love, are who they appear to be."

"That's just it." They had been creeping along the sidewalk, Joyce urging with her own body language to move them towards her Porsche. They were at the car now. The gun throbbed in the back of Joyce's mind. She needed to get Simon out of this predicament. "Simon doesn't love me. It's me who loves him."

Susan shook her head. "Why love someone who can never love you back?"

Joyce's eyes locked on Susan's for a beat. "Get in. I'll give you a ride back to your car." Joyce unlocked the doors.

After a moment, Susan climbed in. Joyce started the engine, planning out the route she'd take in her head.

They weren't going back to the park.

CHAPTER FORTY

LAURA

Rosie would stay with Laura at the trailer tonight. After the man left and Laura received Addy's message about Trina, she called Rosie. Laura didn't know what else to do, besides sit on the cheap carpeting and weep. Laura wasn't done with her shift until an hour later, and by the time she arrived at her trailer it was starting to get dark.

Laura glanced around the woods by her home. She couldn't be certain that the man, or anyone else, hadn't followed her from the hotel, although she'd driven around in circles for a while just in case any of the headlights behind her were more than people running errands and heading home from work. She put her key in the lock and stepped inside the trailer, which was warm and smelled of stale coffee from this morning. Laura went over to the coffee pot and turned it off. She'd forgotten to flip the switch before she left today, and the coffee had been burning off slowly in the urn. She was lucky the trailer hadn't caught fire.

A hum in her pocket signaled she was getting a call. Her heart thudded as she reached to answer it, thinking that it couldn't be more bad news, because almost everyone she loved was already dead.

It was Rosie.

"I'm sorry I'm not there yet. I'm waiting for my cousin to get home from work so I can borrow the car," she explained.

Laura assured her it was fine. That she was fine.

Although Laura had no way of knowing if that were true.

"Do you want to stay on the phone until I can come over?" Rosie asked.

Laura sat down on the couch. She chose the same spot where Dermot's sister sat when she delivered her revelations about her brother. Susan was so polished and elegant. Like the ballerinas in the *Nutcracker* play Laura went to once with her mother at Christmastime. They'd looked like angels, dancing on the stage, and all Laura could think was that she'd never feel or be as pretty as those women.

She'd never said that to her mother. Her mother was the kind of woman who assumed the world knew she was gorgeous, and that everything would always be okay.

"It'll work out," she would say to Laura any time she came to her mom with a problem, whether it was a boy pulling her hair in the playground or an F on her math test. It was only now, that Laura's life was imploding and she was totally, utterly alone— except for Rosie—that she realized her mother's nonchalance was more carelessness than trust in the goodness of the world. She simply didn't want to be bothered with her children's worries, Laura thought now.

"Are you really going to have this baby?" Rosie asked, not waiting for Laura to answer her first question.

"Yes," was Laura's automatic reply.

"What are you going to do with a baby?" Rosie wasn't accusatory. She seemed genuine in her question.

Laura wasn't sure how to answer her.

Laura leaned back into the cushions of the couch. She felt a deep, dark hole humming inside her, and poor Rosie was going to get sucked into it if she wasn't careful. "You mean, now that my boyfriend and brother are dead? And the one person who I thought could help was murdered too?" She meant Trina, of course.

Rosie's voice became urgent. "What do you mean?"

Laura nodded, and then remembered Rosie couldn't see her over the phone. "Trina's dead. Addy texted me. She found her in her apartment. Strangled, apparently."

"Oh my God."

"I got the message right after I spoke to you. After that man came to the hotel and threatened me." Laura forgave herself this small lie to Rosie. She didn't have the energy to tell Rosie earlier when they spoke. She looked out the window and thought she saw a light flicker, somewhere deep in the woods. People knew where she lived.

"Come over now," Rosie insisted. "You can stay with me. Or we can stay in a hotel."

"Okay." Laura wasn't sure where she'd be safe. She was mainly certain she couldn't be in this trailer for a second longer. "I'm on my way."

"I should have told you to come over as soon as you were done with work," Rosie chided herself.

Laura thought about the coffee pot she'd left on. If she'd gone straight to Rosie's, her trailer would have surely burned down. No, she was glad she'd come home for the few moments that she had.

But it was time to leave.

She told Rosie she was headed over and ended the call.

Laura went out into the freezing night again, but before she stepped off the makeshift porch a stream of headlights shone from the end of the lane as a car swung onto the drive.

Fear lit up through her spine. She couldn't go back inside until she knew who was there. The only certainty she had was that it wasn't Rosie.

Or Dermot. Terry. Trina.

The list was so long.

It was freezing outside. Laura's feet were shod in sneakers. Her coat was from three Christmases ago, a gift from the foster parents she was living with at the time. It had fur around the hood, but the seams were coming apart and the zipper gapped if you didn't close it just right.

Laura made a decision. She slipped back into the trailer and grabbed a flashlight. She disappeared into the dark, just as the car pulled up in the drive and two figures in long coats slinked out the doors. It was like Laura had never been there, except for her footprints in the snow.

CHAPTER FORTY-ONE

SIMON

If you asked him, he couldn't tell you when it started. Not the feelings—those had been there as long as he could remember. But the actions, that was all a blur in his mind that wouldn't clarify, no matter how hard he tried to remember. It was after he came out of his depression, his body singing again like it wasn't trying to just wither and die. He remembered being at the grocery store, and having another man purposefully bump into him in the bread aisle. He was gorgeous, dressed like a summer island in cashmere and chinos, his hair combed just so. The man had beautiful green eyes, and Simon followed him into the back alley behind the store and kissed his perfectly plump lips. It wasn't the first time. There had been other men, but that was in the fog of alcohol and dark bars he'd stumbled into after a long shift at the hospital. He could barely remember what happened in those places, except for the soreness of his lips and legs the next day.

Simon thought about that man in the grocery store—he didn't even know his name, and yet his face was indelibly marked in his memory despite everything Simon had done to forget him—as the detectives asked Simon for details about his confession.

But, of course, he couldn't give them anything. Not that that made him any less guilty.

It was after a question regarding Dermot's body, asking about where he'd struck Dermot and with what, that Simon knew it wasn't going to work.

"Just lock me up. I don't deserve my freedom." Simon was being maudlin, but there'd always been a flare for the dramatic inside him. If this wasn't the time to let it out, he didn't know when was.

Detective Bechdel rolled her eyes. "This is getting us nowhere. He didn't do anything."

"Why did you come here?" Detective Kirkpatrick straightened his posture.

"I have a drinking problem," Simon said. "I black out. I can't remember things I've done. Places I've been. Entire evenings are lost."

The two detectives shifted in their seats. Kirkpatrick made to leave, but Bechdel held out her hand as if she were going to touch her partner's shoulder, and he settled back in.

Simon wondered if perhaps they were lovers, the almost-touch was so tender. But, then again, they worked together in high stakes situations. Life and death. Simon did the same thing with countless colleagues, seeking out a platonic closeness with them after an eight-hour surgery, bumping knees under the table while getting something to eat from the lackluster cafeteria.

"So you knew Dermot before he met Trina?" Bechdel tried again. She'd decided to go back to the beginning, as though they hadn't been speaking in circles for the last thirty minutes.

"Yes. We'd been intimate, several times." Simon's last several texts to Dermot were ignored. He'd become more distant over the last week or so, ignoring Simon's calls and messages. It wasn't the first time Simon had been ghosted—such a strange, perfectly descriptive word. Like a person had never existed. Even though you'd seen each other naked, and smelled their scent after they'd woken up, suddenly they were gone. At least from the world you lived in.

"Sunday evening, I was lonely. Joyce was out, and I'd spent the afternoon doing paperwork in the office, drinking myself through a very expensive bottle of Scotch. I wanted to see him." All of that was true, Simon noted.

"So you and Dermot had been together?" Kirkpatrick asked.

"Not together, as in a couple. He didn't want that."

"Where did you meet?" Bechdel's eyes flicked to the side. Something was bothering her.

"I frequent a few online forums. Dermot had an account at one of them. They cater to older men looking for younger..." Simon paused on the word. "Friends," he finally settled on.

"And you messaged him first?" Bechdel was taking the lead on this interview now.

"I did."

"Can you show us your account?"

"Yes, of course." Simon waited while Kirkpatrick pulled a laptop out of his bag, opened the lid, and slid it over the table to Simon.

Simon tapped a few keys and his account showed up. He'd taken the photo himself with his phone, in their backyard. Roses bloomed behind him. He wore a crisp white shirt, and he'd filtered the photo to make his eyes seem bluer.

"Would you like to see our messages?"

Simon turned the computer around so the detectives could view his conversations with Dermot.

"Where did you meet up for the first time?"

"In the parking lot behind the bowling alley. He met me in my car. It wasn't terribly romantic."

Simon's palms had gone sweaty waiting for Dermot to show up. He'd been one of the few younger men to have a picture that was wholesome on his account. The photo showed Dermot in the woods, looking up at a bright sky. It was a photo far enough away that someone else must have taken it for him. Sometimes, while Simon was kissing his neck and waiting for Dermot to slip his hands down his pants, he'd wondered about the person who took that picture.

"Did it become more romantic?" Bechdel asked.

Simon didn't hesitate. "It did. We started meeting in hotels. We went away for the weekend once. I told my wife I was at a conference."

"Does your wife know about you and your extra relationships?" Simon could tell Kirkpatrick was being particularly careful with his wording.

"I'm not sure," Simon admitted honestly. Joyce was a smart woman, with a quicksilver mind and a cruel streak that she contained just below the surface of everything she did. Simon knew what she was capable of. "This past year has been difficult. Both she and I have struggled."

Kirkpatrick scrolled through the messages. Simon waited for him to find it.

He saw precisely when the detective read the message.

Simon still recalled the words appearing as he waited for Dermot to respond to his first message.

Hi there. I'm happy to meet up. You're gorgeous. Does it matter that I'm also doing your wife?

Simon had replied that it didn't, although of course it turned out to matter very much.

CHAPTER FORTY-TWO

LAURA

The woods were dark and life throbbed out of the shadows as Laura made her way down the path towards the stream. Birds settled into their shelters and night creatures ventured out for their evening's adventures. There was a large oak tree nearby, its trunk almost as broad as a car, that Laura could hide behind. From that vantage point she could still see the trailer and whoever was visiting her on this cold night, but it was nearly impossible to see the ground in the dark, and she'd turned the flashlight off to avoid having herself discovered before she was ready.

Laura's legs were freezing. She wished she could afford a better coat.

She peered towards the trailer, trying to make out who was there, but all Laura saw were the two shadowy figures standing on the doorstep. The darkness leached color from everything around it, and the outer light above the trailer door gave no clues as to who was looking for Laura.

Laura wrapped her arms around her chest. Her teeth were beginning to chatter. A woman's voice broke through the air.

"Laura? Laura, are you out there?"

She didn't recognize it.

"Hello?" a second woman called out. "Laura, are you there?"

This voice registered in Laura's brain somewhere, but she couldn't quite place it.

I can't trust anyone, Laura reminded herself. Except Rosie, she corrected. She wondered how long it would take for Rosie to start worrying when Laura didn't arrive at her apartment. And then Laura wondered if Rosie might come to the trailer, if it were safe for her friend to come here in the first place.

Something yowled in the distance. A fox or an owl, Laura wasn't sure.

Dermot would know what it was, she thought. Her feet stumbled along the path.

"I'm here!" Laura called out to the two figures. She hoped she was right about the voice she recognized. "I'm coming."

Laura came into view of the two women waiting for her. She swallowed hard.

"What are you doing here?" she asked.

"I came to see you," the taller, darker woman said, her voice smooth as silk but unfamiliar. Although Laura recognized her face immediately. She'd seen pictures of her on Dermot's phone. Not those kind of pictures. Pretty pictures, of her standing out in the woods or in front of a trail sign. Laura had thought she was a coworker of Dermot's, or maybe an old family friend. She was just so much older, Laura never even thought she was a threat. "I'm Joyce. And you must be Laura."

She couldn't help it—Laura blushed hearing such a posh woman say her name, like it was a special award announced only for her.

It was easy checking Dermot's phone when he'd go to the bathroom at the diner. Laura watched Dermot log in when he checked it and she memorized the passcode. It was simple. He didn't even try to hide it from her, which made her think it meant he trusted her more than anyone else. What she realized now was that it hadn't even occurred to him that she could be so smart.

Standing next to Joyce was Susan, looking nervous. She kept fidgeting with something in her hands and wouldn't look up to make eye contact with Laura.

"Want to come inside where it's warm?" Laura offered.

"That sounds lovely," Joyce said.

Joyce gingerly took a step forward, and Susan moved with her. That's when Laura noticed the gun, held between Susan's hands like a cancer. She held it against Joyce's side, her finger looped through the trigger and the entire set-up almost entirely hidden by the baggy folds of Susan's pink coat.

"Why do you have a gun?" The sight of the weapon made Laura want to scream. Laura had never seen a gun in real life before tonight. A small part of her mind wondered if maybe it was just a toy, and this was all a misunderstanding.

Susan finally looked up. A large bruise was forming over the crest of her left eye. "Because this one here was going to kill me with it," she said, jabbing the barrel into Joyce's side.

She flicked her head towards the door. "Now open up. We have a lot to talk about."

CHAPTER FORTY-THREE

ADDY

She woke up in the musty dark. A dim light streamed out from around the edges of wherever she was, so dim that she could barely see her hand in front of her face. Addy reached up, but her hands met with a hard surface above her. She was crouched into a fetal position, her knees up around her mouth.

Her brain was foggy, and she couldn't place at first where she was or what had happened. Just that she was alone and aching all over. And trapped.

It was that word which stuck with her. Trapped.

She'd been in her office, ready to move out of the door and into the safety of the hallway when she'd felt a hand on her shoulder and screamed. A hard edge had met the nape of her neck and she'd fallen over and then away, into unconsciousness, by the time the second blow had come. She hadn't been able to see her attacker's face.

And now she was here, inside a cramped space. If she could move her arms around more freely, she'd feel the base of her skull to see how badly she was hurt. It felt slick on her neck, and Addy wondered if it was wet with blood or just sweat, although it was freezing wherever she was. It could be tears, dripping down her face. She felt like she'd been crying in her sleep, her throat aching from the effort of it.

Addy tried to move her arms and legs apart and found that her hands weren't tied together. Her feet were bound with some sort of loose rag, and it slipped off over her tall leather boots easily. A shiver ran up her back as the adrenaline from waking up in a dark, locked box leached out of her and was replaced with a full awareness of her situation.

She could barely see anything.

She didn't know where she was, or what was enclosing her.

Panic started to work at the back of her mind, and Addy found her breath ratcheting up into faster and faster intakes. *What if she ran out of air in here?* Her mind played tricks on her, fear overtaking reason, so she fought back. If light could seep in, then air was getting in too, she reminded herself.

She told herself to be steady. Work the problem. *Do you want to die in here? Do you want to wait for whoever put you here to come back, and then do horrible things to you?* Of course, the answer was "no".

Figure out what you need to do to get out.

It was no different than standing in front of her committee at her comprehensive exams, some of the professors supportive and others intent on making any student look ill-prepared and idiotic. It was a very different level of harm, but harm all the same. And how had she handled that? She'd focused her mind on her abilities, reassured herself that she could do it. She'd ignored the fear clawing at the back of her mind and steadied her thoughts into the logic of her preparation.

She hadn't prepared for this, but any woman can tell you that their entire life has been an act of courage against the dangers of the world. You walk home in the dark, carrying your keys between your knuckles because that's what your parents and teachers taught you. You listen for footsteps behind you and avoid dates at a person's house until you know them better. You use the buddy system at parties and carry pepper spray in your purse. You don't go running alone on the fire trails in the woods by your town, no matter how much you'd like to be alone, because women are never really alone in this world.

Addy stopped first and listened. Could she hear anything distinctive? Wherever she was, she was certain she wasn't moving. There were no sounds coming from outside. Except— she held her breath. There were soft rustlings, like someone wrapping themselves in a blanket on top of wherever she was. And then there was the sharp snap of a door closing.

She felt around, her fingers brushing something hard and plastic with bristles along one side. Addy inhaled deeply, smelling beyond the mustiness the sure scent of gasoline and snow. She was in the trunk of a car. Her fingers brushed against the bristles of a basic ice scraper. She moved her feet, hoping to find more. She pushed against something soft and crinkled, rectangular in shape.

It was a stack of reusable grocery bags. Addy had used them often enough herself.

It was an odd juxtaposition her mind caught on. Someone would take the time to store shopping bags in their car, to carry an ice scraper for winter weather—such normal, well-intentioned things—and then carry a woman in the back of their car after knocking her unconscious.

Relief seeped in as Addy considered these were signs she wasn't in the hands of someone insane and sadistic—how could somebody who brought their own shopping bags not be somewhat reasonable?—when she thought about something one of her professors said in her first abnormal psychology class.

"Nobody is normal."

What she'd meant was that human beings were by nature layered creatures. Someone who was kind to their child and baked them a cake for their birthday was also able to murder a man for looking at them the wrong way. Someone who shook their baby could be an excellent employee and always give customers a smile. People could be incredibly kind to strangers and then call their spouse a cunt for forgetting to buy more milk at the store.

Someone might be perfectly capable of reusing grocery bags and dumping a body in a vacant lot.

The irrational relief she'd felt a moment ago was replaced with urgency. Addy needed to get out of there.

She tried to latch onto something she'd read in the newspaper, back when she was a kid. There'd been an article about car trunks, and a new feature to pop the trunk door open in case a child got locked in accidentally. They'd started manufacturing cars that way after several children climbed into trunks and were hurt when they couldn't climb back out.

Addy needed to find that latch, but she couldn't move her shoulders up or flip herself around comfortably. She'd have to feel around with her hands, hopefully popping the trunk open and then climbing out before whoever had put her there noticed.

Her fingers searched, feeling the cheap felt of the trunk's interior and the cool metal of the mechanisms for the trunk door, but no latch. She tried to think if she'd put her phone in her pocket. Was her purse there?

Not that she could feel.

And then her hands landed on a switch. It felt like cheap plastic, with a cord attached. She prayed that it wouldn't crack or rip apart as she pulled.

The trunk door flipped open and Addy blinked as bright artificial light poured in. Someone stood in front of her, their features blocked out by the light shining from behind.

"I was just coming to get you," the figure said. They moved slightly and Addy saw a stylish woman, her clothes and haircut expensive-looking. Her face was drawn, shadows darkening the skin beneath her well-groomed eye makeup and brows.

"Hurry up," someone shouted from behind her.

"I'm Joyce," the woman said, before she yanked Addy from the car.

CHAPTER FORTY-FOUR

How exactly had this happened? Joyce couldn't quite believe it herself. She had her gun in her glove compartment, certain Susan was clueless.

Although, there was the situation with Simon showing up at the police station. Had that prompted Susan to search Joyce's car, hoping to find something incriminating?

Joyce had landed a decent defensive blow to Susan's forehead before Susan pointed the gun at her. It was satisfying to see the bruise swell up, marring Susan's well-maintained face.

At least Susan hadn't done a thorough search. It was a small pleasure seeing Susan's face react to the revelation that a young woman was stowed in the trunk of Joyce's car.

"Just another count of kidnapping," Joyce told Susan coolly after informing her of their extra cargo. That had earned Joyce another sharp jab in her ribs.

In reality, Joyce would have figured something out, gun pointed at her or not, if Susan had insisted she drive them somewhere out of Joyce's way. Joyce wasn't in the habit of doing things she didn't want to.

Joyce learned about Laura a while ago—Dermot could barely

shut up about the girl. How damaged she was, chaotic, desperate for love. The exact opposite of Joyce, which she'd assumed was part of her own appeal to Dermot. Although she hadn't thought Dermot and Laura were actually intimate.

The girl, now that they were here, had all the signs of being a mother-to-be. Sickly pale, shying away from Susan's expensive and potent perfume, a greenness around her chin and eyes that suggested food poisoning. But no, just a fetus growing inside.

Dermot's baby. *How quaint*, Joyce thought.

They sat in Laura's living room, waiting for Susan to convene this meeting of the women of Dermot's life, apparently. Laura, Joyce, and that grad student whose name Joyce could never remember.

Had Dermot managed to seduce them all? Or had he been seduced at some point by each of them? Looking around at the women, Joyce considered it a sign of how the internet was changing the world. Not through the sharing of information or culture, but the sharing of bodies.

"What are we waiting for?" Laura asked. She had a petulant look, which made her appear younger. It was disturbing almost, to see her pretty face pouting like a four-year-old.

"Stop talking," Susan said, waving the gun in the air. It annoyed Joyce no end that this halfwit was holding *her* gun. And it made Joyce burn with fury that Susan was able to out-maneuver her. She shouldn't have assumed Susan was so stupid. That was Joyce's first mistake, and her main one in life in general: Underestimating other women.

She'd found you could really never underestimate a man. They always disappointed you.

Joyce should have kept the gun on her. She couldn't put it in the trunk, because that simpering graduate student had been there. She wished she could have hunted her down herself, but there was no time. Between juggling Susan and Simon, the police and Trina and Laura—good Lord this was a messy network—

Joyce needed to delegate. Victor was a great friend, and good in bed when she needed an extra oomph. He hadn't minded heading over to campus after confronting Laura at the hotel earlier that day. It had actually been perfect. He was able to retrieve Joyce's favorite lipstick she'd left in the hotel room after a recent rendezvous with some nameless stud, all while giving Laura a good scare.

Joyce suspected there were more layers to Laura than she let on and her reaction to Victor's visit suggested Joyce was right. She had her suspicions about Laura.

Joyce met Victor at his home before she drove to the park for her appointment with Susan. He lived in a gorgeous McMansion on the edge of town—Russian mafia money, Joyce had no doubt —and transferred Addy from his car to Joyce's. She didn't ask for details regarding how Victor successfully retrieved Addy, although he couldn't help mentioning his luck at tracking her to her shared office and using a hard-earned set of campus janitorial keys for the service elevator. Joyce figured he was hoping for a quick lay, but there was no time.

She really needed a vacation.

As she drove Susan to Laura's, Joyce should have realized her mistake. Susan was too quiet, too appreciating as she sat in her passenger seat. In fact, Joyce should have been suspicious when Susan climbed into the car with her to begin with. Her husband had just confessed to killing her brother!

Oh, Joyce was getting sloppy. This past year wore on her like a rough stone dulling a blade. Her mind was getting too frenetic.

Focus, she reminded herself. Do what you should have done when Susan opened the glove compartment, pulled out the gun, and demanded Joyce drive her to Laura's house. Joyce hadn't mentioned they were already headed there.

After failing to retaliate against Susan, grab the gun, and steer the car simultaneously, Joyce had resigned herself to being beaten. For the moment.

Somewhat.

"Do you even know how to use that?" Joyce couldn't resist baiting her.

To which Susan promptly flicked off the safety and cocked the barrel.

"Would you like to find out?" she asked Joyce.

Joyce shut up and drove until they pulled up to the run-down trailer. It was even worse than Joyce had imagined. She'd only seen it from a distance, when Dermot met her on a trail to play out a "hiker in distress" fantasy. Of course, he'd taken her along a trail that brought Laura's home into view. He'd pointed it out from the crest of a hill, and then Joyce kissed him and unbuckled his pants.

It'd looked like a small home from that viewpoint. Up close, though, she saw how derelict it was. Siding stripped off in parts, exposing the insulation like rolls of fat exploding from the inside. Cracks in the windows repaired with duct tape and seams along the roof gaping so wide she could see the one outside light through the ceiling's edge from her current vantage point on the sofa.

Joyce looked over at Addy, who stared out into nothing. She seemed drained and woozy. Addy probably had a concussion, not that Joyce could do anything about that now. It was a shame, really, that Addy had to be involved. But if there was one thing Joyce learned over this last year, it's that loose ends were the undoing of us all.

"What are you going to do with us?" Laura said. Her voice was steady, and a feeling flashed in Joyce that was close to appreciation. The girl was definitely tougher than she appeared.

Susan didn't answer Laura. Her phone buzzed in her pocket, and Susan pulled it out to glance at the screen, keeping the gun aimed at their small group. Her face instantly turned anguished. She pushed the button and silenced her phone, tucking it back into her coat's pocket.

Joyce saw an opportunity.

"Is it your family?" she asked.

Susan refused to look at her.

Joyce kept her voice sweet and untarnished. "You can turn back from this. You haven't done anything undoable. You could still go home to your family."

It wasn't entirely true. Kidnapping. Theft. Assault with a deadly weapon—that's what Joyce would call this woman waving her own gun at her from the passenger seat of her Porsche. Joyce felt a bruise forming on her ribs.

But Susan didn't need to consider all of that now. She just needed to think about her darling family, waiting for Mommy to come home.

Joyce was banking on motherly love to come through for her in the end.

Susan looked up at Joyce suddenly, her eyes flashing. "You know," she said. "That's easy to fix."

Dermot's sister turned to her left and shot Addy.

CHAPTER FORTY-FIVE

SIMON

"We're releasing you," Bechdel told him, her face a neutral mask.

"What?" Simon hadn't planned for this, which probably showed more his own naivety than his ability to anticipate the dark turns of life. If he wasn't going to be taken into custody, then he would have to go home. A crack opened in his chest, and he wanted to scream out at the unfairness of it all.

"You are no longer a suspect," Kirkpatrick reiterated. "You are free to go."

"I don't understand. I confessed. I have information for you." Simon realized he was begging.

Bechdel moved to the door of the interview room and pushed it open with her right arm, her papers balanced in the other. "Actually, you don't. You seem confused by the events of the last few days, and for some reason think confessing to a crime you did not commit would help our situation." She looked pointedly at him. "Or yours."

"I don't understand," Simon repeated to himself. "Why don't you believe me?"

Kirkpatrick was clearly annoyed, sighing into his coffee cup as he bit into the soft lining of the Styrofoam and gathered his papers from the desk. He shoved them into his bag, along with his laptop. Simon waited, and the detective moved his cup from his mouth and stood up from the cheap metal table. "Because you couldn't tell us how Dermot was killed. You were mistaken about the means of his death. And you were seen in video footage at another location, where another man was killed—*not by you*, around the time Trina Dell was murdered. Based on the updated coroner's report, there's no way you could have killed Trina, been a hostage in the shooting, and received the follow-up care at the hospital. The timeframe doesn't fit. We need to find whoever is doing this and stop wasting time on you."

A dark chasm opened up in front of Simon. He couldn't go back home. He didn't want to see Joyce, to climb in bed with her and listen to her breathing in her sleep while he waited to die. His work tortured him, leaving him vacant inside because he couldn't tolerate the imperfection of it all. He drank to alleviate the despair of losing patients, and he lost patients because he drank. He'd killed Tom, if not by his own hands then by his own actions, and now Trina was dead and there was no point in trying to make up for what he'd done.

There was only resignation.

Nothing made him happy.

Except considering what he could do to Joyce. *For* Joyce, he corrected himself. Because, of course, she was his wife and he was working to make up for the pain he'd caused her.

"I can tell you things," Simon offered as a last resort.

Bechdel gave him a raised eyebrow and motioned with her hand through the door. "Nothing we don't already know."

Simon bristled at this. As beaten down as he was, he still didn't tolerate being told he wasn't the smartest person in the room. That was a lesson Joyce learned early on in their life together.

"My wife hated Trina Dell." He said it like an oath, the words sturdy on his tongue.

"Everyone knows that." Kirkpatrick stood at the door with Bechdel, but Simon remained seated. He knew he was irritating them, not following the silent rules of body language to leave their space.

"My wife was sleeping with Dermot."

"As we confirmed from your messages." Kirkpatrick checked his watch. It was an old-fashioned movement that made Simon feel nostalgic in a way. So many young people just looked at their phones instead. "We're examining all possibilities."

"Joyce tried to kill me," he said.

This made the two detectives move away from the door, and a flutter of satisfaction gave way in Simon's stomach.

He'd been holding onto this memory, willing it to stop appearing in his mind, desperate to get out. The reason he'd come here was to help his wife and doing this would help, in the end. He told himself he was certain of it, and that he wasn't offering up this revelation just to delay the inevitable of going back to her.

"When?" Bechdel asked, her eyes keen on him again.

"Almost ten years ago. It was in my food. She put arsenic into a soup she made for me—butternut squash, my favorite. But she didn't get the ratio right, and I was only terribly sick for several days."

The two detectives looked at Simon for a moment, and then silently came back to their chairs. Kirkpatrick's squealed as he pulled it back across the linoleum floor. Simon waited a few more seconds for them to settle before he continued. They didn't need to ask him to go on. He was ready.

"We never spoke of it."

"Then how do you know it was an intentional poisoning, instead of just food poisoning or some other coincidental illness?" Bechdel's skepticism flared again. She seemed intent on ignoring the facts about his wife.

"I'm a doctor. I know the symptoms of arsenic poisoning."

"And you stayed with her?"

"Yes," Simon said simply.

"Did you eat one of her meals again?" Kirkpatrick seemed almost amused by his question as he asked it, and Simon realized that he might not believe what Simon was saying.

"Yes, I did." Simon thought about the next time Joyce made butternut squash soup. He came home from a long day of surgeries he'd scheduled purposefully to avoid making special plans for their wedding anniversary. When he walked in the door, the smell of the soup wafted from the kitchen and almost brought him to his knees. He was never meant to eat it.

It was a warning.

He turned around, headed to the nearest florist, and bought as many flowers as he could carry. And then he came home and apologized over and over. That was what Joyce wanted.

He didn't make the same mistake again next year.

"Why? I don't understand. Why are you still with her?"

"Do you know why she did it that day? It was because a man I was seeing had called the house—he'd found my number in the phone book—and then left a message on the answering machine that was a bit graphic. We'd been seeing each other for a few weeks, and I missed one of our meet-ups because of an emergency surgery. He thought I was blowing him off, and when I didn't answer my cell phone he decided to call my house. He was upset and said some revealing things."

"What did she say about it?" Kirkpatrick asked.

"She didn't ask me about it. I found the message later, after I was recovered from the poisoning. You see, my wife is very, very smart. She didn't get the proportions wrong. If she'd wanted me dead, I would be dead."

"So it was a warning," Bechdel surmised.

"Yes. For me to be more discreet."

"Why are you telling us this now?"

"Because I wanted you to know what my wife is capable of, and how that might have given her enemies who would do awful things to pay back her cruelties."

"You think your wife is being framed for murdering Dermot? And Trina?"

"I think my wife is capable of a lot of things, including killing. And I think Joyce is too smart to have left such a mess in her wake. Whoever is doing this is an amateur. My wife is a professional."

CHAPTER FORTY-SIX

LAURA

None of this was happening. None of this was real.

Laura wiped her hand across her face, and when she pulled it away it was streaked with red.

Blood, Addy's blood, had sprayed across her face.

A few seconds ago Addy had sat across from Laura. Susan and Joyce brought Addy out from the trunk of the car after Susan insisted Laura go inside and wait in the trailer. Addy had looked pale and drawn when they sat her down, and she'd shivered with big jolting bursts for the first several minutes as she warmed herself off the meager heat.

And now Addy was bleeding out.

Someone gasped. Laura wasn't sure who it was. Joyce or Susan. Maybe she did it herself. A moment later, someone else started laughing. The sound of it echoed in the trailer, where the air was almost solid, like you could take a chisel and break off a piece if you hammered hard enough. Laura forced herself to look up from the blood on her hand and examine the women around her. The laughter pitched higher, growing more hysterical, and Laura realized it was Susan.

Susan's face contorted into a horrible grimace of pleasure and pain, like she was trying to convince herself to be happy she'd just shot someone who never did anything to hurt her.

And then the screaming started. Addy wasn't dead yet.

Susan had shot her in the shoulder. Blood poured out of the wound.

Laura looked around for something to staunch the bleeding. She settled on a blanket thrown haphazardly over the back of the sofa.

Addy screamed again as Laura held the fabric against her shoulder. There was so much blood.

"This is insane," Susan said between gulps of air to feed her laughter. The gun hung loosely at her side. Laura looked to Joyce for help, but Joyce wasn't paying attention to Addy. Joyce was eyeing the gun.

The elegant woman remained calmer than everyone else. Joyce reached up with a hand, her wedding and engagement rings glinting off the ceiling light, and brushed a strand of sleek chestnut hair out of her eye. You'd never know, looking at Joyce, that a woman had just been shot in front of her, or that the gun had been wedged into her side only an hour before.

"Susan, put the gun down." Joyce said it like a command, the way Laura's schoolteachers would tell her to sit up straight in her chair or stop chewing the ends of her pencil.

Laura considered her options, even as part of her wanted to give up and curl into a ball on the couch and let the world spin out of control around her. So much death. So many terrible things.

And of course, Laura felt that small flutter in her stomach, and remembered she wasn't just responsible for herself anymore. She had another life she was guiding into this world, and she couldn't let anything or anyone hurt it. It was the last piece she still had of Dermot.

Susan ignored Joyce's instructions. She began to pace the small aisle between the couch and the door of the trailer. Susan pulled her hands to her forehead, the gun dangling from a fingertip. "No, no, no," she murmured to herself. "No, no, no."

Joyce sat up even straighter in her square of the couch.

"Somebody help me," Laura cried out, but both women ignored her. Addy mumbled something, but Laura couldn't hear it.

The blanket was doing nothing to help stop the bleeding. Laura's hands were warm with Addy's blood, and a metallic scent clung to the air. A wave of disgust clambered up Laura's throat, and she fought the urge to vomit. She needed to keep herself calm.

"You can't take this back," Joyce advised Susan. "You've done this. You killed her, just for the spite of it."

Susan and Joyce were both acting like Addy was already dead.

Susan locked eyes with Joyce, terror written clearly across her face and her eyes wide with shock. Pale streaks ran down her cheeks where tears had washed away her heavy foundation.

"I didn't think… I didn't think I could do it." Susan's voice strained at the edges.

"That's right." Joyce stood up, and Laura held her breath. "You didn't think. That was your problem."

"So much has happened. I didn't mean for any of this to be real. I can't believe it's real."

Joyce edged closer to Susan, her hands raising slightly as though she were about to comfort her.

Something shifted in Susan's face. "She was always a bitch, you know?" she said.

"Who was?" Joyce asked, her hands almost to Susan's shoulders, playing at an embrace for comforting her. The gun was limp in Susan's hands and very close to Joyce.

Laura kept pressing down on Addy's shoulder, all while trying to make sense of what was happening between Joyce and Susan. A second flashed where Joyce tried to snatch the gun, but Susan was quicker than that and she sidestepped from Joyce's reach.

Joyce's cheeks flushed, with fury or embarrassment or both, Laura wasn't sure.

Susan cleared her throat. "Trina. Trina was always a bitch."

Joyce was quiet for a moment. "You knew her?"

"We went to school together. I knew her and her fiancé."

"You didn't say anything about that before."

Susan didn't respond.

"You grew up together?" Joyce prompted, still standing so close to Susan.

"Trina was four years younger than me, but she was in the popular crowd at school, and for some reason she decided to single me out. She made my life a living hell. My parents were very religious, and she convinced the entire school we were in a cult. She said terrible things. Things that ruined my life."

Susan took a deep breath. Joyce looked bored already.

"In college, I thought I had left all of that behind. I was seeing a wonderful guy, and I brought him home to meet my parents. I made the mistake of accepting an invitation to a house party a high-school classmate was having—they'd sent the invite through Facebook—and Trina was there. Once she walked into the room, all fresh and wild, there was no stopping her. Tom was a goner."

"Tom?" Joyce was paying attention again.

Susan stared out into space, but Laura noticed a twitch in her jaw. "Tom Hovisky. You have to realize, I wasn't the way I am now." Susan held up an arm to gesture to her rich clothes, her expensive haircut. "I was still so much under my parents' influence. I thought dressing nicely and flirting were sinful. I was lucky to have Tom even be interested in me in the first place. I couldn't believe my luck when he sat next to me in the library and introduced himself."

Tears formed in Susan's eyes. "He congratulated me on earning the highest grade on our calculus exam. One thing led to another, and I offered to help him with his homework in the class."

Joyce made a small noise in the back of her throat.

Susan cut a discerning look at both Joyce and Laura. "I *knew* it might have started off as him using me. But then we fell in love. We enjoyed spending time together. Tom was the first man I slept with. He was going to propose soon, I was certain."

Susan shook her head. "Until that *bitch* showed up back in my life." She paused. "I didn't become *this* Susan until well after he left me for Trina. It took years to transform myself."

Joyce glared at Susan. "Did you kill her?"

Addy moaned, and Laura snapped her attention back to her patient. The bleeding seemed to be slowing down.

Nobody spoke.

CHAPTER FORTY-SEVEN

SIMON

Simon sat in the parking lot, his expensive car resting beneath him like a beast waiting to be summoned. Where was he going?

For the second time that day, he left the police station.

The detectives took his information, said they'd follow up, and now he was alone again. He checked his phone to see where Joyce was. They set location tracking up a long time ago, and he rarely used it because he'd prefer to not know where his wife was. He mainly checked it on his way home from the office, to see which type of emptiness he was coming home to.

Kirkpatrick and Bechdel assured him they were working the case for Dermot. And for Trina. There were moments where Simon felt normal, and his mind forgot the terrible things he'd seen, and there were others where it suffocated him. Like a wave crashing into him, uncontrollable as it molded itself out of his grasp.

Joyce was somewhere out in the trailer park that skirted the edge of town. Her green dot beckoned from the screen of his phone.

Why was she there? What was she doing?

Simon decided to find out. The engine purred seductively as he turned the key. Money bought little that could bring happiness, he'd discovered, but it did buy good engineering.

Simon had always been a good driver, enjoying the process of directing a massive machine with his hands. It's why he became a surgeon in the first place, because what are our bodies if not self-aware machines?

And there it was, pushing down on him again. The memories of what he'd done.

So much of what he touched now turned to death.

He'd been sure Tom had a rupture in his spleen. The bleeding, the hardening of his abdomen from where the blood pooled from the impact. He needed help, and Simon had offered it. He'd used a penknife, one that he kept in his pocket as though he were some old-fashioned twee gentleman. Simon's father always liked being the best-dressed man in the room, with a sliver of malice underneath.

At the hearing in front of the hospital board, Trina said Simon slit Tom open like he was a stray dog. That had stung more than the other accusations. From his colleagues. From the police, who knew the law of being a Good Samaritan applied, even if the bystander was drunk. From Joyce, although hers were silent. Quick actions behind his back.

One time she left her gun on the kitchen counter, next to a loaf of bread and a grocery receipt, just for him to see it when he came home from the office. Neither of them mentioned it, and the gun was gone by the time she called him from his study for dinner.

The gun didn't need to stay. It had served its purpose, which was to show Simon that she had it. That she'd use it.

Simon thought about the whiskey flask he kept in the middle console, but pushed it out of his mind. He could stand this pain. He just needed to bite back, let it ride him empty and then nothing would be there to hurt.

He was so close to that already.

The streets were nearly empty, all the lights turning green for him as though they were welcoming Simon on his journey. Keep going, find your wife and let her consume you.

An image of that man's body shattering as he looked at Simon from across the convenience store came next, unbidden and fragrant like a corpse flower.

Simon turned off the main highway onto the gravel road leading to the trailer park. He imagined Joyce watching his dot move towards her, delighted by the fact he was seeking her out this one last time.

CHAPTER FORTY-EIGHT

JOYCE

This Susan was a real piece of work.

Joyce let go of Susan and took a step back, putting space between herself and the other woman. She asked the question she already knew the answer to. "Where's Tom now? Did he and Trina break up, after all that?"

Susan grimaced. "Tom was killed on the side of the road last year by some drunk."

A sharp edge sliced through Joyce's chest. Nobody talked about her husband that way.

"You just shot a young woman for no reason," Joyce said, stating the obvious. She wanted to get Susan angry, angrier than she already was.

"I did that because I had to," Susan snapped. She held the gun straight at her side. Her finger sat idly on the trigger. "You don't know what it's like, getting up in the morning each day, taking care of your husband and your kids, hoping for some little break in routine, some small bit of appreciation. But no, there's always the next meal, the next pile of laundry, the next toilet bowl full of shit to scrub. It doesn't matter how many nice things you buy for yourself, or how many special recipes you clip and recreate. It doesn't matter that they love you, really, and you love them. Because every day is the same slog!"

"And it wouldn't have been like that if you were with Tom?" Joyce had to work hard to keep the sarcasm out of her voice. Because none of that was true.

"Of course not. If Trina hadn't stolen him from me, my life would be totally different. Better. Trina deserved to be miserable." Susan nodded her head. "I'm glad she's dead." Susan lifted her eyes to Joyce's. "Aren't you?"

CHAPTER FORTY-NINE

LAURA

Laura shifted where she was, holding down on Addy's wound. "You shot Addy because you're a bored housewife?"

"No," Susan replied. "I shot her because there's no going back for me now. Either I kill you all, or I kill myself." Susan lifted the pistol. Joyce held her distance. Laura held down on Addy's shoulder, feeling useless and small. Addy mumbled something under her breath.

Susan pointed the gun at Joyce, who refused to back down. Laura heard the distinctive click as Susan cocked the revolver. Laura took her hands from Addy's wound and leapt towards Joyce.

She wasn't going to let another person die.

The loud bang of the gun went off. Laura landed, her body covering Joyce's.

Just then the door whipped open, and a man Laura thought she'd never see again ran in.

"Laura!" he shouted. "Get off my wife."

Another loud crack shook the air around them.

CHAPTER FIFTY

SIMON

Simon ignored the blast of the gun. He trained his focus on Joyce, who had climbed out from under Laura.

He reached out and put his hands on Joyce's shoulders, shaking her with as much force as he dared. "Get out! For God's sake, Joyce, get out!"

"No. Stop it!" Joyce's voice pummeled his ears. She shifted back to move his hands off and away from her.

Simon surveyed the scene in front of him. A young woman lay on the floor by the couch. Blood soaked her clothes and a blanket someone had used to staunch the bleeding. She was very, very pale. Her lips almost blue in color.

Laura remained crouched on the floor next to Joyce. Susan stood close to the kitchenette. She pointed the gun in the air, and Simon saw the corresponding hole in the roof of the trailer.

Joyce wasn't injured. Laura seemed okay. The first bullet had missed. He didn't know what to do about Susan, or why she'd fired up into the ceiling this time.

But the young woman bleeding on the ground. He could help her. He could make up for what he'd done to Tom.

This was why everything had happened. Why Trina was dead,

and Dermot too. Or, at least, part of the reason. Simon didn't pretend to believe these horrible things happened because the universe wanted to give him a chance at redemption. A small part of him was simply relieved that he might be able to correct in some small way the many mistakes he'd made in his life.

Sound swirled around him.

He was sober. His hands were trained and knew what to do.

He'd save this woman, and in that he'd save himself.

His self-congratulation was broken by a primal cry from Susan.

The sound leaked from her mouth in a howl, something broken cracking the air around them. "Stop it!" she cried. "Stop helping her!"

"Why?" The word lifted from his lips like a prayer.

"Don't listen to her." Laura pointed a finger at Susan. Blood was buried underneath her nails. "She shot her. She shot Addy. She wants us all dead."

"What do you mean?" Simon held his hand over the woman, losing precious seconds in helping her. He felt his chance slipping away. Anger seethed underneath his impatience.

"She killed Dermot." Laura almost choked on his name.

"No, that's not true!" Susan's fury surged across the room, and the gun wavered in her hand. Simon wondered how many bullets were left.

The woman below him—Addy—let out a gasp and her eyes fluttered. Simon sprang into action, forcing the distraction from his mind.

"Get off her, I said." Susan's eyes bored into his. "You need to listen to me this time."

Simon turned his chin upwards and fought the urge to stand and smack his forehead into Susan's. He wasn't a violent man, but he could learn.

"I need to help her."

From the corner of Simon's eye he noticed Joyce's body tense.

"How do you know her name?" Susan asked.

"She's my wife," he replied distractedly.

"No, not her. I mean Laura. When you came in, you said her name. How do you know who she is?"

"What do you mean? Why does it matter?" Simon returned his focus to his patient, working swiftly. He still kept a pocketknife in his coat—for his sins—and tore strips from his shirt to staunch the bleeding.

Joyce pulled her hands up in surrender. "I'd like to know as well."

"We met once, at Dermot's," Laura offered. Her cheeks were bright red, two red blooms against her pale skin.

"At Dermot's?" Joyce's voice sounded incredulous, and if Simon was being honest, he'd also say a bit impressed.

"He was my lover." Simon didn't look at his wife as he said it.

"I know," Joyce replied, quietly. But Simon didn't have time to take in her full expression. He was doing important work. None of these other pieces of his life mattered right now. He ran his hands over the woman's shoulder, feeling for pressure. She gave a yelp of pain as he touched her side, and Simon knew he was being tested.

"How many of you were sleeping with my brother?" Susan's voice had lost its edge, although Simon couldn't guess what about this piece of information regarding Dermot's sexuality—given everything else going on—was the trigger. He needed to remove the bullet and stop the bleeding. Otherwise she'd rupture and bleed out in a hemorrhage. Simon directed his words to Susan. "She's going to die if I don't do something."

"Good," she said, but her voice was less steady than before.

"Don't do it," Joyce pleaded with Simon. "Don't make this same mistake again."

The gun was still pointed at them. Simon couldn't take the time to see if her hand was shaking. He only observed the dark hulk of it from his periphery.

"Everyone but you, it seems," Joyce said, answering Susan's earlier question. "Dermot was sleeping with both me and Simon. Separately," she clarified. 'And Laura. And I believe Addy, as well." Joyce nodded towards the woman under Simon's working hands. "He loved sex," Joyce explained.

His wife crossed her arms over her chest. It was a movement Simon wasn't familiar with—Joyce allowing herself to be seen as vulnerable.

In the back of Simon's mind, he understood Joyce was admitting to her affair in front of him, hoping for a response. But Simon couldn't offer it.

He had work to do.

CHAPTER FIFTY-ONE

LAURA

Addy's blood was drying into the cracks in Laura's hands. They were chafed from the long winter, and ripe for splitting.

Laura didn't know how she was going to get out of this. Her heart pulsed with two beats. She knew it was too early to feel the baby ticking away like a clock inside her body, but she felt it anyway, like a phantom limb or a broken heart.

She thought about telling Susan she was pregnant. With her brother, Dermot's, baby. Maybe Susan would spare her.

But then Laura recalled how Susan spoke about her own family, her children and husband. Her parents. Laura realized telling Susan about her pregnancy might make Susan want to hurt her more.

Dermot's face rose in her mind. Not the way he looked when they made love, or when he took her out in the hills and wrote their initials in the snow. It was the final time she saw him, in that hotel room. Fear shining back at her from his eyes, his mouth curled into a horrible half-smile like he couldn't believe she was capable of anything but following his lead.

She'd shown him, for once.

Laura looked at Simon, tearing at Addy's clothes and opening her like a gutted fish with his penknife, and then Joyce, pulling away from him with a fatigue Laura thought had to go deeper than the cluster bomb they'd found themselves in.

Was that love? Cheating, coercing, pretending everything was okay day after day, just because it was easier than living life uncertain and alone?

She wondered if Terry knew what she'd done, all along. Could he read her that well?

The night after it happened—not the night Dermot died, but the night she must have conceived the baby she was carrying—she came home to the trailer, her hands still shaking from the adrenaline. Terry was home, making something on the stove. Laura couldn't remember what it was. All she could smell was that acidic tang of something burning, which might not have been from Terry. It could have been a remnant from Dermot's place still clinging to her brain.

Addy cried out, and Simon moved over her, pressing with his hands and calling out to someone to boil water, like he was a midwife bringing life into this world.

Laura wept that night, after Dermot's. She'd wanted to be with him so badly. They'd kissed in his apartment, holding each other tight. Laura stopped by unannounced and found Dermot alone with a bottle of beer in his hand.

"Are you okay?" he'd asked. The question caught like a ragged edge drawn across her skin. He wasn't happy she was there, she thought.

"I wanted to see you," she told him. She'd followed him into the kitchen, letting him take her jacket. They'd danced around the idea of being together long enough, she'd decided. He was being too cautious. She'd come to his apartment, ready to show him how she felt.

He got her a glass of water, and as he handed it to her she let her fingers linger on his. Dermot coughed and moved away, sitting on one of the bar stools, but Laura followed him. She took a deep breath, and in a swift movement she'd practiced at home in front of her spotted mirror, she slipped off her shirt. She'd put on a deep burgundy bra, the padding pushing her breasts up into an impressive shelf despite how tiny she was in real life.

"Laura," Dermot said, but she was certain she heard it in his voice. He wanted her, just like she wanted him.

Laura moved over and put her lips against his, soft and gentle. He didn't move away. She opened her mouth and he pushed his tongue against her teeth, a hunger taking over that she'd felt for so long but wasn't sure he felt too. Her heart shot off a burst of happiness.

She searched with her hands for the hem of his shirt, not wanting to take her attention away from his face—oh, his gorgeous face, so close to hers. When she found it, she pulled it up, greedy with anticipation. Dermot let out a sigh, his hands moving down her torso. They lingered on her breasts and then found the snap of her jeans. She'd thought about wearing the dress she'd bought with him but decided at the last minute he'd want her to be like herself. He preferred women who were natural, she'd thought.

Although now she knew there was no truth in that. Dermot didn't prefer natural women any more than he preferred glamorous models or old men with sad eyes. Dermot wanted everyone and no one.

Which explained to her what happened next, at least in some small way.

They were knotted together, limbs and mouths and hot breath twisting around each other. Laura was naked and Dermot was only in his briefs, his hardness pressing against the side of her hip. They hadn't said a word to each other since she kissed him. Their bodies pulsed together, each movement a question and the following one an answer.

She reached and slipped off his underwear, exposing his

excitement. She'd never seen one in real life, and it thrilled and appalled her in equal parts. "I love you," Laura said, just as he was reaching between her thighs, ready to guide himself inside of her.

The air around them shifted, and that welcome pressure of his body on hers moved away. "I'm sorry. I can't." He lay alongside her. "This is wrong."

She didn't know what he meant. She couldn't understand it.

She reached over, and just like she'd seen on the internet when she'd explored in the hopes of being a good lover for Dermot, she gripped him in her hand and moved up and down, rubbing the tip and cradling him below.

Dermot moaned, maybe in protest. His hands gripped her wrists, but then loosened as she brought him closer to the edge. He'd love her, if only she could show him how good she could make him feel.

When he finished, he didn't offer to touch her again. Instead, he pulled his pants up, and started tapping at his phone. She went to the bathroom to clean up.

Laura stood in the bathroom, her hands slick with his cum, and instead of washing them off she shoved her fingers inside herself. She'd never touched herself like that before, and the angle of her wrist as it went inside cricked at her hand, but she pushed forward until she was as deep inside as she could go. When she pulled her hand out, she checked for any left on her skin, and then washed her hands well.

At least he was inside of her, she'd thought.

She came out of the bathroom, hoping to see Dermot waiting for her.

Instead, the bedroom was empty. She gathered up her clothes, holding them up to her exposed skin, and walked down the hallway towards the kitchen. She heard their voices too late, and when she emerged past the bookcase Simon was there at the door, looking desperate as he tried to explain something to Dermot.

They both turned as she entered the room.

When she looked at Simon, she thought she'd never seen someone so broken in her life.

"Simon, this is Laura," Dermot said. "Laura's a friend of mine."

Simon blinked, turned, and left without speaking.

It was that word that stuck in her throat. *Friend.* Her thighs ached from where he'd pressed against her.

It was the first time she'd wanted to kill him.

CHAPTER FIFTY-TWO

JOYCE

Apparently nobody had any self-control anymore. Her husband was playing God and Laura was useless. Susan held the gun in the air like it was a magic wand that would grant all her wishes, namely to erase this entire mess from existence.

Joyce sighed, accepting that if you wanted something done right, you had to do it yourself.

"Simon," she said. Her voice floated like its own shadow across the space between them. He didn't look at her. Blood pooled in the crease between Addy's clavicle, which had been exposed when Simon tore her shirt to address the gunshot wound.

Joyce should have been able to tell if he'd been drinking, but she wasn't sure. His hands were steady at least.

She said his name again, and this time he turned his head slightly towards her, an expression of intense irritation on his face. "I need to focus," he told her. "Leave me alone."

"You need to stop." She let the words drop into the void of space between her and Simon, Simon and Susan, Susan and the gun. Laura and the rest of the world.

"I can save her this time!" Beads of sweat broke on his brow, and Simon wiped at his face with the edge of his forearm. He didn't even have gloves on. He hadn't thought to wash his hands.

Joyce moved towards him, putting her hands out to steady him away from Addy, but a voice cut in.

"Don't touch him!" Susan shouted, pointing *Joyce's* gun at *her*.

Joyce turned to her coolly. "Stop waving that thing around. You're going to hurt someone. Again."

Susan didn't move. The barrel remained pointed at Joyce's chest.

Simon turned back to his patient.

Joyce figured there was no harm in taking a moment to explain what needed to happen next. "Susan killed Trina," she began.

Simon ignored her. "I need clean towels. Thread. A sterilized needle." He barked out the orders like he was in his surgery.

Nobody moved. Susan looked expectantly at Joyce. Laura stared at the ground.

Joyce continued, letting her eyes fall on Laura. "And Laura killed Dermot."

"What?" Susan flinched.

She thought about Susan poking the gun between her ribs earlier.

"Why would I kill Dermot? I was in love with him. He's the father of my baby." Laura walked over to the kitchen counter and started rattling around in the drawers.

"What are you doing?" Joyce asked.

"I'm looking for a needle and thread." Laura bit the words between her teeth.

"You killed my brother?" Susan wavered on her feet. She gave a quick glance to Joyce and then leaned back against the kitchen counter. "What am I going to do?"

"Why else would anyone kill him?" Joyce's feet hurt. She should have worn more comfortable shoes. She sat down on the couch, which was tilted back with its cheap frame. Her knees bumped up above her waist, so Joyce stood up again.

"I don't know. Drugs. Revenge. Irritation." Laura came back to Simon with a plastic hotel sewing kit, a roll of paper towels, and a lighter. She snapped the lighter open and brought out the flame, running the needle through until it burned an angry red.

Laura passed the materials to Simon, who snatched them without a word. He kept his focus on his patient. This time.

"Irritation?" Joyce echoed. "What about jealousy?"

"Well, if it's jealousy, then why wouldn't it be you? Or your husband? Or Addy, even?"

"Because none of us were in love with him." Joyce only loved one person, and he was slowly killing the woman underneath him.

"What about the initials in the tree trunk, by the trailhead Dermot always liked? The initials were J.L. It must stand for Joyce…" Laura's thoughts trailed off.

There was a long pause where no one spoke.

"Joyce Lynch. That's her maiden name." Simon leaned back on his heels. A neat incision with black stitching covered the left side of Addy's shoulder. He took a deep breath and leaned down to listen to his patient's breathing. His eyes locked on Joyce's. "I think she's going to make it."

A glimmer touched his face. "I did it," he said quietly to his wife.

"So you *were* in love with Dermot." Laura pointed a finger at Joyce.

"No, no I wasn't. It was just a stupid carving, something we did after a day spent outside on the trails. Playing out fantasies. Being passionate. It was something silly." Joyce thought about the other passionate things they'd done.

"I'd thought it meant he was in love with me." Laura's brow furrowed as she spoke.

"The only person Dermot loved was himself." Joyce couldn't believe she had to remind everyone of this.

"Is she going to be okay?" Susan asked.

Joyce snapped her attention back to the woman with the gun. She couldn't tell if Susan was hoping Addy would live or die. Joyce wasn't sure which outcome was more likely from her husband's frantic treatment.

Simon silently held his fingers to Addy's wrist on her uninjured side, taking her pulse. He frowned, then stood to move past Susan and wash his bloody hands at the sink in the small kitchen.

Joyce could have screamed at him for moving so close—within grabbing distance—of Susan.

Susan, who'd killed Trina. Susan, who'd stolen Joyce's gun and shot Addy. All because she was a dissatisfied wife and mother.

Figure it out, she wanted to scream at Susan. We're all miserable in our little lives. Figure out what makes you just a small bit happier and do it.

Susan stared ahead. Joyce could almost see the wheels turning in her brain.

Having Simon show up was unfortunate, but Joyce could work with this. Her eyes trained on the lighter, considering her next move.

Originally, she'd planned to bring Addy here with Laura and Susan to have a supposed big meet-up about Dermot and all his faults. Addy would be horrified after Victor's visit to her office, and once Joyce pulled out the gun she knew Laura and Susan would have to listen to her instructions just as carefully.

Joyce saw Laura go into Dermot's room that night, after Trina left. She'd followed Trina that evening, as she'd been in the habit of doing over the past year. Sometimes to follow Simon during his surveillance of Trina's life. Sometimes just to feel a hidden control over the woman who was ruining hers. Joyce stayed at the opposite end of the hall, but in view of Dermot's door, even after Trina left, because she didn't want to admit to herself that she was jealous of Trina in a way she'd never been jealous of her husband.

Trina had to ruin everything, even Joyce's fun.

If she'd known Laura was going to kill Dermot, Joyce would have stepped from out of the shadows and put herself between the girl and her lover. Dermot was promiscuous, but he was sweet in his way.

He didn't deserve to die. Not from Joyce's perspective, at least.

As it stood, she'd left after she saw Laura go into the hotel room. Joyce had thought there was no point in staying. She'd thought she already knew the ending.

Joyce had also suspected Susan was the one who killed Trina. She'd asked Victor to do some checking up on Dermot when she first realized both she and Simon were sleeping with him—one can never be too careful about potential blackmail—and Victor had uncovered Dermot's lingering family connections, including an older sister with a history of institutionalization at a mental hospital. Meeting Susan at the nail salon had been a magnificent stroke of luck and meant Joyce didn't need to track Susan down herself and lure her to town.

After that, it was easy for Joyce to see an ending to this year of hell.

Technically, she hadn't needed to include Addy in all of this—what did the girl know about Joyce's life or have to do with Trina and Tom? And Addy's only mistake with Dermot was sleeping with him. But then Joyce noticed Addy's growing interest in Trina, and Addy was the one who discovered Trina's body. There was no way to be certain Addy didn't know about Joyce and Simon's double-dipping with Dermot, or what Trina may have told her about Simon's accident with Tom. It would be so easy to wipe the slate clean entirely without her in the mix too.

Plus, controlling other people was an adrenaline rush like no other. Just like she would tell Susan, if she would only listen: You need to make your own happiness in this life.

Every woman for herself.

Simon and Joyce could start their life without any reminiscences of their past mistakes, and anyone who would connect them to Trina would be dead. As would anyone who could remind Simon about Dermot.

Susan had been the perfect scapegoat for Joyce's plan.

And she still was.

CHAPTER FIFTY-THREE

SUSAN

No one answered her question, so she asked it again.

"Is she going to be okay?"

Simon finally looked up towards her, but his eyes wouldn't meet hers. Instead, they fell on the gun held nimbly in her left hand.

"Why do you want to know?" he asked. "So you can shoot her again?"

Susan felt her face crumple. She should have taken her medication today.

She should have taken it for the last month. Her husband thought she was at a spa, "getting better." Her children had parent-teacher conferences next week. Riley, her second-grader, wasn't doing well in school and her teachers were worried. Susan needed to be back in time for that.

"What?" Laura asked.

Susan must have been mumbling under her breath. "I have a meeting for my children's school next week."

"I don't understand." Laura looked dumbfounded.

"Are you serious?" Joyce coughed down her mean laugh.

"I should be home by now," Susan reminded herself. "I haven't packed lunches for the week yet."

"You should have thought of that before you shot an innocent woman," Simon reminded her. He stood behind her, drying his hands at the sink. Susan waved the gun to motion him back in front of her.

"You think I don't know that?" Fury flared in her stomach. "You think I don't understand that all of this was one huge mistake?"

"No, I don't," Joyce replied coolly.

"What's wrong with you?" Laura was trying to sound confrontational, but Susan heard the fear in her voice.

"Nothing is wrong with me!" Susan held her hands up to her ears and pressed them down hard. Sometimes the world buzzed around her too much. So much it hurt.

"I need to figure out the ending."

Addy moaned below them, and Simon knelt to check on her again.

"Didn't it seem a little too unbelievable that I showed up to this derelict town where Dermot had been hiding out and found Trina Dell skulking around? What were the odds? Pretty good, I suppose, since a year ago I found Trina in the same place. And that I sent Dermot to seduce her that night at the wedding."

"Ah, there it is," Joyce murmured.

"What about the letter? It only arrived a week before he died," Laura said. "The letter where Dermot got back in touch with you, and confessed that he'd killed Tom?"

Susan was only half listening…

Mom, give me a drink! Mom, why are we out of milk? I don't like this casserole, honey. Maybe you overbaked it? Stop bothering me, I'm busy working. I have better things to do than listen to you prattle on about your boring day going to the grocery store. Mom, I wet the bed again. Mom, Mom, Mom, pay attention to me!

All of these are things that had been said to Susan in recent months. *All* of them.

There was something about living a life for others that makes murder seem a reasonable alternative.

"I love my family," Susan replied. "I just also hate them."

And why did she have *this* family? Because of fucking Trina Dell.

And because of her brother. Because of Dermot.

"Okay…" Laura held onto the last syllable. "But the letter?"

Simon was still fussing with Addy. "Get away from her!" Susan barked. "Go stand by Joyce."

Simon obeyed. Now Susan could see everyone. Addy on the floor. Laura near the edge of the couch. Joyce and Simon around the other side, by Addy's bandaged shoulder.

"Dermot sent a letter to me, but it was almost a year ago that I received it. He felt himself spiraling out of control, he said. He'd done something terrible. A hit and run. He couldn't stop—he'd been drinking and driving way too fast. It was after a party with some friends where he shouldn't have been driving home, but did anyway. Reckless. He couldn't go to the police. He had his entire life ahead of him. He needed to trust someone, so he came to me. He knew I'd had difficulties in the past. He thought I could help him.

"And all of this I could handle. I was reading the letter, thinking to myself that I could be there for my little brother. I'd help him through this awful thing that he did and help get his life back on track.

"But then, in the second to last paragraph of his letter, he said the man's name who he'd hit. Tom. And I knew. From the bottom of my soul I knew what he'd done. I'd kept track of Trina and Tom for years. Social media made it so easy to stalk people behind the curtain of Facebook posts and Instagram selfies. Dermot was too young, and then too separated from our family, to remember what happened between me, Tom, and Trina. When

I was hospitalized after Tom left me, Dermot was just starting high school. My parents told him I had really bad depression, but didn't say anything about *why* I was so depressed. I knew Dermot was living in the same town as Tom, but I had no reason to think they'd ever run into each other."

A sharp bleat of laughter escaped her mouth. "Run. Hah!"

Susan paused, feeling the four sets of eyes in the room tunneling into her. Something like a siren shrieked in her brain and she shook her head side to side to release it.

She continued. "Plus, Dermot was using my mom's maiden name as his last name at that point—he was so messed up from my parents that he didn't even want the same name as them anymore—so Tom wouldn't link the two of us. That's why Trina never connected Dermot back to me and who I was in high school. That, or she didn't even remember me."

Susan gulped down a sob. "I checked the news as soon as I finished reading his letter. I'd been busy with family stuff that week, and hadn't gone onto Trina or Tom's accounts for a while." She laughed, mixed with her sob. "I actually thought I was getting better. Getting over it."

"You weren't," Joyce interjected, stating the obvious.

Susan shook her head. "No, I wasn't." She continued. "But I didn't blame Dermot. Not really. I blamed Trina." She paused. "And I blamed you." She turned her gaze on Simon.

CHAPTER FIFTY-FOUR

SIMON

If this wasn't hell, then Simon didn't know what was. Blood on his hands that wouldn't come off in the sink. Blood seeping through Addy's bandages. So much blood. Susan stared at him from above, telling him this was really all his fault.

He couldn't wait any longer for Susan to *just shut up.* "She needs to go to the hospital." He was begging, and he didn't care.

"Be quiet." Joyce's voice was firm.

Her hands gripped his wrist. Joyce's hands were icy. "Stop touching me," he cried out.

Joyce froze next to him. He looked at his wife, and there she was, looking back at him like a dog that had just been beaten, only to realize its teeth were sharper than the stick.

"Don't you talk to me like that, ever again." She shifted away from him.

Joyce bent over and picked Addy up from underneath her arms. Addy groaned, and Simon choked back a caution that moving her would cause more damage and rip the stitches.

"Stop it," Susan commanded. "Stop moving. Stay where you are." Simon glimpsed the gun moving in the cheap overhead lighting of the trailer.

And his eye caught on something else. The lighter, nestled underneath a pile of bloody paper towels by Addy's leg. He had to accept that nothing he'd done in his entire life had mattered, including trying to save this broken woman.

Not Addy.

He meant Joyce. He meant his wife.

CHAPTER FIFTY-FIVE

ADDY

She was only twenty-six years old. She couldn't die this way, like an animal on the floor of this awful trailer. All because she was lonely and stupid and decided to sleep with a guy who she knew was bad for her anyway.

Addy thought about meeting Laura, just two days ago at Dermot's apartment. How she'd looked so fragile and young. Like a child, almost. She'd been worried about her, about what all of this would do to such an innocent person.

But Laura hurt people. She hurt Dermot.

Kill, Addy corrected herself. Not hurt. *Kill*.

Laura killed Dermot.

She'd overheard them talking through the haze of pain shooting from her shoulder through the rest of her body.

And Susan. Susan was a killer too. She killed Trina. She'd almost killed Addy.

Susan wanted Addy to die.

People above her were arguing. A hand grabbed at something by her knee.

Addy wished she'd had more fun with her life. She wished she'd kissed more good boys, and sung more songs and drunk more wine in the evening and coffee in the morning, and had one dear friend who loved her perfectly. She wished she'd never met Dermot Carine. She wished she'd seen the Great Wall of China.

But most of all, as Addy struggled to remain conscious, she wished she'd called her mother back, just to hear her voice one last time.

CHAPTER FIFTY-SIX

JOYCE

So this was how it was going to end? Joyce thought. Listening to this woman babble on and on about her "terrible" life while she died of boredom?

Not a chance in hell.

As if reading her mind, Simon reached down and grabbed the lighter. The roll of paper towels was there beside him.

Now she needed to figure out the timing. If she did everything right, she and Simon could be home in less than an hour.

Alone.

If she did things right, there'd be no graves to dig. Which was ideal, because she'd just had her nails done.

CHAPTER FIFTY-SEVEN

SUSAN

*T*om *and I should be together, holding hands on a beach somewhere,* Susan thought.

"My husband never holds my hand anymore," she gave as way of explanation to the four people she held at gunpoint. "He barely kisses me during sex. The most action I get to validate myself is when I call out 'Thank you!' to the FedEx delivery guy and he says back, 'Have a wonderful day!'"

She held her hand up to her forehead, wiping at some unseen hair caught on her face.

"After Dermot told me about the accident, I wasn't sure what I would do. I was only certain I was going to do something. I kept tabs on Trina. It was easy to see her downward spiral through her Instagram posts. Honestly, the same was true for Dermot. They were both reeling from what happened."

Susan cut a look at Simon and Joyce, who were next to Addy near the couch. He stared at his hands, too weak to even meet her eyes.

Susan kept talking. Nothing like a loaded gun to hold someone's attention—something it felt like she hadn't had for years. It felt good to talk about everything instead of letting it stay jumbled and searing inside her mind.

"I figured out she was crashing weddings. When I saw on Facebook that one of Dermot's friends from high school was getting married in town, I knew he'd be invited. I also figured Trina would choose that wedding over any of the others in town because the Marriott had a reputation for the better booze. When I floated the idea by Dermot, explaining how I was trying to get back at a high-school bully and really he would be helping to serve justice, he was all too happy to spend a night out on the town, bedding a would-be train wreck. His standards for ethical behavior were really slipping after the accident, although I'd assured him that I was only going to scare Trina. He didn't know I'd planned to kill her. I was going to make it look like an accident."

Susan caught her breath. "Anyway, when Trina stumbled home, with plenty of proof Dermot was still safely in his hotel room, I was planning to help her walk off the edge of a bridge or stumble down a flight of stairs. People die every day from stupid mistakes. Right? I mean, just look at the five of us?" Susan knew she was starting to talk a little too fast, but she couldn't stop now.

"But when Trina came home she wasn't drunk—or not drunk enough—and I lost my nerve. It was a moment of weakness. Just like when we were at the party all those years ago, and I let Trina take Tom away from me. I never expected Dermot to be the dead one, and for Trina to survive."

Susan brushed at the phantom hair, this time leaving red marks across her cheek from where her nails scratched the skin. "But I was stronger the second time. I was all ready to have to pick her lock, but that neighbor boy of hers with the weird tics let me in without a question. I'll tell you—the look on her face when she realized I was hiding in her apartment was priceless. I didn't say a word. I just choked the breath out of her until she couldn't do one other thing to hurt me."

Nobody spoke. Susan started tapping her leg up and down, making a soft rap on the linoleum floor of the kitchen.

"Now the only other piece of the puzzle is Simon," she explained.

"Then why are you here?" Laura searched Susan's face. Susan's mouth twitched up into a half smile. She was getting excited now that it was almost finished.

"I needed Joyce to lure Simon. And Joyce was heading here." Susan shrugged her shoulders. She turned to Joyce. "I knew you liked that nail salon. I also knew which cafés you preferred. And where you got your hair done. My private investigator offered a bulk package, as you can tell." Susan gave a short bark of a laugh that ended as abruptly as it started. "It was just a matter of time before we ran into each other, and I gave you my sob story about my dead brother."

Susan looked back at Laura. "You and Addy are just collateral damage. Sorry about that."

"You didn't bring Addy here?" Laura asked.

"Joyce had some thug stow her in the trunk of her car."

"What?" Laura turned to look at Joyce. It was the first time she'd moved her eyes away from the gun.

Now, Susan told herself. Do it now while she's not looking.

But before Susan could bring up the courage to kill this innocent girl—she didn't believe for a second that she killed Dermot; her money was on Joyce for that—Joyce stood up fully and shouted to Simon.

"Now, Simon. Do it now!"

The words echoed in Susan's head.

There was the scrape of metal against metal. Then a flicker of flame. Something hard and sharp smacked against Susan's legs, knocking her down. Her head cracked against the floor.

The door to the trailer opened, letting in a shock of cool wind that urged the flames on.

Susan's head pounded. Something warm dripped down her

forehead and she knew it was blood even before she reached up to touch it. She tried to stand up but her eyes wouldn't focus.

People were leaving the trailer. Smoke began to fill the small set of rooms.

Everything went black for Susan. A moment passed. Then two. Then longer.

She woke up coughing. Smoke billowed around her.

Susan got as low to the floor as she possibly could and took a deep breath of air that was somewhat clear. She felt for the gun next to her thigh where she'd dropped it when she fell, but it wasn't there.

The couch was engulfed in flames now. As she moved along the floor from the kitchen to the doorway, she was blocked by fire. The air in the room was so hot, it hurt Susan to breathe. She coughed again, this time from deep inside her chest.

Susan couldn't get air into her lungs. There was smoke all around her. Her body rioted against her attempts to breathe. Her legs gave an involuntarily jerk and her chest burned from inside.

She pushed her body further down to the floor, trying to find a pocket of air. Susan took one more breath and choked on the smoke. She heard the door slam closed. She sensed she was alone in the trailer.

Everything around her burned. Everything she felt was pain.

She clutched her hands to her throat, but no one was there to see. The smells around her were violent, singed hair and skin.

She lay down and curled her knees to her chest. Susan's last thoughts weren't of her children. Or her husband.

They were of Tom.

CHAPTER FIFTY-EIGHT

LAURA

Through some unspoken understanding, Simon and Laura worked together to carry Addy out of the trailer. Joyce screamed for Simon to leave them behind, but he wouldn't listen.

Laura had noticed Simon fold the lighter into his hand. The paper towels were left from triaging Addy.

And her home was a tinderbox of cheap construction.

As the flames grew brighter, their group made their way to the oak tree Laura hid behind earlier that evening, when Joyce and Susan first arrived unannounced. Which made her think for a split second of Rosie and wonder how much time had passed. Laura had no way of knowing. She didn't wear a watch, and the surges of adrenaline in her body were confusing any natural sense of time she might have.

Laura sent up a quick prayer to anyone who was listening that her friend wouldn't stumble into this mess. Laura was going to fix all of this before another one of her friends was hurt.

She didn't want to think about Susan inside.

She turned her attention to Simon and Joyce, who were wrapped up in a tight knot of limbs next to Addy. Simon was crying. Laura had pegged him for a crier, from the moment she'd spotted him at Dermot's apartment. He'd seen her appear around the corner, and his face looked so stricken by the fact that a nearly naked girl was with Dermot that Laura almost felt sorry for him. His mouth collapsed in on itself, and after Dermot introduced her as a friend, Simon turned away, wet streaks staining his cheeks.

It didn't track, she thought. Dermot bringing everyone in to love him, and not loving a single person in return.

Addy moved slightly, perhaps from the pressure of Joyce and Simon tangled so near to her. Simon struggled against Joyce's arms, and she kept whispering in his ear that it was going to be okay. Just listen to her and let her fix everything. A rush of sick rose in Laura's throat.

She wasn't safe with Joyce. Neither was Addy.

"What should we do with Addy?" she asked Joyce, motioning down to her.

Joyce looked at Laura, although she kept her hold on Simon's shoulders firm.

Laura needed to think fast.

No one told you, when you were a child, how quickly life can shift. Everything seems to stretch in time when you're a kid—long afternoons where nothing happens, hours at a desk at school wishing for class to be over. And then the universe snaps its fingers and suddenly, in one space between breaths, someone dies or someone is born or an elegant woman shows up at your door and wants to destroy every bright piece of your life.

Laura didn't just have herself to worry about anymore. She thought about her baby. She'd read online that this far into the pregnancy it was still only the size of an almond. But it would get bigger, he or she. Her baby would need her more than anyone had ever needed her.

Joyce approached Laura, her face resolving in Laura's field of vision like a bad reception on the television finally tuned.

"Simon and I are going to leave," Joyce replied coolly. "We're the only people who haven't killed anyone here." Joyce held the gun at Laura. It was like an old silent film, with the gun poised at Joyce's waist level and her mouth barely moving as she spoke.

Of course Joyce grabbed the gun. Laura watched her take off her fancy high heel and whip it at Susan's knees while she was distracted by Simon's firestarting. Laura had been too focused on getting Addy out of harm's way to pay attention to the gun.

Stupid mistake. Now she and Addy were both in trouble.

"Didn't Simon kill Trina's fiancé?" Laura knew she'd struck a nerve, because even in the gloom of the evening she could see Joyce's jaw clench.

"That was an accident," Joyce responded. Simon gave a small yelp.

"Just like Dermot was an accident." Laura said it as firmly as her cold lips would allow.

"Oh was he? You didn't purposefully kill the man who got you pregnant and then abandoned you?" Joyce tipped her chin.

Laura took a step towards Joyce, ignoring the gun pointed at her.

"Move back," Joyce commanded.

"No." Laura stayed where she was. "If you want to shoot me, you're going to need to do it to my face."

"I said, get back!" For the first time all evening, Joyce's voice wavered, and Laura realized that Joyce might not be as callous as she wanted everyone to believe.

"Put the gun down." Laura took another step forward and held her hands out. The toe of her boot brushed against Addy's arm, which felt limp and lifeless, and Laura choked back a scream. She was a normal girl, once. Before her parents died. Before everyone in her life decided to leave her.

Laura wished Terry were here. He was a bull in a china shop of a world, but he was her brother and she loved him. He didn't want her to become a mother. Maybe he even suspected what she'd done to Dermot. Love was a funny thing. Terry had gone to rob a store—the store who wouldn't give him a job—to get the money she'd need for an abortion and give Laura a fighting chance. She wanted to believe that, at least.

It was better than thinking he'd died a senseless death trying to get money for drugs.

"You're not going to shoot me," Laura cautioned Joyce.

"Oh really? Why's that?"

"Because then you'd be a killer. You'd be just like me."

"I'll never be like you," the older woman replied.

Laura lunged at Joyce. Her fingers clasped the cool metal of the gun.

In that motion, Laura remembered all of it. Every moment that ticked by after she found Dermot in his hotel room, alone. Trina had left for the evening, her hair tumbled and her face and neck red from Dermot's five o'clock shadow. Laura watched her go, hidden in the edge of a doorway by the front stairwell.

She hadn't gone there with the intention of hurting Dermot, although she was trembling with a certain rage when she knocked on the door and he gave her a look like she was the last person he'd wanted to see.

He was drunk, stumbling around the room in hastily drawn-up boxer shorts and his skin slick with sweat or drained bourbon. Someone had smashed the champagne bottle she'd ordered for him. The carpet was soaked underneath the silver stand.

"What are you doing here?" he asked, turning his back to her and rifling around the bedstand for something. There were some pills scattered along the surface, but no prescription bottle.

"I came to see you," she said.

"I can see that." He raised an eyebrow and smiled at her, and for a second Laura thought that everything was going to be okay. The words rushed out of her mouth before she could stop them.

"I'm pregnant," she said. Saying it out loud made it feel real, and she wanted it so much to be real. They'd take a test together tomorrow, take a photo of it for the scrapbook they'd make for the baby.

The emotion that flashed across Dermot's face was a mixture of horror and disgust Laura had never seen on anyone before. "Really?" He sounded incredulous.

That was the moment Laura finally realized how much of a fool she'd been. For years. For far too long.

"Yes, really," she told him.

"How?"

"From you, *Dermot*." She punched the emphasis on his name. "I'm in love with you."

"But we never had sex." He said it like he was schooling her in some basic logic.

"But we were together." Of course they were. But then she thought about Simon's visit to Dermot's apartment, and that word. *Friend*.

"Not like that. We stopped, remember. I can't sleep with you. I'd get into trouble. If work found out, they could think I'd been sleeping with you back when you were a client of mine. I could get fired. I could lose my license." Dermot was getting agitated, waving his arms around. "I need my job, Laura. Those kids need me."

"Your kid is going to need you," Laura told him. She reached out to put his hands on her stomach. Maybe, just maybe, it could still be all right.

"How do I know it's even true?" he asked, pulling away from her. He stumbled over his shoes, which were tossed in the middle of the floor between the bed and the television.

"Do you think I'd lie to you about something like this?" she asked.

"Of course I do! You're magically pregnant, even though we never had sex? Even though we were never a couple? None of it makes sense."

"I did it myself. When I went to the bathroom, after that time we were almost together."

"You did what? Fucked yourself?" And Laura couldn't believe it, but she swore she saw him sneer at her, like she was some neighborhood slut. Like she was some stupid girl he'd made the mistake of taking home.

"Yes!" she shouted into his face. Her pulse pounded in her ears. She put her hands on his chest and shoved him.

Dermot stumbled back. His feet caught the broken glass on the floor from the champagne bottle. "Ow, fuck!" He steadied himself by putting a hand on the cheap dresser. "I always knew you were crazy."

Laura pushed him again. His head cracked open on the jagged edge of the broken champagne bottle tipped up like a toothy grin on the ground. She heard the soft slip of Dermot's skin when the shards cut through the base of his skull. His face went blank almost immediately.

That was how she'd killed him. The man she loved. The man she was crazy for.

The fire ripped through the roof of Laura's trailer. Her home. Laura's lips felt warmer from the heat the blaze gave off.

Joyce was stronger than she looked, and Laura had to push as hard as she could to get her to fall over onto the ground. A streak of mud snaked over the white of Joyce's blouse, mixing with blood from when she carried Addy out of the trailer.

Joyce started to stand up. Both women still held onto the gun. Laura would let go soon. Just a few more seconds.

She couldn't see Simon.

The fire roared on. Simon might be a doctor, and Joyce might be rich, but one thing Laura was betting on was that neither of them knew how a trailer like Laura's was heated in the winter.

In fact, she was counting on it.

Headlights flashed from the driveway of the trailer, catching everyone in their glow.

CHAPTER FIFTY-NINE

SIMON

Simon couldn't be around Joyce any longer. He should have helped Laura get the gun off his wife, but he was just so tired. The headlights snaking down the driveway drew him further away from the violence happening beside him, like a moth seeking solace from the dreadful dark of night.

"It's you," Simon said as she climbed out of the car. His heart did an odd flip-flop in his chest that he forgot the medical term for. He just wanted this day, this life, to be over.

Even though he'd summoned her, he couldn't believe she was standing in front of him. Seeing her here, in a context that he'd never expect, outside of the familiar and routine, left him disoriented. If she was here, then who was back in the spot where she should be? His mind pinged strange thoughts back and forth like a video game he used to play as a child.

Right now, he'd give anything to be that young again.

"I'm here to help," she explained. She pulled on a pair of gloves. She'd drawn her hair back severely, pulled tight into a knot that sat at the back of her neck.

There was a smash and a scream behind them. A hiss sounded

for a few seconds. Something cracked the night air like a bomb exploding, throwing Simon down into the snow. Stones and grit ground into the heels of his hands. When he managed to stand up again, he'd lost her.

CHAPTER SIXTY

JOYCE

That hissing. What was that hissing?

Joyce couldn't place the sound. While she swiveled her head to look, Laura slipped out of her grasp.

Joyce started to go after her, but then the hissing stopped.

The trailer exploded.

The flames expanded from nothing to covering her entire field of vision in a few seconds. Where she was standing, the wall of heat smacked into her and made her stumble back until she could steady her feet again.

The light of the fire was so bright Joyce almost missed the beam of headlights flooding from the driveway. A glimmer of hope sounded in her mind.

Poor, manic Susan. She hadn't thought to take Joyce's phone.

Because who could you hurt with your phone?

Joyce's body crumpled to the ground in a tangle of pain.

But, despite the pounding in her ears, Joyce was able to think about those headlights. About the possibility that, even if she failed, she wasn't going to lose.

CHAPTER SIXTY-ONE

LAURA

Even though she'd dragged Addy and hidden them both behind the oak tree for protection, Laura still felt the wave of energy from the propane tank exploding. Her head pounded from the roar of the flames.

Her hands immediately went to her stomach. She was bleeding, not from a wound, but from inside.

The baby. Was she losing the baby?

Someone was crying. Her home burned.

Laura thought about her parents, and what they might have looked like after that car accident. How they would have been husks of who they were a few moments before that truck hit them.

That's what she felt like. A husk that was once human.

Addy took steady breaths below her. At least she'd helped protect her friend from the explosion.

Something snapped inside Laura's abdomen and a fresh flood of blood soaked her pants. Surveying the wreckage around her, Laura didn't know what to feel. She needed to get to a hospital.

A numbness began to creep from her core to her limbs.

Someone walked up to her, a woman she didn't recognize, and in an instant, the numbness went away. And then there was nothing.

Sweet nothing.

CHAPTER SIXTY-TWO

SIMON

"Clara." He said her name like a curse and a prayer.

She pointed her gun at him, the metal glinting in the light of the flames. "Mr. Morgan, you shouldn't be standing so close to the fire." She flicked the gun with her wrist to propel him backwards. Simon noticed white edges peeking out from the hem of her coat. She still had her apron on.

"We need to get out of here," he reminded her.

He'd called the house when he left the police station, after the questioning left him unsure of what his next steps were. He didn't know why he'd called. Part of him hoped Joyce would answer, that she would come and find him and tell him what to do. The other part must have hoped Clara was there, because when she answered his whole sordid story spilled out of him like a dose of bad milk coming back up.

She listened quietly on the other end of the line, and Simon waited for her to exclaim surprise or disappointment or something else on her part. He'd just told her he was having an affair with a young man who'd been murdered, that Joyce was also sleeping with him, and that he'd told the police Joyce was dangerous.

Now, watching Clara hold the gun in her hand, he realized none of it was a surprise to her. The explosion hadn't rattled her in the slightest, her body like steel against the flames as the fire grew to consume the trailer.

"I need to find Joyce," he told her.

"I have her," Clara replied. She bent down and, in the smoky fog of the fire he saw that what he thought was just debris over the ground mixed with the now-melting snow was in fact his wife and two other bodies.

No, not bodies. They were both breathing. Laura and Addy. They were dirty and bloody. Laura had a pool of blood spreading from the crotch of her pants. But they were both moving, ever so gently.

Susan was dead. He felt the weight of that fact deep inside. She'd looked so different from the photo he saw once at Dermot's apartment. Susan's face was round and joy-filled, blowing out candles on a birthday cake in the picture. Life had given her a rawness by the time he met her in person.

It was the only personal photo Dermot had up in his apartment when Simon visited him there. He'd commented on it to Dermot, remarking about how lovely the young woman was in the photo, just a small sliver of jealousy sitting in the back of his compliment.

The next time Simon visited Dermot, the photo was gone.

Clara held Joyce by the shoulders, and although Joyce's face was covered in dirt and red scratches from when she was pushed by the explosion to the ground, she was alert and able to stand up with Clara's help. Simon surveyed her and didn't register any major wounds. She wasn't bleeding anywhere.

His wife was indestructible.

Simon helped Clara move the three other women further away from the fire. He'd parked his car far enough away there was no danger of it catching fire from the trailer. Clara was parked even further back.

"Be careful with her," Clara told Simon as he bent to pick Laura up. "I injected a sedative to help with the pain." When Simon met his housekeeper's gaze with a questioning look, she shrugged. "Sometimes Mrs. Morgan has trouble sleeping. I prefer to be prepared."

Simon considered Clara might have brought the sedative with other purposes in mind as well.

Finally, when they were between the two cars and clear of the fire, Clara set Joyce down where the snow wasn't as thick. Joyce hadn't said a word as they moved, but now she cleared her throat and doubled over in a string of raspy coughs.

"Are you all right?" Clara asked Joyce as she bent down to bring them face to face.

Joyce coughed again. Simon heard the rattling of phlegm in her lungs.

"I'm fine. I'm fine." Repeating only convinced Simon that Joyce wasn't. Her skin was growing pale and her hands trembled as she raked them through her hair.

She tried to take a deep breath, but it ended in another fit of coughs.

He sat down next to Joyce. Rocking back and forth helped his head settle into firmer thoughts. "What took you so long?" Simon asked.

"I was nearly killed," Joyce snapped, and then doubled over to catch her breath.

"Not you. Clara. I called you just as I left the police station. What took you so long to get here?"

Clara was silent, staring out into the darkness.

"Clara?" Joyce asked, and in those two syllables Simon realized how full his mistake was.

How long had it been since he'd watched Clara and Joyce together? He'd been avoiding home, working from the office, drinking from the office.

He thought about the soup Joyce made. Had she made it? He

pictured Clara standing at the stove, wishing him dead while she stirred in the poison, all so she and Joyce could be together, undisturbed, in the big, beautiful house they'd shared. The three of them.

Clara turned from where she'd been staring. She locked her eyes onto Simon.

"I had to see my cousin."

And then she pointed the gun, took a breath, and let Simon give a little prayer of thanks that this nightmare was over.

"Stop!" Joyce shouted.

"Do it!" Simon called out at the same time.

CHAPTER SIXTY-THREE

JOYCE

"I'm sorry, Mrs. Morgan. I misunderstood." Clara lowered the gun.

Joyce couldn't catch her breath. "Why would you think I wanted you to kill Simon?"

Clara looked away. Flames danced in the dark pupils of her eyes. "Like I say, I misunderstand."

Joyce realized her mistake instantly. Her attempts to keep Simon under her control, the help she'd requested from Clara. Clara would have thought it was because Joyce hated her husband. But Joyce had done it from a place of desperate love. A love she couldn't live without.

Another roar sounded in the night. Not low and thunderous, but a high-pitched wail. Blue and red lights bounced against the trunks of trees.

The police were here. And fire trucks and an ambulance. Someone must have spotted the smoke from the fire and called it in.

Clara offered to drive away right now with Joyce, along the back trails. She had another cousin, one who was a doctor back in Croatia. They could get Joyce drugs, new lungs, a new life.

"I don't want any of that." She looked at Simon. He nodded back at her.

She reached out and grabbed Clara's hand.

"Thank you for coming to save us," she told her only friend.

She took the gun from Clara. Joyce didn't have to fight against her wounds.

It fell from Clara's grip with ease. Trust.

She couldn't let anyone hurt Simon. If they went back to their life, Joyce could never be certain Clara wouldn't try and do it again. That there wouldn't be another misunderstanding.

She gave one last look at Clara. In her mind, she whispered those words she so rarely allowed herself to feel. I'm sorry, she thought.

In that moment of weakness, Simon grabbed the gun and shot Clara himself.

It was only through some strange law of physics that Joyce could hear the shouted commands of the police officers above her screams.

They'd seen everything. They'd seen her husband kill a woman in cold blood.

Just to get away from his wife.

EPILOGUE

Laura
Six Months Later

She was hungry. So very hungry.

All the time. She made herself a plate of cheese and crackers and sat down on the couch in their apartment. Rosie's cousins would be home soon. Rosie was working today, but they'd have dinner together later.

The baby was kicking like crazy now. The doctor said she could go into labor at any point. Rosie wouldn't let her drive by herself anymore.

It was a girl. Laura was going to name her Clara, in honor of the woman who helped save her and the baby. The doctors at the hospital said the sedative Clara gave her helped calm her body down and stop the contractions brought on by the explosion.

Laura couldn't remember much from the rest of that night when her trailer burned down. She only remembered waking up in the hospital bed, with wires and tubes coming out of her, and Rosie sitting by her bedside.

"You're okay." It was the first thing out of Laura's mouth when she saw her friend. In her dreams after the fire, she'd imagined her friend screaming for help. Calling her name from a dark abyss.

"I'm fine." Rosie smiled. "How are you?" She reached out and held Laura's hand.

It was over the next few hours that Rosie explained what she'd learned. Simon had been arrested. He confessed to killing Dermot, Susan, and Clara. It was hard for the police not to believe him about the other two deaths when an officer saw him pull the trigger at Clara.

After some explaining by the survivors of the fire, the police accepted the knowledge that Susan killed Trina. Four murders solved was a hard triumph to resist.

Laura didn't tell Rosie the truth about Dermot. She'd never tell her.

Laura rubbed her swollen, pregnant belly. She had another life to worry about. Who needed her.

A small part of her loved Simon for his sacrifice.

And in her darker days since everything that happened, a more than small part hated herself.

Addy had been in the hospital room next to Laura's. The doctors sent her home only a few days later. Apparently, Simon had done a good job cleaning her up in the trailer with the sewing kit Laura gave him. Addy lived with her parents now. Laura messaged her a few times over Facebook. She said she was in therapy.

Laura wasn't sure if Addy knew about Dermot and how he died. Addy may have been unconscious when they had that conversation in the trailer. She might not have been. Laura was only certain Addy was grateful Laura pulled her from the trailer when the fire started. Addy had messaged her every day to say thank you, until Laura explained it would be better if she stopped. It was upsetting to be reminded again and again of the fire, and everything that happened before and after. Addy should move on with her life, and Laura needed to. The baby would be here soon.

Laura came home from the hospital around the same time Addy did.

Well, not home. Her home was gone. She came to live with Rosie.

Laura finished her snack and stood up to put her dishes in the sink.

Simon was in the county jail still awaiting trial. Rosie said he'd refused having a lawyer and insisted on representing himself. He wouldn't see Joyce and refused all her visits.

If there was one thing Laura had learned from all the death in her life, but especially in the last year, it was that love wasn't simple. Especially when it was the killing kind.

There was a knock on the door. Laura assumed it was a package being delivered. She'd been ordering a few things to get ready for the baby.

Just simple things. Onesies and bottles and a stroller.

Laura opened the door.

Joyce stood in front of her. Laura hadn't seen her since the night at the trailer. Joyce was discharged from the hospital well before Laura was ready, and they'd been called as separate witnesses on different days for the preliminary hearings for Simon's trial.

Laura had hoped she'd never see Joyce again.

The two women stared at each other.

Joyce held a large basket wrapped in cellophane in her arms. She looked thin. Too thin. Ragged around her polished edges.

There was lipstick on her teeth.

"You look radiant," Joyce announced, sauntering into the apartment. "I heard through the grapevine you were having a girl."

Laura stared at her in disbelief.

"Close the door," Joyce motioned to the apartment's entrance. "We have a lot to talk about."

Laura stared out into the hallway, but it was deserted.

She thought about what had been said in the trailer. What Joyce could tell the police if she wanted to. Laura remembered the feeling of Dermot's shoulders as she pushed him onto the shards of the champagne bottle.

She closed the door and sat down next to Joyce.

The baby kicked inside, and Laura reflexively put her hand up to it.

"Oh, can I feel?" Joyce asked. "It's amazing how having that huge empty house of mine has encouraged me to think more about family."

"What?" Laura said. Joyce reached out and touched Laura's stomach.

Joyce sighed. "You know, I was pregnant once. A long time ago."

Laura said nothing. She couldn't bring herself to say anything past the dread swelling in her chest.

"I hadn't told Simon yet." Joyce cast her eyes to the side. "It wasn't his baby, but I'd hoped we could raise it as our own. He always wanted children."

"Why are you here?" Laura finally managed the question.

Joyce ignored her. "After the miscarriage, I had a D&C. It can be a type of abortion, but sometimes expectant mothers need to have them done when tissue remains. I bled a lot afterwards. Too much."

Joyce shook her head. Her voice was quieter as she continued. "Whatever happened to induce the miscarriage, and to treat it afterwards, caused permanent damage. The doctors told me I couldn't have children after that."

"I'm sorry." Laura didn't know what else to say.

Joyce stared off into the distance. Laura noticed a missing button from her silk blouse. Underneath, Joyce's beige bra peeked through the gap. A small brown stain discolored the fabric just above where it tucked into her pencil skirt, as though Joyce had spilled coffee and never cleaned it.

"Simon thought I didn't want children. I never told him the truth."

"You could still tell him," Laura offered. She didn't know why she was trying to help this woman.

Joyce shook her head. "No, no. That's all in the past. We need to think about the future! Obviously you'll move in with me. I have all that room and no one to share it with."

She looked pointedly at Laura's swelling stomach.

Laura swallowed.

"I was thinking 'Joyce' would be a lovely name," Joyce said. "And she could call me Auntie, when she's able to."

Laura started to say something, but the words caught in her throat.

"Don't worry. I'll teach her everything I know." Joyce smiled, but it didn't reach her eyes.

THE END

ACKNOWLEDGMENTS

Thank you to the excellent team at Bloodhound Books for bringing this book into the world. Many thanks go again to Ian Skewis for his skills as an editor.

Thank you to all my writing friends, but especially Brian Centrone. We'll do that romance novel one day!

Thank you to Katrina Kasper and Robina Rader for not only being my friends, but for agreeing to beta-read *The Killing Kind* (both did it in record time!). This novel is so much better thanks to your keen eyes and thoughtful feedback.

Thank you to my beloved friend, Jennifer Crissman-Ishler, for being my work wife and emotional support person through everything.

Thank you to Dr. Sharon Stringer, my developmental psychology professor at Youngstown State University. I try to emulate your kindness, empathy, and passion for the field every day I am in the classroom.

Thank you to my students, who give me courage to look towards the future. Being with you all, I know the world is in good hands.

Thank you to my mom for everything she does. My first reader, my cheerleader, support system, and my friend.

Thank you to my brothers, Jacob and Ben, who are wonderful human beings.

Thank you to my late father, Stephen. He was the best dad any child could ask for.

Thank you to my children for being who they are and seeking out adventures in the world.

Finally, thank you to my husband, Joshua. Everything is better with you by my side.

ABOUT THE AUTHOR

Sarah K. Stephens is the author of six novels and a developmental psychologist at Penn State University. Her writing has appeared in *LitHub*, *The Writer's Chronicle*, *Hazlitt*, and *The Millions*. Aside from *The Good Life*, her books include the psychological thrillers *A Flash of Red*, *It Was Always You*, *The Anniversary*, *Isolation*, and *The Good Life*. Sarah lives with her husband in Central Pennsylvania.

Follow Sarah on Twitter (@skstephenswrite), Instagram (@skstephenswrite), or Facebook (@sarahkstephensauthor) and read more of her writing on her website (www.sarahkstephens.com).

A NOTE FROM THE PUBLISHER

Thank you for reading this book. If you enjoyed it please do consider leaving a review on Amazon to help others find it too.

We hate typos. All of our books have been rigorously edited and proofread, but sometimes mistakes do slip through. If you have spotted a typo, please do let us know and we can get it amended within hours.

info@bloodhoundbooks.com